Repeat
Performance
William O'Farrell

Black Gat Books • Eureka California

REPEAT PERFORMANCE

Published by Black Gat Books
A division of Stark House Press
1315 H Street
Eureka, CA 95501, USA
griffinskye3@sbcglobal.net
www.starkhousepress.com

REPEAT PERFORMANCE
Originally published by Houghton Mifflin, New York, and
copyright © 1942 by William O'Farrell. Revised and published
in paperback by Pennant Books, 1954. This edition is a reprint
of the original hardback version.

ISBN-13: 978-1-951473-42-6

Book design by Mark Shepard, shepgraphics.com
Cover design by Jeff Vorzimmer, ¡caliente!design, Austin, Texas
Proofreading by Bill Kelly
Cover art by Raymond Pease

PUBLISHER'S NOTE:

First Stark House Press/Black Gat Edition: August 2021

For
My Wife

One

There was a smell of disinfectant in the room and the cot on which I was lying had no sheet. I didn't have to open my eyes to know that I was back in the HIGHLAND HOTEL, REAL BEDS TWENTY-FIVE CENTS. I knew the place well; I'd been hitting it off and on for four months now, on my good nights. The nights when I had a quarter.

The room felt empty; the other sleepers had wandered off already. And pretty soon, unless I stirred myself, someone would come along and toss me out, too. Feeling the way I did, I wouldn't like that.

So I pulled myself into a sitting position and tried to think. No luck; my head was still foggy with the fumes of two-bit shake-up, the stuff they sold in a delicatessen on Twenty-Fourth Street. I looked around the room.

There were a hundred cots there and they were all exactly like mine. But the others were all mussed; the grimy blankets thrown aside. The sleepers had gone, and that meant it was after eight o'clock.

I got to my feet and waited until the room stopped shaking. My overcoat was lying across the foot of the bed, and I pulled it on over my wrinkled suit and felt, not really hoping, in the pockets. There was a pint bottle in one of them, but, as I expected, it was empty, and I started to throw it away.

Then I stopped and looked at the bottle again. There was a label on it; it had originally contained an expensive imported brandy. That was funny. I took the cork out and smelled it; the brandy odor was still there. Somehow I, who had to hustle to get enough money for a drink of cheap shake-up, had got hold of a bottle of cognac that must have cost somebody at least three bucks. How?

Let's see:

I'd been standing on the corner outside of Fritz's Place down in the Village. I'd gone there, stupidly forgetting that Fritz was dead, that he'd died months before, and that his bar was being run by someone else. I'd been standing there and a taxi had come along and—

The bottle slipped to the floor, and I sat down suddenly on the bed. I remembered, now. The whole thing came back to me.

I started looking for my hat. It wasn't there; it wasn't on the bed and it wasn't under the bed. I looked all around and it wasn't anywhere.

Someone was coming up the stairs, and I straightened up and waited. The footsteps climbed slowly, and then Tommy's unshaven face came into view and I relaxed. Tommy was the man who got a free flop and a couple of dollars a week for running the second floor. He stuck his head over the handrail and called, "Hey. Your name is Page, ain't it?"

"Yes."

"Barney Page?"

"Why do you want to know? What's it to you?"

His dirty face grinned at me. "Nothing, pal. There's a guy downstairs wants to see you."

I waited.

Tommy shook his head. "Don't get in an uproar," he said.

This guy's okay. Friday, he says his name is. John Friday. Where does John fit into this? I wondered. How did he ever find me, anyway?

And then I remembered something else. I had been running somewhere. Along Park Avenue, it was, late at night, and running I'd bumped into John. God only knew what I'd told him.

I said, "Thanks, Tommy," and started for the stairs. My knees were wobbly and my stomach turned over when I walked, but I made it. I went downstairs into the big, evil-smelling room that passed as a lobby, and John was there waiting for me. He looked out of place among all the misfits: stocky, well dressed, and capable; his very presence in this place was an unspoken reproach. But he didn't seem to be aware of it. He smiled when he saw me and came over to the foot of the stairs.

"Hello, Barney."

I looked at him and saw at once that he knew. I'd talked. And, abruptly, I was glad that I had because now I wasn't alone anymore. John wasn't going to let me down.

It was such a hell of a big relief that I turned away from him. I didn't want him to see how I felt. He took me by the arm and said, "Come on, kid. I've been waiting for you to wake up. Let's get outside."

"John—"

"Save it." He led me toward the door.

Fifteen minutes later, I was gulping a double Scotch-and-soda and staring at my face in the mirror over the bar in a place on First Avenue near Twenty-Sixth Street.

It was a miserable-looking face. I can talk about it objectively because I'd never thought of that particular face as actually belonging to me. I'd carried it around with me for something like four months at this time, but in sheer self-protection I still thought of it as an unfortunate temporary appearance which could and would disappear at any given moment. Then my own face, my real face, would come back again. My real face I always thought of as rather nice-looking.

This thing in the mirror wasn't. It needed a shave, and the hair that sat up on top of it was stringy and disheveled and dirty-looking. The mouth was a grayish white, and the lips were cracked and covered with broken peelings of hard, dead skin. The eyes were dead, the skin was dead, and there wasn't enough blood or grace in me to blush about it.

John's eyes met mine in the mirror. He smiled consolingly.

"Never mind, Barney," he said. "I knew you when."

"You're the only one left who'll admit it," I said. "Why do you bother?"

He shrugged. "I'm a sentimentalist. You're an old keepsake I've packed away in moth balls."

"What's the real reason?"

"I've been rummaging in the attic," he meandered. "You're an old toy I played with when I was a kid. I loved you. You're dirty and you're rusty, but I don't think you're broken. So I dust you off and oil you up."

"Nuts."

"Maybe." He turned around and stared at me. "I've known you since you were knee-high to a duck, Barney. I knew your father and mother before you were born. A friendship like that has its obligations. If there's any truth in this story of yours, I'll have to try to help you—somehow."

"There's truth in it."

"So," he said. He motioned toward my drink. "Finish it off. We've got things to do."

I tried to look unconcerned. "What things?"

"We have to get your hat." He turned toward the swinging doors.

I grabbed his arm. "Listen, John," I said. "I can't go back there. Maybe they've already found out. Maybe they're waiting for me."

"Maybe," he agreed. "That's a chance we'll have to take."

"Look at my clothes. The doorman wouldn't let me inside."

"You got in last night, you said."

"Fern took me in," I explained. "We went through a

side entrance. I forgot about it when I came out."

"We'll use it." He propelled me toward the door. "Now don't give me an argument. We'll have to work fast."

We went over to Second Avenue and started walking uptown. I must have been in pretty much of a stupor because, once we had started, I lost all consciousness of the reality of the situation and got interested in a game John seemed to be playing. It was the same game I always played when I had a long walk ahead of me. First we'd walk five or six blocks uptown and then we'd walk one block west. The game was to plot your walk so you came out just on top of your destination. It killed time and made the walk seem shorter.

Once I came back to earth long enough to say, "Fern was a friend of yours. You shouldn't be trying to help me."

He looked at me with a hard, set smile. "She was a friend of yours, too, Barney," he said, "only you both got twisted somewhere."

"I hadn't seen her for such a long time," I said. "I'd kept away from her. I should never have let her take me back to the apartment."

He shrugged his shoulders. "But you did go back. We'll have to start from that point."

Then I went back into my daze and didn't come out of it until we were standing on the side street across from the private entrance to the apartment house.

John had me by the arm. "Give me the key."

I didn't have any key, but, obediently, I felt in the trouser pocket that didn't have a key, and one was there. I brought it out. "How'd I get that?" I asked.

He didn't answer; he just kept hold of my arm and led me across the street. We walked into the side entrance as if we had a right to, crossed the little hall, and stepped into the automatic elevator.

"What floor?"

"Three." My voice was functioning as automatically as the elevator. I don't think I felt anything at all.

The elevator stopped and we got out. "Which way?" John asked.

I turned left toward the Park Avenue side where the stairs were that I'd gone down the night before. Opposite the stairs was an ivory-colored door with a push-button and, neatly framed over the push-button, was the name, "Miss Fern Costello."

John put the key in the lock and I walked past him into the room. I heard him close the door after me, but I didn't turn around.

I couldn't have turned. I was walking slowly, plodding in a straight line across the untidy room. I wasn't conscious of the daylight filtering through the venetian blinds, nor of the overturned chair, nor of the empty bottle of cognac lying on the floor by the little table. All I could see was the door, slightly ajar, that led into the bedroom, and I walked to the door and pushed it open and went inside.

The reading lamp over the bed was still on just as I had left it, wan and sick-looking in the morning light. And Fern was stiffly lying on the bed just as I had left her, her body half-covered by a silk nightgown and the blue bruises were still upon her throat where I had choked her to death.

I nodded to myself in a stupid sort of way and turned around and went back into the living room.

John was busily working in there. He had my lost hat tucked under his arm and, with a handkerchief, he was going over the furniture, wiping off the fingerprints.

He didn't look up, he didn't make a sound. But his shoulders were drawn in over his chest like those of an old, old man, and his eyes were filled with tears, and he was silently crying as though his heart had broken.

Two

"I don't like this place anymore," I said. "It isn't the same since Fritz died."

John agreed silently. It was late in the afternoon, and we were sitting at a table in Fritz's Place down in the Village. The new Fritz's Place, that is, with its carefully authentic atmosphere that has nothing of Fritz in it anymore. Nothing but his name over the door.

We were waiting for something. Ever since we had left Fern's apartment, we had been waiting for time to pass, but I didn't know why. John had taken complete charge, and he hadn't volunteered any information or asked any questions. And I was content to let it ride at that.

There was a drink in front of me, and when I picked it up my hand was steady. That was a definite improvement, but it had one drawback: the better I felt, the clearer my thinking became. I didn't want to think clearly yet. So I downed the drink and waited until the warm glow began to creep up inside me. Then I smiled across the table at John.

"What are you laughing at?"

"I'm not laughing," I said. "I just feel better."

"Drunk?"

"Not drunk. Resigned. I'm not going to worry."

John nodded. "I'm going to try to fix things. You're looking better, too."

The bar's new decorations included a large mirror near the entrance to the back room. I could see myself in it, and, from a distance, John was right. My clothes were good and, by a miracle, they fit me; my linen was clean, and, although it was hard to do very much about my face, it had, at any rate, been shaved. It was only when you got up close that you noticed the sagging jaw muscles and the lusterless eyes.

"I don't know how I'm going to pay you back, John."

"Right now," he said, "you're in no position to talk about paying things back. So forget it until you are."

"Will I ever be?"

He didn't answer immediately. Then, "I'll do my best for you, Barney," he said slowly. "Maybe I'm a fool, but I can't help it. You're sick; this thing would never have happened if you weren't. I can't let them take you while you're this way. You ought to have a chance. You haven't had much luck this last year."

"Just give me orders, John. Just tell me what to do."

"I'll let you know," he said, and, for a little while, he was silent, leaning back in his chair. His eyes went from floor to ceiling, and I knew that he was thinking the same kind of things I always did when I came into Fritz's Place: of what a waste the months had been since Sheila died, of what sickening changes had been made in this place and in my life, and of what wouldn't I give if she were alive and I had a chance to do it over again.

John gestured over his shoulder as he sat down. He had just come from the lavatory in the back room.

"There's a friend of yours in there."

"Who?"

"William and Mary."

This was surprising and I said so. "It can't be."

"It is, though."

"I thought he was upstate on the nut farm."

"He's here now."

"How do you suppose he got out?"

"Why don't you ask him? He saw me. He'll be here in a minute."

I turned toward the back room. In the doorway a short, stocky figure-with tousled dark hair and a swarthy complexion was looking over the interior of the bar with a pair of brilliant black eyes.

I called, "William" and he turned at the sound of my voice. An amiable smile unfolded over his moon face and he started toward us with that peculiar waddling gate which had earned him the latter part of his name. He oozed himself into a seat at the table and waved a fat hand at the bar.

"Barkeep," he piped. "Drinks for these gentlemen and a whiskey sour on the rocks for myself. And step on it."

The surly-looking barkeep growled to himself and reached for his tools. William and Mary called our attention to him.

"Note," he said, "the pained expression on his ugly merchant's face. If Fritz were still alive, he'd have clouted me with a wet bar rag. But there's no manhood left in the world."

"You," I asked him. "I thought you'd been confined for the good of society and the peace of your relatives. When did they let you out of the booby-hatch?"

William and Mary grinned. "They didn't. I just walked out the gate and got on a bus."

John and I sat up straighter. Holding a conversation with an escaped lunatic was something new even in Fritz's Place. William and Mary sensed our strain and his grin widened.

"Don't be a couple of merchants," he soothed. "I'm harmless. Besides, they'll catch me before long. I'm not trying to hide. I like it up there."

This was quite likely to be true; a lunatic asylum was one place where our old friend would feel completely at home. So we relaxed again and considered him speculatively as the barkeep approached and doled out the drinks. William and Mary, perfectly at ease, tossed four quarters on the table and waved away the change.

He lifted his glass to us and we drank his silent

toast. Then he set his glass down and looked us over deliberately.

"I shan't ask you where you've been or what's happened to you," he said at last, "because you'd only tell me the nonessential things. It's pitiful how little most people know about themselves, and how difficult it is for them to stammer out even that little. That, God be praised, is where I come in. It is my profession, as a poet, to understand what makes people tick and to interpret their inarticulate mumblings."

He gazed for a moment at John and nodded his head gravely. "I have a theory about you," he said, "and at some other time I should like to talk to you about it. You are a phenomenon in which I am greatly interested. But just now we will pass you over. Agreed?"

The two men sat looking at each other for a moment. Then John said drily, "You're right, William. It would be more convenient for everyone concerned."

William and Mary shifted his bulk around to face me. "So we come, then, to Barney. The questions, in order, are, "What is Barney?" and "Why is Barney what he is?""

I fidgeted under his penetrating stare. "Who cares?" I asked. "Why bother?"

"Because," my fat friend insisted, "I am a poet and it is my business to bother."

"My God," I said wearily.

"You're a character," he went on, unabashed, "in a play I wrote a long time ago and was never able to sell. And when I look at you now, coldly, objectively, and dispassionately, I understand why the producer hesitated."

"I wish you'd rewrite me, then," I said.

William and Mary didn't laugh. He turned to John. "Could I, John?" he asked.

"I don't know what you can do." John was staring at

the ceiling. "I don't even know what I can do. A guy like Barney certainly needs a rewrite job done on him. I'm going to see if I can't fix him up with one."

William and Mary pursed his lips and slowly nodded his head. "I see," he said. "Yes, I think I see. That, I believe, calls for a drink."

"For Christ's sake, yes," I said, and rapped for the barkeep.

I lifted my head from the table and let my eyes travel up the stiff white coat to the surly face. The barkeep stood by my table in the back room and looked down at me disdainfully. I suppose I must have been a mess, but, after all, that was my business. His attitude annoyed me.

"Feeling better, Mr. Page? You've had a little rest."

Nuts to you, I thought. "Where are my friends?"

"They went out for a minute," he said. "They'll be right back."

"Where's Mr. Hershey?"

"Jake Hershey?"

"The guy I was just talking to."

The barkeep shook his head. "There's been no one in here since your friends left," he said. "I haven't seen Mr. Hershey today. Maybe you've been dreaming."

That was possible. I had been doing a lot of dreaming lately, and Jake Hershey had figured prominently in all my dreams.

"Get me a whiskey sour," I said.

He cleared his throat and looked pained. "Don't you think—?"

"Never," I stopped him, "if I can possibly avoid it. Get me a whiskey sour."

He walked away, slapping at the tables with his bar rag and muttering to himself.

It's funny how I'm getting these days, I thought. Falling asleep like that all of a sudden. And it's not as if I were drunk. I wasn't drunk. I'm not drunk now. I suppose, when you get a certain amount of alcohol in your system, you reach the saturation point and almost anything is likely to happen.

Take Jake Hershey, for instance. Why did I have to be thinking about him so much? Jake was nothing to me. Sure, I'd been jealous of him once—when Sheila was alive. But God knows there was no reason for jealousy now. It wasn't his fault he'd fallen in love with Sheila; anyone might have done that. He hadn't forced a whole bottle of sodium amytal tablets down her throat. She'd done that herself. On purpose.

It wasn't your fault, Jake, I said. It's all finished with now, anyway. I'm not jealous of you anymore.

Jake pursed his lips as though this were a little difficult to believe. Well, maybe, he said, but if that's so, why do you always keep thinking about me?

I can't very well help thinking about you when you're always following me around, can I? Who asked you to sit down here, in the first place?

Nobody asked me, Jake said. I just sat down because I felt sorry for you because you looked so lonesome. Sheila's dead and Fern's dead and you haven't any friends left and you're all alone. What are you going to do now?

My God, I thought, I'd forgotten about Fern. Imagine forgetting about a woman you've just murdered. That just goes to show you what kind of sieve the human mind really is. Imagine.

Then I thought, just where in hell does the Bronx's Gift to the American Theatre get off at coming in here and talking to me about Fern? What happened between Fern and myself was private. It never had been and never would be anyone's business but our own. Who the hell ever told him about Fern, anyway?

Who the hell ever told you about Fern anyway, I asked him.

Why you did, Jake said. I didn't want to know. I never cared about you and Fern. All I ever wanted was for Sheila to be happy. You've made Sheila very unhappy acting the way you have.

Oh, I've made Sheila unhappy, have I? How do you know?

She told me so. She told me so in my sleep. She said your actions have made her very unhappy.

What actions? I asked him.

You haven't been worth a hoot in hell since she died, Jake said. In four months you've become a tramp and a drunk and a bum and a murderer, although, as you said, it was strictly a private murder. But you ought to do something about yourself.

What would you have me do, my little Pulitzer?

You used to be a good actor before you started playing this circuit, Jake said. It was your acting that pulled more than one John Friday production out of the hole. Get hold of yourself and I'll give you a job. I'll get you a job in my new play.

Get out of here, you lecherous bastard, I told him.

I'll do it for Sheila's sake, he said, because I loved her.

Get out of here, you God damned ghoul, I said. And I picked up the glass from the table and threw it at him.

The glass crashed against the wall with a merry little tinkle. The barkeep grabbed my arm.

"Listen—!" he said. "If you don't like the drinks, tell me so. Don't throw them at me."

I saw my mistake.

"I'm sorry," I apologized. "I'm a little nervous. Get me another whiskey sour. My friends will be coming back soon."

John Friday and I stood outside Jack Delaney's on Sheridan Square. The street lamps were on and the neon lights looked very pretty in the soft May dusk. I was humming to myself and jingling three pennies which had somehow got into my pocket. They were all I had, but that didn't worry me.

"You damned fool," John said, "shut up and listen to me. This is important."

Across the Square two pansies came swishing out of a bar and stood in the middle of the sidewalk calling names in shrill voices. They stood in brittle attitudes of refined haughtiness and shrieked their contempt of each other in a barrage of mincing, high-pitched lisps and elongated vowels. It was very funny, and I laughed.

John grabbed my arms and jerked me toward him. His face was within a few inches of my own, and he said, very distinctly, "Now pull yourself together, will you?"

I broke from his clinch and stepped back. Then I looked at him, turning the thing over in my mind.

"Okay, John," I said. "Go ahead. I'm listening."

He handed me a half-dollar which I put in the pocket with the three pennies. "You'll need that," he said, "for subway fare and cigarettes. I'd give you more, but I want you to stay sober until I see you again."

"When will that be?"

"Tonight," he said. "You'll see me again tonight and we'll go on from there. I know how this thing happened, Barney, and I don't think you're too much to blame. You got caught up in something that was too big for you. Now I've got to pick up the pieces. I'm going to fix things if I can."

He was looking at me intently, and I saw that he was trying to impress something upon me, so I nodded gravely and repeated, "You're going to fix things."

"Remember this," he said. "I'm staying at the Ritz Carlton and I want you to call for me there at eleven-thirty. Take the subway here at Sheridan Square. Get off at Times Square and take the shuttle over to the Grand Central. I want you to take the shuttle at eleven o'clock, so you'd better leave here about fifteen minutes before that."

"Okay," I said. "But I'm not drunk. You don't have to tell me how to get to the Ritz. What difference does it make how I get there as long as I show up at eleven-thirty?"

John didn't say anything for a moment. He looked away from me as if he were framing his answer. "I'm doing the best I can, Barney, and you'll have to trust me. Don't ask questions. Just do as I tell you. Is that good enough?"

"I'll take the shuttle at eleven o'clock and call for you at eleven-thirty," I said. "Anything more?"

"Yes. Keep your mouth shut. You've been talking too much."

That scared me. "When? How do you mean?"

"You were drunk," he said, "this afternoon in Fritz's Place. So for God's sake, watch your step."

"What do you want me to do now?"

"Go over to Madame Céleste's and have some dinner. William and Mary is waiting for you and I've given him enough money to pay the checks. Don't tell him anything more than he knows already. He'll see you through."

"I'll be all right, John," I told him.

"I hope so. I hope to God you'll be all right." He put his hand out and I took it. "Good luck, Barney," he said, "until I see you again."

He turned then and, before I could say anything more, he stepped off the curb and hurried across the Square to the subway entrance. He walked with his head bent down like a man with a lot on his mind.

I watched him until he came to the other side and stood, for a moment, a black silhouette in the yellow light of the subway entrance. I half-lifted my arm to

wave, but, before I was able to, he had hurried down
the steps and was out of sight.

I turned to the right and walked quickly down
Christopher Street to Madame Céleste's.

Three

Madame Céleste greeted me from the deep dusk of
the unlighted street, her exotic dress a challenge to
the gloom, her opaque eyes an acknowledgement and
placid acceptance of it.

"He's here," she said, "your friend. Giving away
quarters. Go upstairs." She touched my shoulder as I
started to pass. "And keep him quiet. No trouble,
please."

I went down three steps into the deeper gloom of
the café. A small room ringed with red-and-white-
topped tables at which not a single diner sat.

But there were sounds of lugubrious revelry from
above. An accordion and a violin wailed faintly, and
down the decrepit old staircase you could smell
Madame Céleste's vaunted tzigane atmosphere
creeping. A mixture of candle grease, cigarette smoke,
onion soup, and sour wine.

I crossed the room and started to climb. On the third
step I fell over a man who was sitting there.

"Henri," I asked, "don't you ever move? Do you live
on that third step? Don't you ever go for a walk, or
move up to the fourth step or down to the second?"

Henri, Madame's husband, raised a face that was
the exact unbelievable color of a plate of borscht. His
one good eye, the piece of cold potato stuck in the
centre, winked at me.

"There is reason in all things," he observed patiently.
"You run here and there, you go places; yet here you
are on the step from which I never move. Which of us

has gone farther?" Then he turned away and forgot all about me.

I squirmed by him and went on up past the telephone and the door to the men's room on the landing, climbed the remaining stairs, and walked past the piano into the upstairs room.

I stood at the top of the stairs and looked the place over. It was like peering through a distorted lens at the face of someone you love. For I'd loved this place once, this place and what it signified. I'd known it for a good many years and I was aware of all its faults. I still loved it. Only, it didn't love me anymore.

It was pretty large as such rooms go, and there were perhaps forty people in it—about two thirds full. A few of these were standing around the piano listening to a girl with a sad, dreary face accompany herself as she recited sadder, drearier poetry. The violinist and accordion player, whom she had temporarily displaced, had retired to a far corner, where they gazed disconsolately out of the window into the depths of Christopher Street. They were uninterested in the sad girl's performance. So were the other people in the room. So was I.

Squinting my eyes to peer through the dim light and the haze of cigarette smoke, I caught sight of William and Mary. He was seated by himself at a table near the window of the ousted musicians, happily playing with stacks and stacks of twenty-five-cent pieces.

My God, I thought, what now? I crossed the room and sat down beside him.

William and Mary waved an arm in proud indication of his wealth. "These," he quoted, "are my treasures."

"How come?"

"In the booby-hatch, one defends oneself. That is from the French verb, 'se défendre.' It means, as you uncultured merchants would say, that one gloms on to anything in sight that isn't nailed down."

"Quarters, too?"

"Particularly quarters. It's practically impossible to nail a quarter down. Especially when one works, as I did, in the commissariat. That's where they put the intelligentsia, or nearly sane patients."

I settled down. Who was I to criticize a little two-bit snatching? "Go on," I sighed.

His voice assumed an ecstatic quality. "It's strange and beautiful," he said, "how Nature has fashioned things to complement each other. 'Male and Female created He them.' Ham-and-eggs. Scotch-and-soda. Quarters and hospital beds."

"Get to the point."

"One is naturally honest," William said. "One never knowingly would gyp a customer. But quarters have a way of slipping through one's fingers and landing unobserved in the dishwater. And at the end of a day of honest toil, when the dishwater is finally drained, what shining treasure is disclosed!" He smiled dreamily. "Strange the number of quarters that can accumulate in a day. And stranger still the fact that, if one removes the roller from the foot of a hospital bed, one finds that the aperture thus revealed is of the exact size to accommodate a stack of twenty-five-cent pieces. Neither too small nor too large." He sighed deeply and gazed unseeing at the wan poetess. "It's beautiful," he concluded.

I agreed with him; it was beautiful. But there were other things on my mind. "What gives now?" I asked.

"And now," William and Mary said, "we dine. But first we drink." He grabbed a drinking glass and pounded loudly on the table.

"Garçon!" he shouted. "Muchacho! Ober! Zwei whiskey sodas vitement!"

It was later, a good deal later. We had finished our

dinners and had drunk a great many whiskeys-and-sodas. The pale chantress of esoteric verse had vanished from the piano, the accordion and violin were wailing their nostalgic music again, and there was a quiet hum of voices in the room.

I leaned back in my chair pleasantly cockeyed and hazily looked the place over. The usual assorted crowd. It was easy to pick the serious workers; they ate, drank, and talked quietly. The others had intent expressions and loud voices.

There were exceptions. William and Mary was one. God knows he always made noise enough, and yet he was, or, at least, had been, a good poet. And there were two men sitting at a table by the piano who didn't seem to fit in. They looked like small-time business men or tourists or something. They didn't belong. I hadn't seen them come in, and consequently I hadn't said anything about them to William and Mary.

I didn't now. Because my eye, rubbering about the hazy room, had lit on something that arrested and held it fixed. I leaned forward and stared. And suddenly all of my whiskey-won contentment was drained out of me, and left me feeling sick.

Why did Pete McCord have to be here at Madame Céleste's tonight of all nights? The sight of him sitting in a far corner affected me like a kick in the stomach.

William and Mary's flow of conversation had broken off. He must have seen what I did, because, after a moment, I became aware of his voice, quietly for a change, saying, "Barney, I seldom offer advice. But on this occasion I feel impelled to break my own rule. And my advice is, leave well enough alone."

I knew he was right, but I couldn't help myself. "You don't understand," I said. "This is the first time I've seen Pete since—since it happened. I was wrong and I'm sorry. I've got to tell him so." I stood up and stepped away from the table.

William and Mary muttered something as I left, but my mind wasn't on what he said. It was on Pete McCord sitting at the long table at the far end of the room. Now that I was on my feet and there were no intervening tables, I could see that he was not alone. All the old gang was with him. Jake Hershey was sitting next to him. But I didn't care for Jake or the others; I didn't owe them anything. My eyes, as I walked toward them, were all for Pete.

He'd grown a beard since I saw him last. A red, well-trimmed beard which, strangely enough, looked well on him. It gave him a virile, robust appearance. But it made me feel bad because here, I thought, is a fellow who has to raise a beard just to make himself feel masculine. Compensation for the loss of Sis, I thought. And I'm the guy who did this to him—to my best friend. It's my fault.

I walked to the table and stood there looking down. There was a sudden hush as I came up and no greetings. I wasn't popular anymore. And then Pete slowly turned and raised his head. He looked at me.

"It's been a long time, Pete," I said, breaking the silence.

He continued to look at me. Finally, "Not long enough, Barney," he said. "Not nearly long enough." His voice was like the voice of someone far away. I kept on standing there. There wasn't anything I could say.

Jake was at my elbow, tentatively touching me. "Barney," he was saying, "don't you think you'd better—"

Suddenly I got sore. Not at Jake, not at Pete, not even at myself. Just at things in general, the rotten way they had of working out.

"Get away from me, God damn you," I said, and brushed Jake aside. He toppled backward into a chair, but I paid him no attention. I was walking back across the room, getting back to my own table as fast as I could.

When I got there, William and Mary was missing. I didn't care. I sat down and went into a huddle with myself.

I was aware of his whispering for several seconds before I understood what Henri was saying. He was bending over me, pretending to brush crumbs from the tablecloth and his old voice was a drone in my ears.

"Your friend is downstairs. He asks me to speak to you." When he saw that I was listening, he went on. "Those two men sitting by the piano. They are detectives. Your friend says they search for you. Me, I know nothing. I only deliver the message."

The fog swept away. Fear is an effective cathartic. I looked across at the two men and saw what I had been too preoccupied to see before. Small business men from uptown? Tourists? Nuts! Centre Street was written in every crease of their clothes and faces.

"Where is he?" I asked, in panic. "Where's William and Mary?"

"Your friend sends you this." He slipped a nickel onto the table. "He says pretend as if you would make a telephone call. He awaits you downstairs." Henri gave a final brush at the tablecloth and picked up a water glass. "Now I return to my step. All that has been said I have already forgotten."

He went off.

I sat there and talked myself into the part. Listen, I said to myself. You used to be an actor. Well, now's the time to prove that you haven't slipped. Those two dicks are after you. If they catch you, they're going to take you up the river and sit you down in a chair designed for the purpose and turn on the juice. They're going to kill you. And the only reason they haven't

taken you already is because they're not quite certain
that you're the guy they're looking for. Your job is to
keep them uncertain until you can get to John Friday.
John will take care of you; he said he would.

I pretended to look at the watch John had loaned
me that afternoon. I registered surprise and called a
waiter. Stage business. "Where's the phone?" Careful
not to overdo it. "On the landing by the men's room?"
I thanked him and ordered another whiskey-and-soda.
"I'll be right back." Then I got up and walked steadily,
unconcernedly, across the room. I lingered a little while
by the piano, looking over the violinist's shoulder at
the sheet music, noting out of the corner of my eye
that the two detectives were watching me closely. Just
another Villager with a few too many drinks aboard?
Or a murderer? I could almost feel their thoughts.
Then slowly, resisting all impulse to run, I crossed to
the head of the stairs and sauntered down to the
landing. Whistling, I spun the nickel in my hand and
caught it deftly.

Then I felt the movement behind me and I didn't
stall any longer. I sailed down those stairs like a bat
out of hell, past Henri mooning on the third step,
across the dining room, and up the three steps to the
street. William and Mary was waiting there. We didn't
speak a word to each other; there was no time. Like a
well-trained football player he swung into position
behind me and we streaked down Christopher Street
toward Sheridan Square. As we hit the curb on the
Square, there was a commotion behind us and I heard
a yell and a couple of shots, but we didn't stop. We ran
across the street, burst into the subway entrance, and
pelted down the steps as fast as we could go. And we
didn't even stop for the turnstiles. We went over them
and into a northbound local just before the door
slammed shut.

The train shot off. We leaned against the side of the

car and gasped for breath. At Fourteenth Street we changed to an express. Then, for the first time, we sat down and compared notes.

"They'll telephone ahead," William and Mary said.

"I know." Now that we were in action, I seemed to be able to think more clearly. "I've got to get to John Friday. There's just a chance that we'll beat them to Times Square."

The train clattered past Twenty-Third Street.

"What time is it?"

I looked at the watch. "Five minutes to eleven."

"You have five minutes," William and Mary said. "John wanted you to catch the Grand Central shuttle at eleven o'clock."

We pulled into Thirty-Fourth Street, Pennsylvania Station, paused for a moment, and clattered on.

That's true, I thought. John insisted on the eleven o'clock shuttle. I wonder why.

"Why?" I asked.

"Answer your own riddles," William and Mary said, and stood up. He moved to the door. "Nobody ever tells me anything. Now get ready to run."

The train stopped and the door banged open. We charged out on a platform filled with people minding their own business. No one suspicious in sight. So far so good; we were ahead of them. We turned right and ran up the stairs to the upper level. We turned right again and, walking quickly, started through the underground cavern toward where the shuttle was waiting.

We were halfway there when we heard them behind us. A plainclothesman and two cops. They shouted to us to stop and we abandoned all pretence. We ran. They couldn't afford to shoot; there were too many people about and too much chance of hitting one of them. So they shouted again and took up the chase not twenty yards from us.

We made the shuttle. The door was open and I plunged inside breathless and exhausted. I brought up against the far side with a bang that left me dazed. Then I pulled myself together and whirled around.

The door was still open and the cops were coming. They were almost there. William and Mary had not followed me into the train; he had stopped outside and turned to face them. He was the only thing that stood between me and capture. Until the door shut and the train started, I was as exposed as if I stood alone and unprotected on a bare stage.

They were on us. And suddenly William and Mary launched himself at them. His chunky body sailed through the air broadside, arms and legs extended, as though it had been shot from a catapult. He caught them just below the middle, all three of them, and then there was nothing but a tangled, swearing heap. I heard the tinkle of silver.

The doors slammed to, the train shuddered and started off. I ran to the window and peered out. The last I saw of the Times Square station was William and Mary sitting on top of the prostrate detective while the two cops had hold of his neck and were shaking him violently. His fat moon face was turned toward me and there was a wide grin spread all over it. His arms were extended toward me and his hands, as he opened them to wave Godspeed, dripped quarters all over the platform.

Then one of the cops let go of William's neck and drew his gun. He levelled it at me so quickly that I didn't have time to duck. I saw his finger tightening on the trigger and then a spurt of flame clouded the muzzle pointing directly at my face.

Four

I must have passed out for a second. I picked myself up off the floor and hung on to a strap while the wheels went round outside and inside my head.

Clackety clackety crash. Clackety clackety crash.

That's the way it sounded. I hung on to my strap and kept my eyes screwed shut and I had the damndest ideas ...

Listen to the subway. Listen to the noise it makes. It's singing a hymn. The subway is Transportation, and Transportation is New York's religion.

It's what the town eats and drinks and swears by. It's the wheels going round. It's Death and Burial, dark burial with a raucous, hilarious wake. And it's Life, an eager plunging into the fertile earth, a noisy rutting and a triumphant orgasm of men and women, human beings, at the other end.

The subway is all that and more; it's transition and rebirth as well. Take a broker, sleepy-eyed, washed-out, impotent. He's sucked into its morning underground flow at Seventy-Second. In Wall Street he pops up a vigorous, back-slapping Napoleon of finance. At five in the afternoon a harried little clerk sneaks out of his office in the wholesale clothing district. Futile, harassed, fearful. Half an hour later he's at home in the Bronx beating his wife. He's master in his own household and a strutting cock in his own chicken run.

What did it? The subway.

It's the *bang bang bang* of jostling purposes and the *clatter clatter clatter* of shuffling dreams. And nobody escapes. A man goes in at one end and, when he comes out the other, something's happened to him; he's changed. Somewhere en route there has occurred a subtle alchemy for better or worse, and the man who is wise enough to know this drops his nickel into the turnstile—symbolically shaped like a cross—with a prayer, and takes his seat, if he can find one, with suitable reverence.

Have you never seen them, these devout subway sitters? Eyes closed, hands folded, an expression of ecstatic peace on their faces? Perhaps you thought them asleep. That's not so. They are at their devotions. Tread softly, you neophytes, for these are the initiates, the true worshippers of the Big City.

When I got on the shuttle at Times Square I was Barney Page, age thirty-two, ex-actor and general all-around son of a bitch. When I got off at Grand Central—

This is the way it happened:

I let go of my strap and looked around and found that I was alone in the car. That was strange in itself because, at eleven o'clock at night, the train should have been jammed with homebound commuters. But that didn't bother me, I had stranger things to think about if I wanted to—the fact, for instance, that that cop had missed me at point-blank range. But I didn't want to; I didn't seem to care. I went over to a seat and sat down and closed my eyes again.

I'm tired, I thought. I can't keep this up much longer. Suppose I do get away? What have I got that makes life so damned attractive? Sheila's dead, Pete might as well be as far as I'm concerned—and now Fern's gone, too. So what have I got to live for? What am I running for—or from?

I didn't know. If there were a chance of starting over again, I thought, there'd be some point in it. But there isn't.

There *isn't*. The wheels of the shuttle clattered it out on the iron rails over and over again. *There isn't. There isn't.*

But if there was?

Something happened. The train gave a sudden jerk and my eyes snapped open. We must have been under the Library just about halfway over to Grand Central. I looked around me.

I was still alone. The car hadn't changed. Everything in the car was just the same. Only I was different.

I wasn't scared anymore. I wasn't panting for breath. My head was clear and I felt calm, relaxed, sure of myself. I felt like a normal human being, and it was all vaguely disturbing because it had been so long since I had felt that way.

The train slowed down and I stood up. We jerked to a stop, the car doors opened, and I stepped out on the platform. No cops in sight. Just the usual bustle and hurry of the Grand Central. I walked toward the stairs. I'd made up my mind that I wasn't going to worry anymore.

A voice from behind halted me. "Mr. Page," it called.

I turned around. A man, a stranger, came running up.

"You dropped this, Mr. Page," he said, and handed me a wallet.

I took it and turned it over in my hand, thinking. Then I looked back at the man still standing there.

"Thanks," I said. "Would you mind answering a question?"

"Not if I can."

"How did you know my name?"

He gave an embarrassed smile. "I just caught your performance in *Say Goodbye* over at the Cochran. Too bad you're closing tonight; it's a swell show."

"Yes," I told him. "Thanks."

"Not at all." He went on past me and up the stairs. There are certainly a lot of screwballs in this town, I thought; *Say Goodbye* closed last May.

I followed him slowly, turning the wallet over and

over in my hand. I recognized it; it was my wallet. I opened it and looked inside. There were a few banknotes, a driver's license with my name on it, and some miscellaneous papers. It was my wallet all right.

The catch was that I hadn't seen it in something like eight months. I'd lost it back in the fall of the year before.

I walked through the corridors and into the huge room at the center of the Grand Central Station. I stopped by the information booth and thought about the man who had returned my wallet.

Somebody slapped me on the back. "Barney!" somebody cried. "I'm glad to see you. I just got in from Boston."

I turned around and looked at him curiously. It was Pete McCord. He wasn't wearing a beard, just a small red moustache. Christ, I said to myself, I must be really drunk. Twenty minutes ago I left this guy down in the Village. He had whiskers. He wasn't speaking to me. Now he's clean-shaven and my bosom pal. I closed one eye and squinted at the hallucination.

"She's coming down from Boston next week," it bubbled on. "Sis, I mean. We're going to be married right away. What do you think of that?"

"Very interesting." I decided to humor my delirium tremens. "Very, very interesting. Pete, do you happen to know what date it is?"

"The twenty-first," he said. "May twenty-first or twenty-second. Why?"

"But what year?"

He started to laugh, but I was dead serious. "I'm not kidding," I told him.

"Why," he said, "the exact date, I believe, is May the twentieth, nineteen hundred and forty-one. You'd better go on home, Barney. You look tired."

"It's not nineteen forty-two?"

He smiled. "Not for another year. Call me tomorrow,

will you?" He slapped me on the shoulder and walked off toward the downtown subway.

I let him go. I went over to the news-stand and bought a copy of the *New York Times*. It was an early edition for the next day, Wednesday, just off the press. I turned it over and looked at the front page.

It was dated Wednesday, May 21, 1941, and the headlines read:

GLIDERS DROP GERMANS ON CRETE
BRITISH REPORT ATTACK CRUSHED
ALL ON *ZAMZAM* SAFE IN FRANCE

It was the name *Zamzam* that got me. That wasn't the kind of name you could make a mistake about. The *Zamzam* had been sunk the year before.

The paper slipped out of my hand and fell to the floor.

I looked up at the ceiling. I looked to the left, and there was the long line of gates that led to the upper-level trains. I looked to the right, and there was the way to the Forty-Second Street entrance. Everything was just as usual.

The newspaper on the floor stared up at me. There it was. *May 21, 1941.* "British and Greek military authorities in Crete are in complete mastery of the situation." I looked at the people who were eddying about me. Crete, I thought. Good Lord! Don't they know about Crete yet? And how about the Russians?

A redcap picked up the paper for me. "Anything wrong, sir?" His brown face was solicitous.

"Throw it away," I said, referring to the paper. Then, as he started off. "What do you think about the Russians?"

He cocked a belligerent eyebrow. "Look," he said. "I was being polite because I thought you was sick. This is a free country. My politics are my own business."

"What do you think of Stalin?"

"You go to hell," he said, and vanished into the crowd.

That settled it. I had the D.T.s and as bad a case as I'd ever heard of. I needed a drink quick. So I left the Grand Central by the Forty-Second Street entrance and hurried to a bar I knew around the corner.

It wasn't there. There was a drugstore in the place where it should have been. I stood on the sidewalk and stared stupidly at the patent medicines in the window. People kept bumping into me, but I stayed there staring at them.

After a while a policeman strolled by. It never even occurred to me that he might be looking for me. I stopped him and, after a couple of tries, I managed to get a sentence out.

"Where's the bar?" I said. "What's happened to Mike's Bar?"

He looked me over and twirled his truncheon. "Keep your shirt on, fellow," he said. "Give Mike a little time. He only got the lease on this place last week; they're starting to remodel tomorrow. Try coming back three months from now." He walked off, swinging his club.

I leaned my forehead against the plate-glass window of the drugstore and closed my eyes. It was cool and felt good against my forehead. Now, I said to myself, let's be rational. Let's reason this thing out.

These are the facts: This is the year nineteen-forty-two and nothing on God's earth can make it any other year. It's been twelve months since Crete was taken and the *Zamzam* sunk, and no magic, black or white, no wishful thinking in the subway, can ever bring that year back again. I'm Barney Page, thirty-two years old, a tramp and a bum and a drunk, and I'll never, never be the Barney Page of nineteen-forty-one again. It's a physical impossibility.

But is it? I asked myself.

I opened my eyes and found that I was staring at a

stranger, a young man about thirty, rather nice-looking with a healthy complexion and clean eyes that were looking directly into mine. I frowned at his frankly open appraisal and, simultaneously, the young man frowned, too.

Then I recognized him and my mouth dropped open. There was a mirror in the drugstore window and I was looking at my own reflection.

I backed away from there and leaned against the side of the building. Idly, the toe of my shoe traced foolish circles on the sidewalk and something inside me kept whispering away, talking away in spite of all my efforts to silence it.

How do you know you're nuts? it said. *How do you know you've got the D.T.s? How do you know you're dreaming this? Isn't it just as possible that this is real and that all of last year was a dream? How do you know you haven't just awakened? What was it John Friday said? ... "A guy like you ought to have a rewrite job done on him. I'll see if I can't fix you up with one."*

Wasn't it possible that he *had* fixed me up?

It wasn't any more impossible, certainly, than that I should be standing here in the middle of a year that was dead and gone.

I ripped into action. There was only one man to settle this. I would have to see him. I would have to see John Friday.

I ran to a taxi stand and plunged into an empty cab.

"The Ritz Carlton," I told the driver. "And kick hell out of that foot throttle. I'm in a hurry."

Five

John squinted at me from his chair in the corner of the room. He was wearing slippers and a dressing gown Sheila and I had given him one Christmas, and seemed very much at ease. The dressing gown, I noticed, looked newer than the last time I had seen it.

He smiled. "If I hadn't known you so long, Barney, this aberration of yours might worry me. But it's been a hard season and anyone's entitled to a few extra drinks on a closing night. Now go on home and get some sleep. I'll call you tomorrow."

"This afternoon," I said, "did you or did you not tell me to take the shuttle at eleven o'clock and meet you here in the hotel?"

John nodded. "I did."

"Ah," I said. "Why?"

"Because I wanted to talk to you about your trip to Hollywood and our plans for next season. Why else?" He spoke as though he were explaining something to a child. "It was just before you went to the theatre. I said I'd either meet you at the shuttle at eleven or, if I missed you there, to come on over to my room."

I stood up. "Is that all you're going to tell me? Is that all you've got to say?"

"What do you want me to tell you?" John rose deliberately and came over and put his arm around my shoulders. "Take it easy, Barney. Look at it this way. You seem to think something miraculous has happened to you. Well, maybe it has for all I know." He shrugged. "So why not take advantage of it? That would be the sensible thing to do, wouldn't it?"

I looked at him, but his eyes didn't tell me a thing. "Now go on home to bed," he said. "If you must make that damned picture this summer, I've got a stack of plays I want you to read before you leave."

He walked me to the door and the next thing I knew I was out in the corridor and there was nothing to do but push the button for the elevator.

I stood on the corner of Forty-Fourth and looked up at the Paramount tower and saw that it was after one o'clock. I'd been walking around longer than I thought, just walking around getting nowhere. I turned then, and walked slowly back Forty-Fourth toward the Lambs Club.

So I was nuts. I had an aberration, as John Friday put it. Well, maybe so. But it was the most beautifully stage-managed aberration I'd ever heard of.

I remembered this night. It was the night *Say Goodbye* had closed at the Cochran Theatre and I'd decided to accept an offer to make a picture out on the Coast. With far-reaching and disastrous results.

For it was in Hollywood that I had first met Fern Costello.

Well, I thought, it's too bad I didn't know what that jaunt to California was going to cost me. I certainly shouldn't have made it if I had. If I hadn't gone to the Coast, I shouldn't have met Fern. If I hadn't met Fern, I should never have fallen in love with her, and sooner or later I might have been able to straighten things out with Sheila. If I'd never met her, I could never have, shaken by Sheila's suicide, gone into Fern's bedroom and suddenly, unbelievably, found myself choking her to death.

Those things would never have happened.

I stopped in front of the Lambs Club and looked down the dimly lighted, deserted street. Or put it another way, I thought. If this night were actually what it seems to be instead of what it obviously is—a delusion—then all those things would never have to happen at all. Knowing what I know now, I could change the whole course of my life. It would be up to me.

Abruptly I started to walk again—east. I crossed Sixth Avenue and kept on toward Fifth. A taxi passed me and slowed down, the driver looking back hopefully. I waved him on. On Fifth Avenue I turned south and headed toward Washington Square. There was one sure way to end this thing, one way to see it out to its bitter conclusion. I was on my way to do just that.

I walked through the spring night and my crowded mind busied itself nervously. I tried to worry about my fantasies, tried to force myself back into the morbid frame of mind which had become my accustomed norm. It didn't work very well. The healthy young body I seemed to be inhabiting shed worry like a dog shakes water off its back. Several times I caught myself actually hoping, but I tried to stop that right away. There was no percentage in kidding myself into a kick in the teeth.

I passed the Library and, after that, the Empire State, and I kept on going. What's got into you tonight, Barney? I asked myself. Why don't you accept this thing for what it is and go to a Mills Hotel and get a four-bit flop and sleep it off?

And then I passed a pet shop where I'd bought a dog once, a little white collie pup I'd taken home to Sheila when we were first married, and which she had loved and been good to. And I knew why I couldn't. As long as there was a chance, no matter how slim or far-fetched, that I could square things with the world and myself, I'd have to take that chance. Even if I'd wanted to stop or turn around, my feet wouldn't have let me. They'd have kept on going.

Twenty-Ninth, Twenty-Eighth, Twenty-Seventh, and Twenty-Sixth Streets. The Flatiron Building, and over, beyond it, the cool green of Madison Square locked in night. It was calm; it looked soothing. I crossed the street and went slowly along the winding paths.

Don't hope, Barney, I told myself. Don't be a God damned fool. Tomorrow morning will come and you'll be back where you started. Worse. You'll have lost something you never had, and you'll very likely be in jail for murder. This last year has played hell with you; you're nothing but a walking case of the nine-day horrors. Why don't you use what's left of your head? You've got a good start now. Grab a ferry and get over to Jersey and hop a freight. Get out of the State. Go to Mexico. Go some place where they don't know you and you can start all over again.

Start what over again? My life? That mess of unadulterated grief? I'd rather get it over with right now, one way or the other. I've got nothing I want to start doing all over again.

At Twenty-Third Street, the end of the park, I crossed the Avenue diagonally to the west side again. I was still headed south.

I was tired now, and a little confused. It was lonely on the corner; I might have been the last person left alive on earth. The only sign of life on the Avenue was a faint glow from Washington Square and the lights of the Brevoort against the black sky. I turned down Tenth Street, walking slowly.

The apartment house was still there just as it used to be. There were spring flowers in the window-boxes, and the white stone facings were soft in the glow of the street lamp. The outer door was unlocked as it always was, and I stepped inside and let it swing to behind me. I looked at the row of brass letter-boxes, at the place over the second one from the left where my own name used to be.

And then the backs of my knees gave way and my heart started pounding. The card over the box still read, *PAGE*.

I couldn't help myself. My hand shot out to the button above the card and I pushed it in the old signal. Two long rings and three short ones.

And I jerked my finger away and cursed myself for being a credulous, idiotic fool. Brother, I told myself, you certainly stick your neck out, don't you? I turned away and started out again.

Then the door latch clicked and I stopped like a steer that has just been hit in the head by the butcher's mallet. And from that time on I acted without conscious volition. I pushed open the inner door and jerkily mounted the stairs. The apartment door stood wide, and I paused outside for a second.

I went on in.

She tossed the magazine down on the couch beside her and smiled up at me a little petulantly.

"What on earth happened to you?" she asked. "I've been getting worried." She stretched her arms out and offered her cheek to be kissed.

I took off my hat and dropped it on the floor. Then I let myself down on my knees beside the couch. I reached out slowly and put my hand on her shoulder.

"Sheila," I said.

After a moment I kissed her.

The telephone was shrill and insistent.

Sheila disengaged herself and rose from the couch where we were sitting. She crossed the room and picked up the phone.

"Yes," she said into the mouthpiece, "he's home now. He just came in.... Thank you, but it hasn't been any trouble at all, really. Hold the line."

"It's for you." She turned to me. "Some man's been trying to get you all evening. He has a nice voice. He says his name is Jake Hershey."

Six

Little things, little things.... We're not free agents, independent men and women with wills of our own. We're just haphazard conglomerations of small happenings.

Sheila leaned back in the boat and let the sun drench

her face. "Tell me a story," she said sleepily. So this is what I told her.

Now look. A young punk takes his girl dancing at the Roseland. She tears her dress on a nail. There's nobody to blame and nobody to get mad at, so she takes it out on him. He takes her home, and she lives way to hell and gone out in Flatbush. All the way there she lets him have it, and he apologizes and she sulks. Finally, on her front porch, they make it up and spend until about four A.M. each one claiming it was his fault. *No, not you, sweetheart. I'm the one that's to blame. It's all my nasty temper.* So he doesn't get much sleep, and next morning when the alarm clock goes off he doesn't hear it. So he's fired.

So times are tough and he doesn't know what to do and he wanders down the street to the waterfront and a kind stranger buys him a couple of beers and he wakes up in the forecastle of a ship. So years pass, and with lots of hard labor and a few lucky breaks he gets to be captain.

So one night he's barging along full speed ahead and runs his ship smack into the business end of a torpedo, and the ship goes down leaving him hanging on a biscuit crate in the middle of the ocean with just enough life left to notice the flag of the submarine that downed him. So he reports what happened, and it develops with other things into an international incident and that leads to war.

So billions and billions of people get killed until finally he's the only man left alive in the whole world. And he's hungry. So he says to himself, if I only had a fish-hook maybe I could catch a fish. So he goes over to the ruins of a building that used to be the Roseland and he searches through the rubbish and he finds the very nail that started all the trouble in the first place.

So he bends it into a fish-hook and he goes down to the Hudson and he catches a big fat fish, and that day he doesn't starve to death.

Sheila looked up from the bottom of the boat and laughed. The sun was on her face and she looked lovely as she always did. I laughed, too, but not because I thought my story was funny. It wasn't, to me.

"Something's happened to you," Sheila said thoughtfully. "Ever since the play closed you've been different."

I became engrossed with the traffic on the lake. This was difficult, since there were only two other boats and the nearest one was fifty yards away, but it served my purpose. I fiddled with the oars and pretended not to be listening intently.

"You're not so ready to jump on me for every little thing," she went on. "You seem older."

"Better-looking, too," I said.

She ignored that. "What happened to you last week?" she wanted to know. "What changed you?"

I'd been expecting this. "Aren't you satisfied?"

She smiled. "Why shouldn't I be? We've had a wonderful season, everybody's raved about your work, and we actually have a bank balance." She examined the polish on her fingernails. "Now if you only wouldn't be silly about not making that picture, everything would be perfect."

I didn't say anything.

"Couldn't we go out to California, Barney? Think what it would mean to have a picture to your credit. It would darn near double your salary. And the weather is swell out there this time, of year." She held her hand out to me.

I took it in mine. It was small and very soft and warm.

"Darling," I said, "we'll go away if you like, but not to California. I've worked hard this year and I have a tough season coming up. We'll go to that place on Lake Michigan. We can have a swell time there. Don't you think you'd like that?"

Sheila shrugged and pulled her hand back. "It doesn't make any difference. Whatever you say." She closed her eyes and lay back in the boat, frowning slightly.

I looked down at her, at her pliable young body lying there at ease. God keep her that way, I thought. God keep her alive and beautiful. Never let me remember how I once saw her: in a hospital bed, grey and stiff before they pulled the sheet over her face.

I bent down and picked up her hand again and kissed it. She opened one eye to look at me. "Well!" she said, and laughed.

"Let's go home, Sheila," I said. "Don't you want to?"

She opened the other eye then and considered me gravely. "All right," she said at last. "Why not?"

I rowed over to the landing stage and we walked to the Fifty-Ninth Street entrance to the Park. I didn't bother with a bus; we took a taxi. I was in a hurry to get home.

When we got there William and Mary was waiting for us on the curb. That's the kind of breaks I get.

We walked down Waverly Place and turned up Gay Street, William and Mary and I. Half a dozen times on the way over from my apartment we said hello to different people, and it was quite an experience. I'd forgotten how many people I used to know and like, and who used to know and like me.

When we came to Fritz's Place, William and Mary started to go in, but I stopped on the corner. He turned at the door and came back to me.

"Love is a wonderful thing, my friend," he said. "But it can be carried to extremes."

"So?"

"So. You may be under the impression that you walked here from Fifth Avenue. You didn't. You sailed here, sitting on top of a pink cloud with lace trimmings.

I had to pull you out from under the wheels of one taxi and three trucks."

"Thanks."

"Don't mention it. But you and Sheila have been all alone in your private dream-world ever since the play closed. Couldn't you park the cloud for a few minutes and climb down to earth?"

I laughed. "Okay," I said. "Go on in and I'll be with you in a minute."

"But Jake Hershey is waiting for us. He's pestered me for a week to fix it so he could have a talk with you."

I knew that only too well, just as I knew why Jake wanted to meet me and what he wanted to talk about. Not that I had got used to being able to foresee these things; I could never accept that calmly. But I'd come to the point where I was willing to play along without asking too many questions.

"Take him in the back room and buy him a drink," I said. "Tell him he's written a great play and that I can hardly wait to take it to John Friday. That should hold him."

"How do you know it's a great play?" William and Mary asked. "You haven't read it."

"I'm psychic," I said. "Between you and me, it's going to win the Pulitzer Prize next year if it's properly handled. I'll see that it's properly handled."

William and Mary turned his penetrating black eyes on me. "Sometime," he said, "I want to have a talk with you."

"You do that practically every day."

"I know." He nodded soberly. "But this time I'd like you to do some of the talking. I have an idea that maybe you could tell me something I want to know."

And he turned and pushed through the swinging doors. I'll have to soft-pedal that sort of talk, I said to myself. I can't be pulling that psychic gag all the time.

But it was a swell spring afternoon; it wasn't made for worry. The sun was warm on the cobblestones and the organ-grinders were out in force with all their monkeys freshly washed and in new clothes. All over the Village the hand-organs were grinding away. And the peddlers had fresh flowers and fruit in their pushcarts and wore clean bandannas around their necks. Nobody knew better than I what a swell day it was.

I hope to Christ I'm not doing the wrong thing, I thought. It seems to me it would be foolish to pack Sheila up and run away with her. After all, I have to work for a living, and New York is the only place I can work. And Jake Hershey does have a good play. If I'm careful I can make enough money out of it to leave town for a long while. And God knows Jake is harmless enough—as long as he and Sheila never meet. All I have to do is keep them from meeting.

So I smiled to myself and pushed the swinging doors aside and followed William and Mary into Fritz's Place, as Fritz's Place was before he died.

It wasn't streamlined and it wasn't antiseptic. It was less like a cocktail lounge than any place you could imagine. It was cool and it smelled of beer, and there was sawdust on the floor and a handsome oil painting of a nude Junoesque female over the bar. The trim, disillusioned barkeep was not there, and, in his place, it didn't seem at all strange to see Fritz methodically slapping suds from the top of foaming glasses with a tongue depressor.

He saw me and yelled to come over and have a drink on the house. His red face beamed and his bald head nodded cheerfully; he looked as much like a Schubert musical comedy bartender as he ever did. So I crossed the room and put my foot on the rail and said I'd have a glass of ginger ale.

He looked at me and sighed. "Come off it," he said.

"I'll fix you a whiskey sour. On the rocks."

"I'm on the wagon," I told him. "Strictly high and dry from now on."

There was a drunk standing next to me who seemed to think this was funny. He laughed.

Fritz leaned over the bar until his face was only a few inches from the drunk's. Their noses were almost rubbing. "Listen," he said; "if my friend says he ain't drinking, then he ain't drinking. See? There ain't nothing funny about that, is there?" His dripping bar rag was held lightly in his hand and he reached across the counter and slapped the drunk in the face with it, "Get out," he said.

The drunk went; in certain moods Fritz wasn't a man to be trifled with, and his customers knew it. He either liked you or he didn't, and, if he didn't, you were better off outside.

Fritz reached for the special bottle he kept under the bar, poured a shot for himself and a glass of ginger ale for me, and set the drinks down between us.

"I've missed you this last week," he said. "Where have you been hiding out?"

I didn't answer. There was a nicely dressed little fellow with white hair and a white moustache standing at the far end of the bar. I recognized him. He seemed to be an innocuous little man, polite and inoffensive-looking, but I knew, nevertheless, that a few months from now he would swear out the complaint which would eventually land William and Mary in the nuthouse.

Unless he was stopped. Unless somebody stopped him. And it looked as though the somebody would have to be me. I turned back to Fritz.

"That little guy down at the end," I said. "Do you know who he is?"

Fritz turned to consider the stranger. "He comes in every once in a while," he told me. "Every six months or so. His name is Roberts. From somewhere out West, I think. He's quiet enough and he's got plenty of money. He don't do no harm."

"Maybe," I said. "I hope you're right."

Fritz looked up sharply. "What do you mean?"

I played coy. "Oh, hell," I shrugged. "There's probably nothing in it at all."

"In what?"

"The story that Roberts is a member of the Bund. Maybe he's nothing of the kind. You can't believe everything you hear, can you?"

Fritz looked thoughtful. "I'll fix the son of a bitch," he muttered.

I raised my glass of ginger ale to him and drank it off. Then I started toward the back room feeling pretty pleased with myself. I knew that things would shortly become too hot for Brother Roberts. He'd go back uptown where he belonged, and the chances were he'd never even see William and Mary.

Jake Hershey's intelligent eyes looked gratefully at me through his horn-rimmed glasses. And his voice was as pleasant as Sheila had noticed it was over the telephone.

"That certainly is decent of you, Mr. Page," he said. "You have no idea how hard it is for an unknown playwright even to get his stuff read."

William and Mary sat between us, saying little. He beamed on us both impartially and from time to time allowed Jake to buy him another drink. He looked very happy.

"Friday will read it, all right," I promised. "In fact, I can almost guarantee you a fall production."

"That would be great," Jake said. He looked at me a little shyly. "You know, I wish you'd consider the part of Everett Stanton. I've admired your work ever since I saw you in *Say Goodbye*."

"I was good before then, too," I told him pleasantly.

"And all this isn't pure philanthropy on my side. The part of Stanton is the one I had in mind."

He jerked his head in enthusiastic agreement. "That makes me feel better. It's nice to think your work is being accepted on its merits alone. I wonder—" he began, and stopped.

"What is it?"

"William was telling me you are married," he went on. "I wonder if you and Mrs. Page would have dinner with me tomorrow night at Madame Céleste's. We could make a little party of it; sort of a celebration, you know."

"Why not tonight?" William and Mary accepted. "Or, for that matter, this afternoon?"

I looked at Jake thoughtfully for a minute before I answered. He's a pretty decent sort of guy, I thought. It's too bad. Then I shook my head slowly and definitely.

"That's out," I said. "I never mix business and pleasure."

"But—"

"Furthermore," I added, "my wife is allergic to playwrights." I didn't like to hurt him, but it had to be done.

"I see," he said.

There was a commotion in the bar and a streak like a rush of wind went past our table. The door to the men's room banged. We all looked at each other.

"What was that?" I asked.

Strange sounds issued from inside, and then a sudden thump as if a body had dropped on the floor. William and Mary stood up.

"I'll see what's happened," he said. We watched him as he opened the door and went inside. In a minute he came back again.

"Get me a taxi," he told Jake Hershey. And when Jake had gone he grinned at me. "Fritz slipped one of his customers a Mickey Finn," he explained. "I'll take him home."

I remembered something. "Who is this guy?" I wanted to know.

William and Mary's grin broadened. "A little fellow who's going to be very, very useful to me," he said. "He's got lots of money; a veritable prince of merchants. His name is Roberts."

He went back into the men's room and picked up the semiconscious figure of the man who would eventually have him committed. He half-carried him out the side door to the curb where the taxi would stop. I sat there and watched him do it. There was nothing else for me to do.

And for a long time after he had gone I continued to sit there, drumming on the table with my fingers and thinking.

Seven

Pete McCord was to be married on the sixth of June and the latest communiqué from the Boston front reported that Sis would arrive on the morning of the wedding. Meanwhile, he was something of a problem. No matter where he happened to be, his mind was somewhere else.

So, on the Saturday night before the big event Sheila and I took him along to see *Life With Father*. John Friday met us in the foyer and we got into our seats just before the curtain rose. It was a swell performance, and it was pleasant to sit back and watch other people work for a change.

After the play Sheila and I were ready to get a sandwich and go home. At least I was. But John and Pete had other ideas, so we all adjourned to a place on Forty-Fourth to talk them over. We sat at a table entirely surrounded by photographs of operatic personages, and John started ordering drinks. But I vetoed that.

"Sheila and I are on the wagon," I said.

"That's the first I heard about it." Sheila flashed a smile at me and quickly looked away. "If you won't take me to California you'll have to let me have my fun where I can find it."

So she ordered a Scotch-and-soda and when it came I tried not to watch her drink it. I felt like kicking myself for not having had this out with her before. I should have known better than to think she might fall into line that easily.

We talked for half an hour or so and then Sheila excused herself to powder her nose. John and Pete had another drink while she was away and it was decided that, since this was practically Pete's last night of freedom, we would finish the evening at Madame Céleste's.

Sheila was gone a long time and, when she came back, we had the bill paid and were ready to go. We took a taxi straight down Sixth Avenue and then over Christopher Street. We got out in front of Madame Céleste's and went into the deserted downstairs dining room. As we passed Henri sitting in the darkness of the stairs, I took hold of Sheila's elbow and drew her toward me.

"Please don't take another drink," I whispered. "Just as a favor to me. I'll talk to you about it later."

She gave me a queer little smile and didn't say anything at all. Then we left her at the women's room on the landing and went on up to get a table. The place was packed, but a waiter in a Russian blouse recognized me and produced a table from nowhere. We sat down at the far end of the room away from the piano.

After we had ordered, John put his menu to one side

and leaned across the table in my direction. I fidgeted. John made me a little uncomfortable these days. I didn't know quite how to take him.

"Barney," he said, "why did you decide not to go to Hollywood?"

"Because," I answered immediately, "I want to play Everett Stanton." And that was the truth even if it wasn't the reason.

"Oh yes." John drummed on the tablecloth with his fingers. "That new play you gave me. I've read it."

"Well?"

He appeared to be considering his answer. "Not bad," he said at last. "Not bad."

"You're damned tootin' it's not bad," I told him. "In fact, it's good. It's a natural and you know it."

"Maybe," he admitted. "Perhaps. I'd like to talk to the author."

Pete chimed in then. "That's easy. He's sitting over there by the piano."

I turned around quickly. Pete was right. Jake was sitting at a big round table with William and Mary and half a dozen others. Jock McIntyre, Bob Evans, Ruth Goldberg, Hilda Fleming, and a couple I knew only casually as Tom Deems and his wife. Damn it, I thought, why does that guy have to show up every place I go? I'll have to step on this before it can get any farther.

Evidently John was of the same mind. "This is no place to talk," he said. "Bring him to my office next week."

I said that would be okay and I got up and walked over to the big table.

Hilda Fleming was giving her forceful and lengthy opinion of the current Harry Bridges deportation order, and everyone was listening intently, hoping for the slightest pause that would give them a chance to air their own views. But they were quiet; Hilda could be cutting if she was interrupted; when she spoke everyone was pretty respectful. Everyone, of course, except William and Mary who had found a mechanical mouse somewhere and was amusing himself by running it up and down the tablecloth.

"Hello," I said. "Hello, Jake. Hello, William."

Hilda stopped talking and told me to sit down and have a drink. Everyone seconded the invitation. Only William and Mary remained aloof. He haughtily picked up his mouse and scowled at me.

"My name is Mary," he said.

He dropped the mouse and it ran off the table. I stooped to pick it up and took advantage of my position to look under the tablecloth and, sure enough, he was wearing a skirt. "Sorry, Mary," I said. Then I turned to the others and told them thanks, that I couldn't sit down, that I wasn't drinking any more, that I had a party of my own, and that we were discussing business. That should stop them, I thought.

I put my hand on Jake Hershey's shoulder. "Friday has read your play and he likes it. He wants to talk to you." I pushed down on his shoulder when I felt him start to rise. "Some day next week," I said, "I'll call you and we'll go up to his office."

He relaxed, beaming at me through his horn-rimmed glasses. "So long, kids," I said. "So long, Mary." I turned back to my own table and everyone started talking at once, each hoping to beat Hilda to the punch. But they were only amateurs. Hilda was halfway through an involved syllogism before anyone else could stammer a first premise. All that talk, I thought. All that talk. If they only knew what I know.

When I got back, Sheila was still missing, but John Friday had something on his mind, so I settled down to listen.

"Now about this Hershey play. Who'd do the woman's part?"

"Any one of fifteen leading ladies," I told him. "It's practically actor-proof."

"That's the opinion you always have of any part you're not playing." He shook his head. "This woman has to be a definite type, and if she's miscast the whole play goes phooey. It's not so easy."

"Don't worry, John," I said. "You have until next fall. You'll have more types on your hands by that time than you'll be able to fit on your casting couch."

I broke off the conversation. Sheila was coming toward us. And she didn't look any too good.

Her eyes were unnaturally large and dark and I saw that the pupils were expanded to fill the entire iris. She was smiling vaguely and walking with extreme care. I stepped away from the table and drew back her chair for her, managing, as she sat down, to brush my hand against her purse. She had a pint bottle in there, all right, but there wasn't much I could do about it now; it was probably empty by this time.

Between two and two-thirty on a Sunday morning Madame Céleste's reaches what might be described as its zenith. Personally, viewing it from a sober angle for the first time in my life, I was more inclined to consider it as a nadir.

Or maybe my attitude was biased; maybe I was just worried. Sheila had spoken hardly a word all evening, just sat quietly in her chair and looked at things with those wide eyes and that vague smile. Sometimes she answered shortly when she was spoken to, but usually she limited her replies to a little nod or a shake of the head. Her conversation, until the present moment, had consisted of totally irrelevant remarks concerning the lovable qualities of myself, John Friday, Pete McCord, Madame Céleste's, dogs, Scotch whiskey, and the world in general. She loved them all. Anyone else would have said she carried her liquor well. I knew better. The only reason I hadn't hustled her home before this was because it would have been sure to precipitate a scene.

And now the first dissatisfied note crept in. She noticed the big party over by the window and felt slighted because William and Mary hadn't come over to speak to her.

"Why hasn't he?" she wanted to know. "I've always been nice to him, haven't I? Why doesn't he speak to me? Doesn't he like me anymore?"

I tried to explain that the William part of our friend was temporarily in abeyance; that one could hardly expect the Mary part to come over to our table and that she'd better keep out of the women's room if she didn't want to be embarrassed. None of it registered.

"You talked to him," she said. "You told him not to speak to me, didn't you? You're always doing things like that, aren't you?" Her eyes were hot.

I hastily excused myself and went back to the big table. I stole a chair on the way, slipped it into place beside William and Mary and sat down. He was quite drunk and the mechanical mouse still claimed all of his attention. I took him by the arm and spoke to him confidentially.

"Hello, Mary," I said. "That's a nice mouse."

He looked up. "My friend," he replied, "you understate the matter. This is not a nice mouse. This is a superb mouse. They don't make mice like this anymore."

"No doubt," I agreed. "Sheila was asking about you."

"Ah," he said; "and how is dear Sheila?"

"She's fine. How about coming over to our table and speaking to her?"

He thought about this for a moment, and then shook his head. "I am afraid that is impossible," he said. "I admire your wife very much. Such a lovely girl. I would do anything for her. I would give her my most prized possession. But I cannot go over to your table to speak to her. Because," he continued, "if at this moment I tried to stand up, I should fall flat on my face, and then they would carry me home. And I don't want to go home yet."

I saw his point. "Well," I said, and got up; "I'll tell her you were asking about her." I started away.

"Come here," he said, and, when I turned back to him, "You will do nothing of the sort. I send my own messages. Go to your table and say absolutely nothing. You will hear from me shortly. Meanwhile"—he plucked a wilted carnation from the vase on the table—"give this to dear Sheila. Tell her it is from an unknown admirer."

I took the carnation and thanked him and went on back to my own seat. When I got there, I found that Sheila had already forgotten about William and Mary and was happily expounding a revolutionary theory about dogs and babies. It seemed that they could infallibly tell a good man from a bad man and that horses had the same psychic gift as well. But not cows. Only dogs and babies and horses.

This developed into a lengthy discussion. It had just reached the point where Pete was advocating the removal of all adult humans from juries and the substitution of animals and babies, when Henri ambled over to us carrying a large bunch of frayed flowers and a little cardboard box tied with a pink ribbon.

"From an admirer of Madame's." He gallantly laid the bouquet in front of Sheila. She gave a cry of pleasure, and I knew that William and Mary had made good his promise. He had sent her his most prized possession, whatever that might be.

Henri meandered off toward the stairs and Sheila untied the pink box. She took off the tap and lifted a layer of tissue paper. We all leaned forward to see what was inside.

Then she dropped the box and froze stiff in her chair, her face a pale, drained mask of horror.

The box lit on the table beside her glass, tilted over, and the mechanical mouse fell out. It landed right side up and scurried straight toward Sheila. It ran off the edge of the table, fell into her lap, and made futile little rushings here and there on her dress. The mechanism was wound up tight.

Sheila screamed. And the room came to a dead standstill. Before I could get to my feet, she screamed a second time, and in the stricken silence it was a horrible sound.

She couldn't help it. I grabbed the mouse, threw it across the room, put my arms around her and held her tight. "Sheila," I said, "for Christ's sake, stop. Sheila!" But she just sat there with her mouth open and that noise coming out of it.

So I slapped her. She shuddered and stared at me, and I slapped her again. Suddenly she burst into tears. "Get me out of here," she sobbed. "Barney, get me out of here."

I nodded to John Friday and Pete, and helped her to her feet. With my arms around her, we moved to the head of the stairs, winding our way between the tables filled with curious people.

A little group of our friends met us at the stairs. Could they do anything? I told them no.

"Can't I help?" Jake Hershey asked.

"No, thanks," I said. "We'll be all right."

We got downstairs and into the street. A taxi was waiting there and I helped Sheila into it. Then I turned to John and Pete waiting helplessly on the sidewalk.

"Thanks for everything," I said. "Don't worry."

They nodded doubtfully and watched me climb into the cab after Sheila. I called our address to the driver and we started off, leaving them standing on the sidewalk staring after us.

I put my arms around Sheila. "Take it easy, baby. You'll be all right now."

She didn't answer. She buried her head on my shoulder and kept it there all through the ride.

When we got home, I helped her undress and get into bed. I took her pulse; it was erratic and very fast, about a hundred and forty. I went out to the bathroom and looked in the medicine cabinet, but there was nothing there but accumulated odds and ends, so I tiptoed back into the bedroom, turned off all the lights except a small reading lamp by the chair, and quickly got out of my clothes and into my pajamas and bathrobe. I knew that Sheila was still awake, but she was very quiet, lying with her face in the pillow.

Just as I was about to settle down in the chair, I heard a tapping on the front door. So I went out through the living room and into the little corridor by the kitchen, opened the door slightly and peered out.

Pete McCord stood there, looking worried.

"How is she?" he whispered.

"She'll be okay," I said. "She's going to sleep now."

"Good." He felt in his pocket and brought out a little round box, the kind they use in pharmacies. "If she's very upset, you can give her one of these. Jake Hershey ran over home and got them for her."

"Thanks, Pete," I said. "Thank Jake for me. But she's in good shape now. Good night."

"Sure," Pete said. "Of course she is. Good night."

He went down the stairs, and I put the medicine box in the pocket of my bathrobe and closed the door. When I got back to the bedroom, Sheila's breathing was deep and regular as if she were asleep. So I took a blanket off the other twin bed, wrapped it around myself, and settled down in the easy-chair and switched off the light. I didn't want to turn in until I was absolutely sure Sheila was going to be all right.

I must have been pretty tired because, when Sheila screamed again, it awakened me from a sound sleep. It wasn't as bad an attack as the one she had had at Madame Céleste's, and the tears came almost immediately. As I sat on the edge of the bed, holding her, I saw by the luminous dial of the clock that it was a little after four. I had slept for over an hour.

"Better, darling?" I asked. "There's nothing to be afraid of. Nothing at all."

She murmured something I didn't understand, but I could feel her lips moving against my shoulder and I bent my head to catch what she was whispering.

"It's those little feet," she cried softly. "They come scratching at me in the dark."

"I know. A lot of women are like that."

"I'm not really a coward, Barney. I'm not afraid of spiders or snakes."

"Of course you're not afraid," I said. "Now I'm going in the bathroom to get something that will make you feel better. Will you be all right for a minute by yourself?"

"Oh yes, Barney. Leave the light on. It's just those little scratching feet."

"We'll fix it," I told her. "Hold tight and I'll be right back."

I got up from the bed and went into the bathroom, closed the door, and switched on the light. I took the green toothbrush glass from its rack, washed it out, and filled it with cool water. Then I felt in the pocket of my bathrobe and brought out the box of medicine Jake Hershey had sent over by Pete.

I took the top off the box and started to pour the capsules into my hand. Then I stopped and just stood there staring at them.

I must have stood there for a full minute doing nothing.

Just counting the capsules over and over. They were

an unmistakable light blue in color and there were three of them. I counted them—one—two—three. And I knew that each capsule contained three grains. Three times three makes nine. Nine grains.

Then I stepped over to the toilet, lifted the seat, and carefully poured the three capsules into the bowl. I flushed the toilet and watched nine grains of sodium amytal rush down the drain.

When they were gone and the toilet was quiet again, I switched off the light, opened the door, and crept into the bedroom. I went over to Sheila's bed, dropped my bathrobe on the floor, slipped into bed beside her and held her tight.

Eight

I was worried, and so, while I waited, I tried to think of things other than the ones I was worried about. I looked out of Doctor Birnbaum's window and thought how Tenth Street, from up here, assumed a different perspective, angular and distorted. The personal touch which comes with living lower down was missing; from the fifth floor things seemed farther away and not nearly so friendly.

The cold heights of science, I thought. All doctors live aloofly, one way or another. But isn't there such a thing as being too objective? I wondered about all these things, but chiefly I wondered what in hell was keeping him so long. Sheila wasn't that sick; she really wasn't sick at all. It was only because I was a little concerned about her hysteria of the night before that I had asked Birnbaum to give her a casual once-over.

He came in, at last, just as I was about to go downstairs myself. He switched his long frame over to a chair in front of me and dropped into it moodily. Then he went into a trance with his legs stuck out in front of him, hands clasped over his stomach and eyes contemplating his hands with all the attention of a rapt Buddha. I waited for him to finish his performance and get down to business. I'd known the Doc for over a year and he was utterly honest. Furthermore, he was young—about thirty-five—and his bedside manner stank. All these things gave me confidence in his judgment.

Finally he snapped out of it. He sighed, and I saw that he was ready to talk.

"Well," I said, "let's have the verdict. It can't be any worse than the face you're making."

He fished a loose cigarette from his pocket and lit it without offering one to me. "There's nothing to be alarmed about," he said. "It's quite common."

"What is?"

"Sheila's condition."

"Is she all right?"

"She's nervous," he said. "Naturally. She doesn't drink much as a rule, does she?"

"Not much," I told him. "Hardly ever, anymore."

"But she used to? You'll have to help me out, Barney. I can't make a diagnosis without knowing something about the case."

"I'll tell you whatever you want," I said. "You mustn't get the wrong impression. She drank a little before we were married—spasmodically. No more than the girls she lived with did." I shrugged. "Less, probably."

"Tell me about them," Birnbaum said. "And about her family. She's not from New York originally."

"She was born in Canton, Ohio," I told him. "But— what with boarding schools and such—I don't think she spent much time there. Her father took her to Europe when she was eighteen, and, on their way home, she insisted on stopping off here. He let her. I guess he let her do what she wanted most of the time. I met her the next year. I can't be very definite about her childhood because there are two stories and they don't always dovetail."

Birnbaum screwed up his forehead and blew out a cloud of smoke. "What do you mean?"

I hesitated. "Don't you think you'd better ask Sheila, herself? After all—"

"I have her version of the story already," he said. "Now, I'd like to hear yours."

I thought about it and made up my mind. "Ask your questions. But give me a cigarette first, please."

He handed me his package and watched while I took one out and lit it. His eyes didn't miss a thing. "Now let's have it," he said. "The whole story. Start from the time you met her."

I took a drag on the cigarette. "She had an apartment up on East Fifty-Second," I told him. "A nice apartment. She was studying art. She lived with a couple of other girls who were supposed to be doing the same thing. They didn't get much studying done. You know the type, Doctor: spoiled kids who had persuaded their families and themselves that they were misunderstood geniuses."

Birnbaum nodded.

"There was a hectic atmosphere in the apartment, but it was amusing. I used to have a lot of fun there before Sheila moved in. But when she did, and I met her, the whole thing soured on me. It wasn't amusing to see her in that setting. She seemed out of place there, and it worried me as to what it would do to her."

"She was very beautiful, wasn't she?" Birnbaum looked at me keenly.

"She's still beautiful, Doctor," I told him. "But she was lovely then. You can understand why I didn't like to see her in that set-up. It seemed such a waste. And the pace began to get her down almost immediately; she started losing weight and looking badly. Sheila's never been the sort of person who does things halfway; it's everything or nothing for her. I tried to get her to go easy."

"What happened?"

"She laughed at me," I said. "She said I reminded her of her father and that she was able to look out for herself. So I told her to go ahead and do it; that I'd already worn myself out trying to keep up with her. I stopped seeing her."

"For how long?" Birnbaum asked.

"Not very long." I smiled ruefully. "I was pretty miserable. I made a point of meeting her accidentally. She seemed glad to see me and I know I was glad to see her. That was when I asked her to marry me."

The Doctor looked at me, but made no comment. After a moment, I went on:

"She didn't say yes and she didn't say no." I shrugged. "And all the time I was trying to get a definite answer we were swinging right back into the old routine. Parties, late hours—my work began to go to pieces. I got mad one day. I told her she'd either have to marry me and begin living like a normal human being, or we'd call the whole thing off. She laughed at me again, and this time I fixed it so I couldn't meet her accidentally or otherwise. I got a job and went out on the road and I didn't hear from her or write to her for four months."

"Would you say that you were in love with her, Barney?"

"Hell, Doctor," I told him. "How should I know? I was sleeping badly and my nerves were jumpy and I had her on my mind. If that's love, I guess I was in love."

"Go on," Birnbaum said. "What happened when you came back?"

"I was staying at the Club. There was a letter from her waiting for me. It scared me and I went up to the apartment right away."

"Scared you?"

"She said she'd been sick," I told him. "She said her father insisted that she come home and she didn't intend to do it. It sounded desperate, sort of, and I started thinking about her mother."

"What about her mother?"

"She committed suicide," I said. "I'll tell you about her in a minute. Anyway, I was scared. I hurried up to see her and she was in bed. She was alone. She'd been ill for quite a while."

"What was the trouble?"

I looked at the glowing end of my cigarette. Then I carefully snubbed it in the ash tray. "She'd taken an overdose of sleeping pills," I said.

Birnbaum's chin jerked up. "Purposely?"

I hesitated. "I don't think so, Doctor. But she was in a bad way. I gathered that, after I'd left town, she'd gone a little haywire. Liquor, you know. She told me it was because I'd left her, and I had no reason not to believe her. As for the sleeping pills, she'd started taking them to get her over hangovers. It must have been a pretty bad situation because the other two girls had gone off and taken an apartment by themselves, leaving her alone. I felt rotten about it."

"Why?" Birnbaum asked. "It wasn't your fault."

"That may be so, Doctor," I admitted. "But I didn't see it like that. Not at the time, anyway."

"About these sedatives—barbiturates, I imagine?— does she use them now?"

I looked at him. "I won't have the damned stuff in the house," I told him, and looked away. "Give me another cigarette, please."

"How did Sheila feel about her father demanding that she go home?"

I lit the cigarette. "She said he'd cut off her allowance to force her to obey. I asked her why she wouldn't do what he wanted—after all, she had a good home; her father had always been kind to her. She said that he was too kind, and that she was afraid of him. I called her on that: I wanted to know exactly what she meant. It was hard to pin her down; the way she put it was that he loved her too much. But what she implied was incest."

Birnbaum was silent and, after a minute, I braced myself to go on:

"I pried pretty deeply into her background then. I felt that I had to, for her sake. I found that her mother had deserted her when she was a baby. Ran off with another man and, later, committed suicide. Sheila didn't blame her mother. According to her, the whole thing was her father's fault. Right now she idolizes a romantic memory of her mother."

"She made no specific charges against her father?"

"No," I said. "She was reluctant to talk about him at all. But she painted a sketchy picture of a man who had terrorized her for years with his advances. It made me sick to think of it. I told her she'd never have to go home to that. I got her dressed and took her to a hotel. We drove up to Greenwich and got married as soon as she was able to."

Doctor Birnbaum drew a deep breath. "So!" he said. "And how about your marriage? Sexual relations all right?"

"As far as I'm concerned, they're swell."

"And as far as Sheila is concerned?"

I spread my hands. "I haven't had any complaints."

"But you have no children."

"No," I said. "What with the uncertainty of my work and—things—we've never felt that we were in a position to."

Birnbaum tapped on his knee with his finger—thoughtfully. "You might keep that in mind as a possible solution to your troubles," he told me. "But

right now I want to go back a little farther. You spoke
of two stories that didn't dovetail. What did you
mean?"

"After we'd been married a little over a year," I said,
"Sheila's father came to see me at the theatre. When
the doorman told me who was calling, I saw red.
During the first few minutes of our conversation I
called him everything I could think of. That was a
mistake. I knew it as soon as I took time to look at
him. He was a good guy, a decent citizen who was
hurt and bewildered by the way Sheila was treating
him. I wasn't bewildered; I saw it clearly enough when
I stopped to think about it. She'd let me believe that
stuff just because it served her purpose; it was a
dramatic excuse for not going home when her father
wanted her to. And Sheila's always had a flair for the
dramatic, regardless of consequences. That's hard to
understand, isn't it?"

"Not necessarily," Birnbaum said. "I knew a medical
student once who was never late to class because he'd
overslept; he'd always been in a train wreck or got
caught in a burning building. We all touch up our
backgrounds for the public view. The only difference
is that we have varying tastes in shade and color. Tell
me this: did you ever tell Sheila that you knew she'd
lied?"

I felt my face getting hot. "I didn't intend to," I said.
"We had word that her father had died shortly after
that; and I thought it was better to forget the whole
thing. But it came out one day in an argument six
months or so later. It was an argument that had been
brewing for a long time. I was pretty well fed up with
the whole situation. When I blurted it out about her
father, she didn't attempt to deny it. She just laughed
at me. I walked out on her."

The Doctor held the ash tray out to me and I put my
cigarette in it. It had been burning my fingers. "I might

as well tell you this too, Doc. As I said, this fight had been under way for quite a while. There were a lot of reasons for it, but jealousy was the chief one. There was cause for it on both sides. When I left Sheila it wasn't just because I was fed up with her. I'd fallen in love with another girl."

Doc Birnbaum smiled to himself. "Love. A little while ago you refused to use that word. You don't seem to have any objection to it now. I take it that this case was different."

I thought about it. "Yes, Doc," I said. "I guess this case was different."

There was a pause then. He unfolded himself and walked over to the window. "Yet you came back to Sheila again," he said. "You left this other girl. Why?"

"I had to."

"Because of Sheila?"

I nodded my head. "She got sick again."

"And your conscience started bothering you again. You have an uncomfortable conscience, Barney."

"I can't help that," I said. "I saw that I'd made a mistake and I did the best I could to set matters right. It wasn't easy. But when I came back, I made up my mind it was going to be for good. I'm here to stay, now."

After a minute Birnbaum came back to his chair. He sat down and faced me. "I'm going to talk to you like a Dutch uncle," he said.

"Go to it. That's what I came here for."

"This is off the record. I haven't enough to go on for a complete diagnosis. I can't help but feel that you're holding back something I ought to know, and that makes it difficult. You understand?"

"I'm sorry you think that, Doctor. I've told you all I can."

"Perhaps." He leaned toward me a little. "To begin with, I don't think there can be any question but that

Sheila is neurotic. I wouldn't go so far as to say the same of you. At present."

"You give me hope," I murmured.

He looked at me. "You dodged this question once," he said. "I'm going to put it to you another way. You know Sheila pretty well now. How do you really feel about her?"

I answered him as truthfully as I could. "I'm married to her. Damn it, she's my wife. A guy feels differently about his wife. Sheila's welfare is bound up in mine in a way I could never explain to you. I'd cut off my right arm to guarantee her a calm, rational, normal life. I mean that." And Birnbaum nodded slowly. I felt a little sympathy oozing out of him.

"You have a tough job ahead of you, Barney," he said. "Sheila's a hysterical type. The episode last night proved that. And she's—well, let's say that she's not emotionally mature. Does that explain things?"

"She's no moron," I told him.

"I didn't mean that. Physically and intellectually, she's a well-developed woman. Emotionally she's a child. She's the kind that can't hear sad music without bursting into tears; she'd throw a fit if you asked her to bait her own fish-hook. She screams at the very thought of a mouse. Isn't all that true?"

It was true, and it worried me more than I cared to admit. All of Sheila's actions in the past proved that she—well, *emotionally immature* was a kind phrase for it. Why else had the sight of those few grains of sodium amytal shocked me so? No mature person, no—say it—sane person kills herself.

I nerved myself for the direct question. "Is Sheila—?" But it was no use. I couldn't get it out.

The Doctor shook his head. "No," he said, "she's not. No more than a lot of us are. We're all a little off, of course. You've done things which, if they were brought to the formal notice of a sanity commission, would put you in the State Hospital ten times over. I have, too. But there's a place for you in society and there's a place for me in society; we've been able to adjust our little quirks to fit everyday life. I think Sheila should be able to adjust herself, too. But she'll need help."

"Help?"

"Your understanding and tolerance. It's quite possible," he said, "that she will go on for years—maybe forever—leading a normal life. From the little I know of the case, I don't see why she shouldn't, provided you keep yourself in hand. You'll have to curb your temper and your very natural jealousy. You'll have to do it for two reasons: for Sheila's sake and for your own. Because, Barney," he told me, "very frankly, you can't stand that sort of thing. You're none too stable yourself."

"I know that."

He straightened up. "Do you think you'll be able to handle it?"

I rose from the chair. "I guess it just has to be done."

"Do you think you'll be able to?" he insisted.

"I guess I'll have to," I said.

I left him then and went downstairs to Sheila. Birnbaum had me worried, all right. But the more I thought of it, the more I realized that, actually, he hadn't told me anything I didn't know before. And there were several things I hadn't told him.

I couldn't very well tell him, for instance, that when I'd left the girl I'd fallen in love with and gone back to Sheila again, it had been already too late. That Sheila had already killed herself. I couldn't very well have told him that. If I'd gone beyond a certain point in my confidences, he'd have brought out the restraints and telephoned for the ambulance. Not for Sheila; for myself.

Even at that I'd got some good out of the talk. I was ready to accept Birnbaum's advice for what it was worth. I thought I knew how to deal with the situation now. If tolerance and understanding would turn the trick, well—I'd had a lesson in both of them. A sharper lesson than any doctor could ever teach me.

Nine

The morning started out badly. Everybody felt tense. I lay on the couch in the living room watching Pete McCord pace a furrow in the rug. He had me in a ticklish spot with this marriage of his.

I couldn't say, "Look here, Pete. This little tramp you're so hot for is going to make life one long merry hell for you. My advice is to go down to the church, spit in her eye, and kick her back to Boston."

I couldn't say that. I couldn't do anything except grin and tell him that, although I'd never met her, I was sure that Sis was a wonderful, wonderful girl and that he and she would be very, very happy.

And they would be, if I had anything to say about it. I was determined that the first time his bride made a motion toward parking her shoes under my bed, they were going to be thrown out the window and she was going to follow them. I wasn't taking any chances on losing Pete's friendship. I knew what it was like to hurt a man you thought a lot of, and to be cut by him and his friends from then on. This time, Sis old girl, I thought, those eyes will roll and those buttocks undulate in vain. I'm pure.

Sheila's entrance put an end to my chaste resolutions. She had been over at Pete's studio to welcome the bride and her messy brother, and she announced that it was time to start for the church. I got up from the couch and felt in my pocket to see if the ring was still there, and sighed. Pete stopped walking around and stood in one place looking at the rug, and sighed. And Sheila sighed, too, just for company.

Then the phone rang. It was John Friday and he wanted me to tell Pete that he wouldn't be able to get to the church, but would show up at the studio afterward. And could he bring a friend along?

"Wait until you see her," his voice bubbled. "She's a natural for the lead in Hershey's play. An old friend of mine and I never thought of her. Isn't that funny?"

"It's a scream," I said. "You can't even go to a wedding without mentally putting the bridesmaids in rehearsals rompers. You have business on the brain. We'll meet you at the studio, and I hope you'll remember it's a wedding breakfast and not a chorus call."

I hung up the phone and turned to Pete. "Well, my lad. You look as though you need a drink."

"I do," he agreed. So I went into the kitchen and poured a stiff one and mixed in half a lemon and a suspicion of water to take the curse off. I was economizing on my guests' liquor since I'd stopped using it myself. I carried it back to him in the living room and was gratified to see Sheila turn away quickly while he drank it. Physically, she was as well as ever, but the moral effect of Saturday night's binge still lingered.

We left the apartment and walked up to Fifth Avenue and caught a cab. They were being married in the Little Church Around the Corner, so we had a nice leisurely ride up Fifth Avenue to Twenty-Ninth Street and I profited by it to sink back comfortably and relax.

It made me feel pretty cocky to be going to Pete's wedding instead of storing up trouble for myself in Hollywood. I congratulated myself on the grief my foreknowledge was saving me. Things had been made pretty easy, I thought. By knowing my bad luck in advance, I was able to sidestep it. By holding my natural jealousy in check, and keeping Sheila and Jake Hershey from meeting, my marital relationship would be kept *in statu quo*. I'd stopped drinking, so I'd never turn out to be a drunk. If I made a point of putting Sis in her place, I wouldn't get into a jam with her, and Pete and I would always be friends. By refusing to go to the Coast, I'd avoided all chance of meeting Fern Costello, and so—

And so—by the time we turned east on Twenty-Ninth Street I'd forgotten all about the morning's bad start. I was feeling pretty good. We pulled up at the church just behind the cab that brought Sis and her brother. Pete caught a glimpse of his bride and started pawing the floor of the taxi like a stallion, but we restrained him until Sis had had time to take her blushes to the retiring room. Then we got out of the cab and followed at a self-conscious pace into the lobby or the apse or whatever they call the foyer of a church.

There were about a dozen and a half of Pete's friends waiting there. Good, hard-working people, all of them, but ill at ease in their present surroundings. They were standing uncomfortably around with their hands in their pockets or clasped behind their backs, staring at the ceiling or pretending an intense interest in the mosaic of the floor. All except Hilda Fleming, who stood with her legs resolutely braced and her shrewd eyes gleaming through her glasses as if she were about to break into her "Religion is the opiate of the people" routine.

Fortunately this was prevented by Buddy's bustling into our midst. Buddy was Sis's brother. He strode over to Pete, grasped his limp hand and pumped it up and down.

"Hello, old boy," he said, and slapped him on the back. "Well, well, well. How's the bridegroom?" Then he sniffed Pete's breath, snorted, and turned his scoutmaster's beam on me. "You're Barney Page," he told me. "Well, well, well. The best man. This is one time the best man didn't win, eh?"

I dodged the poke in the ribs I felt was coming and he turned to meet the bleak barrage of eyes that had fastened upon him. The silence was painful, but he ignored it. "We'll all have a chance to meet later," he promised, "and have a good old get-together. No time now. Let's get on with this business. You ready, McCord?"

"I guess so," Pete whispered.

"Then go along." Pete and I walked into the church and down the aisle.

The studio was on the south side of Twenty-First Street a few doors from Sixth Avenue, and, in the best Chelsea tradition, it consisted of the entire top floor of an ancient brownstone front. The building sat at the top of a flight of steps like an old man dozing in the sun. Twenty-First Street went about its business down on the pavement; other old houses were pulled down and garages built in the places where they had stood, and sooner or later its time would come, too. But meanwhile, it would be obliged if you'd just go away and not disturb it. Or, if you must come in, do so quietly and don't make any noise.

Some of the parties that were thrown there must have given it violent internal pains.

The staircase was of dark wood, wide, ornate, and rather beautiful. On each floor was a niche where a statue once had stood, but the two lower landings were bare of decoration these days, and the one on Pete's floor was used as a receptacle for empty bottles. Sometimes the pile of bottles got top-heavy and slipped, and then there would be a great to-do, bangings and crashings and thumpings down the stairs and a chorus of complaints from the tenants below.

On the floor immediately beneath Pete lived an uncountable number of Italians of both sexes, all vaguely related. On the first floor was an institution, known cryptically as the Chelsea Social Club, run by two sharp-eyed, tight-waisted young gentlemen addicted to spats and conversing out of the corners of their mouths. All three floors carried on a continuous, desultory warfare with each other; sometimes two floors united themselves against the third, but, as a rule, it was strictly catch as catch can.

There were times, of course, when the intramural guerrilla activities were called off by mutual understanding. For instance, on the first of the month all the tenants presented a united front against the landlord, and on certain holidays and state occasions they all spontaneously got drunk together and were the best of friends.

That was the way they were when I arrived. I'd stayed behind at the church to square things with the minister and I was only putting in a polite appearance before I shoved off again to join Sheila. She had agreed with me that it was sure to be a brawl and that we'd both be better off at home. I was relieved that she felt that way; it made things a lot easier for me.

So I pushed my way into the big dusty room and stood for a moment trying to get my bearings. The place was packed. People were overflowing through the open windows to the fire escape and up the ladder to the roof. Everybody was there. Fritz was one of the invited, and the Italian family had chipped in with ten gallons of wine. They all seemed to be having a swell time.

Except Buddy, of course, who sat alone in a corner with a sour look on his puss, waiting for someone to get together with him.

And myself. I had everything pretty well shaken out

of me as soon as I walked in the room. One of the first things I saw was Jake Hershey and Sheila sitting together on the fire escape.

They didn't see me and I didn't interrupt them. The damage had already been done; a too hasty move on my part now might only make things worse. I got hold of a glass of ginger-ale so I wouldn't have a flock of drinks forced on me, and retired to a corner where I could talk some sense into myself.

It was unfortunate that I took that particular corner. It was right in Buddy's line of sight. He spotted me immediately and swooped down. The first thing he did was look disdainfully at my glass.

"Drinking?" It was a snort rather than a question.

"Ginger ale," I said.

He didn't believe me. He had to take the glass out of my hand and sniff at it. When he had finished grimacing, he gave the glass back to me and I tossed it into the fireplace. It made no impression. He just gave me a fond look which intimated that I had been raised to social parity with him.

"That's great," he approved. "That's fine." He glanced aloofly over the heads of all the others present. "What do you think of this sort of thing, Page?"

"What sort of thing?"

"These Bohemians."

I looked around, too. If it had been anyone else but Buddy, I'd have agreed with him. They didn't look so hot. But, after all, in a different and more depressing way, neither did he.

"Those aren't Bohemians," I told him. "There are some Wops here, and some Hunkies and Polacks and a lot of Jews, and I think the guys from the first floor were originally Armenians. But no Bohemians. I don't think I know any Bohemians."

He didn't hear me. I was leaning against a heavy pedestal, and he had caught sight, for the first time, of the statue the pedestal supported. For the moment he was too occupied to do anything but stare.

The statue was one of those damn-fool things that are kept around chiefly for the laughs they get. They start out legitimately enough, but somewhere en route the artist goes a little haywire and, having committed himself, keeps on just to see how screwy he can really be when he lets himself go. Pete had let himself go thoroughly. This particular *objet d'art* was the product of an extremely frivolous moment.

It was about three feet in height and, from the top of the head to the navel, it was as sweet a piece of sculpture as you could find. But from there downward it got very piscatorial; the nude lady became a mermaid, a mermaid the sight of whom would have caused the Argonauts to plunge overboard and swim strongly in the opposite direction. There was nothing particularly enticing about the nether half of this daughter of Lir, no matter how instructive it may have been to the morbidly curious, and the whole thing proved nothing and settled nothing except Pete's idea of what the anatomical structure of mermaids, under certain conditions, should be. Nevertheless, the statue had, in the past, provoked a good deal of interesting speculation and furnished a number of laughs and I had become fond of it in a minor way. I resented Buddy's mystified ogling.

"You like that?" I asked him. "One of Pete's best pieces of work."

"Well," he said doubtfully, "well—"

"Pete's second wife did most of the posing," I said. "If you know her, you can see the resemblance around the eyes. But the breasts are Hilda Fleming's beyond question. While down here," I pointed, "it's easy to see when Ruth Goldberg came into the picture. If you know Ruth, of course. Isn't it interesting," I asked, "how an artist's private life is reflected in his work?"

That got him. "Look here"—he was quite fierce about it. "Do you mean to tell me that Sis will be subjected—?"

"Oh, now that Pete's married," I said, "things will be much simpler. Sis can do all the posing for him and save him that much expense. As long as she keeps her figure, of course; and after that he'll have to find someone else, younger and better-looking. It's the way of the world."

He didn't seem to agree. In fact, he looked as though he were about to do something drastic about it, but, luckily, our conversation was broken off. Someone in the crush got pushed against him and stepped painfully on his instep. Buddy gave a squeal and hopped around on one foot while I made my getaway in the confusion. I wasn't very proud of myself; I knew that, actually, I'd proved myself more of a snob than Buddy, without Buddy's naiveté to excuse my snobbishness. But that was his hard luck; he shouldn't have annoyed me when I was upset about Sheila.

She was still sitting with Jake out on the fire escape at the far end of the room, and I pushed my way toward them. It was slow work in the crowd and I wasn't more than halfway there when I ran into John Friday. His face was split by a smile so wide it seemed to run from ear to ear, and he grabbed my arm and dragged me over to the bar that Pete had built in the alcove by the door. "I've been looking for you," he said. "Have a drink."

I leaned against the bar. "Thanks, I'm not drinking."

He busied himself with bottles and a glass and then turned back to me. "Well," he asked happily, "what do you think of her?"

I looked around the room until I located Sis. She was engaged in what looked like intimate and provocative conversation with a good-looking young Wop from downstairs. I pointed her out to John. "See for yourself."

He shrugged Sis off his private earth. "Oh, hell," he said. "She's a tramp; anybody can see that. I wasn't talking about her." He smiled again and his voice got that ecstatic note. "I'm talking about the girl for the Hershey play. I told you about her on the telephone."

"Is she here?"

He drained his glass and set it on the bar. "She's here some place. You'll meet her. It's the damnedest thing."

"What is?"

"Running into her. I told you that part would be tough to cast. It was. So I'm running around in circles and pounding my brains out when the door of my office opens and in she walks. I knew her on the Coast, but I'd taken it for granted that she was under contract. Imagine."

"Remarkable," I agreed.

"As a matter of fact," he rambled on, "she only came East for two days; she was flying back tomorrow. Had her reservation and everything. It's funny. If you'd gone out to Hollywood as you intended, you'd have probably met her there."

"Sure ... sure ..." My mind was on Sheila and her companion, not on John's meanderings.

"Well, it's settled anyway. I got her signature on a run-of-the-play contract."

"Good work," I told him. "What's her name?"

"Oh yes." John was a little embarrassed. "Of course you're being featured in this play, Barney," he said. "But I know you won't object to my giving her equal billing. She's well known in pictures and—"

Suddenly I tightened up. "What's her name?" I repeated.

I suppose my voice must have sounded a little queer. He looked at me strangely. "Why," he said, "you know her work. Her name is Fern—"

"Costello?" I interrupted. "Her name is Fern

Costello?"

"Yes," he said. "That's right. How did you know? Have you met her?"

I turned away from him and leaned heavily on the bar. After a second I answered him, quite calmly, I think. "No, John," I said. "I haven't met her. Not yet."

Ten

William and Mary had followed me up to the roof and we sat side by side, now, on the parapet overlooking the dusk of Twenty-First Street. The by-streets of the Chelsea district go to bed early; it was about ten o'clock and there was little action down below. Up on Sixth Avenue, to the right, an occasional taxi raced by and, down near Seventh, the street lamps drearily illuminated the fronts of garages and small factories.

By turning around and looking down through the skylight we could see what was left of the wedding breakfast that had started that morning. It wasn't much. Pete and Sis had sneaked out sometime during the afternoon, their departure making no noticeable difference. But now the party had run its course. John Friday still hung on and so did the Italian family. Buddy hovered about, a disapproving ghost. Sheila had gone home and, shortly after, Jake Hershey had gone, too—in the opposite direction. I had made sure of that. Hilda Fleming lingered and a few other die-hards had stuck it out. And Fern Costello was still there, too. That was why I was up on the roof.

I turned away from the skylight and thought of that grim charade, my presentation to Fern. I remembered the thickness of my voice, the unwieldy weight of my arms and legs as I stood before her. I remembered John Friday's voice as he broke off in the middle of his introduction ...

"Fern, this is Barney Page who's doing the Stanton part. I know that you two ... What's the matter, Barney? Are you sick?"

"I'm all right ... How do you do, Miss Costello? I'm glad you're going to be with us ... Leave me alone, John. I'm all right, I tell you. I'm all right ..."

I wasn't all right. I was sick. Fern's eyes made me that way. I'd forgotten about her eyes, the friendly way they had of quirking up at the corners when she smiled at you. I'd forgotten how her black hair hung low about her neck and the frank manner in which she carried herself and walked. It sounds funny to say that a girl has a frank walk. That's because so few of them have. Fern was one of the few.

Oh, I was in bad shape, all right. I was remembering a lot of things it would have been better for me not to have known in the first place. When William and Mary lit a cigarette and gave a prefatory little cough, it almost came as a relief.

"Listen," he said abruptly, "I want to talk to you."

I looked at his broad, intent face high-lighted by the soft glow from the skylight, and I knew what was coming. He had been working up to this for days, ever since that afternoon at Fritz's Place.

There was nothing I could do to help him, I knew. I couldn't answer his questions; I couldn't even answer my own. But—

"Go ahead," I told him.

"What's it all about?"

"What's what all about?"

"Everything," he said. "Look here. I'm supposed to be a poet and, as such, to have an insight into things which lesser mortals are blind to. I'm supposed to have an understanding of large, nebulous, and knotty problems like Life and Love spelled with capital letters. Well, I ain't got it."

"That's tough."

"Yes," he said, "it is. And what makes it tougher is the fact that, every once in a while, Somebody or Something drops the veil, and, just for a fraction of a second, things get clear. I'm able to see what it all means. Then, before I'm able to take it in, up goes the veil again and I'm just as much in the dark as ever."

"Sort of a celestial strip-tease," I suggested.

"Exactly," he agreed. "And that's what I'm driving at. In a burlesque show, a strip-tease act, there are people working backstage. They know how and why the show works; they see the things the audience never sees. They're on the inside." He paused for a moment, thinking.

"Well?"

"Well," he said, "the point is this. How did they rate their jobs? How come they're backstage and I'm in the audience? Why are they allowed to know more than I am? How, to be explicit, did you rate your job?"

That surprised me. To be strictly truthful, it startled me. William and Mary was shrewder than I had given him credit for being. I didn't know what to tell him, so I stalled around.

"I?"

"You," he said bluntly. "There's something up and I'm not in on it. I don't like that. Why have I been given just enough insight to know there's something going on, and not enough to know what it is? Why am I left out in the cold? I've got a hunch that you could answer those questions for me if you wanted to, Barney. Couldn't you?"

"No," I answered truthfully, "I couldn't."

"I suppose you don't even know what I'm talking about?"

"I didn't say that."

"I see," he said. "Well, maybe you're telling the truth. Maybe it's a sort of guild secret. I suppose it must be."

He glanced at me speculatively. "Anyway," he went on, "it's nice to know I have a friend at court. You are a friend of mine, aren't you?"

"I'm a friend of yours, William," I told him. And then, because he was a guy with a lot of savvy who could get more out of a footnote than most people could out of a headline, I dropped him a hint.

"Look here," I said. "That gag of yours about the burlesque show. Well, it takes a lot of people to run a theatre, doesn't it?"

"Yes," he said. "Go on."

"What I mean to say is, all kinds of people go to make up a performance. More than just the audience, the actors, and the stage hands. There are candy butchers, ushers, box-office men, all kinds of people, see?"

"I see."

"And even your audience is made up of different types. There's the out-of-town visitor who's never seen a burlesque before. There's the man who's never seen this particular show, but who knows enough about the business to pretty well tell you what's going on next."

"I follow you."

"And then there's the guy who's catching the show for the second time. If he wanted to, he could tell you all about it."

"Why doesn't he want to?"

"Because," I said, "it wouldn't do any good. It would spoil the show. And then there's always the chance that the management has changed the routine or slipped in a new act. Do you see?"

He nodded his head thoughtfully. "I see that that's all you're going to tell me," he said. "It is, isn't it?"

"Tell you?" I became surprised. "I haven't told you anything, William. I've just been talking through my hat—like you were."

"Okay, pal." He got up. "It wouldn't be so bad," he said reflectively, if every once in a while I didn't get a sort of hunch that—"

"Yes?"

"Well, that I know more about this particular show than anyone else does. That I'd sort of—produced it, or maybe I was the author. Only, I've forgotten." He laughed. "Wouldn't it be funny if the guy who wrote and produced the show went off and forgot about it?"

I looked at him gravely. "It would be very unfunny," I said. "It would be sheer hell."

"I think so, too," he agreed. "I also think I'll go get a drink. Anything I can do for you down there?"

"Yes," I told him. "Ask John Friday to come up. I want to talk to him."

"Your wish," he said, "is my command." And started down the ladder. Just before his head disappeared, he stopped and looked at me. "I forgot to tell you," he said, "I think your show stinks."

I watched John Friday come across the roof and I stood up and waited for him. I put my hands in my pockets so he couldn't see the jerky way they were acting and waited until he sat down on the parapet.

"Hello, Barney," he said. "Feeling better? I told Fern you've been under the weather lately. Why don't you come downstairs?"

"I want to talk to you."

"That's what William said. What's on your chest?"

"John," I told him, "I've changed my mind. I don't want to work in the Hershey play. I'm going to the Coast."

He shook his head. "Sorry, Barney. You should have told me sooner. The *Halfway House* cast is set and I've built the play around Everett Stanton with you in the part. Contracts are signed and everything; it's too late. You should have told me sooner."

"Sooner!" That made me mad. "How the hell could I tell you sooner? How the hell could I know you were going to put Fern Costello in the play?"

He didn't look surprised and that confirmed my suspicions, the suspicions that had never wholly left me. John knew. Only he wasn't admitting it.

"Let's see your hands," he said; and when I had drawn them from my pockets, "You're off on your old tangent again, aren't you? I should have known there was more to this than professional jealousy. Sit down, Barney, and pull yourself together." He waited while I sank on the stone parapet beside him. "I wish you'd get over this thing, kid. You've been acting queer ever since the play closed. As if you suspected me of holding something back from you. That's ridiculous, you know. Believe me, I'm only trying to do one thing—to put this play on. I want you to give a good performance in it. If there was anything I could tell you that would settle your doubts and improve your performance, I'd certainly do it."

He paused for a moment. "Keep it up," I prodded. "Keep talking. Maybe you'll let something slip."

He shook his head and rested his hand on my shoulder. "I haven't anything to say," he told me, "except maybe this: You needn't be afraid of Fern. You needn't be afraid of anyone in the world except yourself. That's where all the trouble comes from— down inside. Why don't you look at things the way you used to?"

I looked up at him.

"Don't you remember how it was when you started in this business—down South in a hick stock company changing bills twice a week? Nothing ever got you down then. You didn't even have time to learn your lines, did you? You just got a general idea of the play and ad-libbed your way through. Think of it like that."

"Like what?" I asked.

"Think of it as though you were just starting in the business again. Everything's ahead of you and you're young and you don't give a damn. Maybe you only half-know your lines. So what? You're working with troupers; they can be depended on to keep up their end. So you wing your part from entrance to entrance and, when you go on, you bluff and ad-lib as best you can. Think of it like that and do your best to give a good performance. That's the only thing that counts. Catch on?"

"Sure," I said. I turned away; there wasn't much use talking to him; I'd have to work this out for myself. "Thanks for the pep talk."

"It's chilly up here," he said. "I think I'll go back to the party. You'd better come along, too."

"I will in a minute."

"Okay." He started down the ladder. I looked down into Twenty-First Street and muttered to myself.

He stopped. "What did you say?"

"Nothing important," I told him. "I just agreed with something William said. I think the show stinks."

He didn't reply. He looked at me for a minute as though he felt very sad about something and then he lowered his head and went on down the ladder.

I stayed up there for a while, looking at the thing from every angle. And at last I came to the conclusion that, regardless of John's displeasure, regardless of signed contracts and the wrath of the entire Actors Equity Association, I wasn't going to work with Fern Costello.

And nobody could make me. I'd get out of the business first.

When I got home that night, I went into the bedroom and found Sheila still awake, lying in bed and reading a manuscript. I sat down on the bed beside her and kissed her.

"Darling," I said, "how'd you like to clear out of town for a while?"

She closed the manuscript sharply. "What's happened?"

"Nothing," I said. "Nothing at all. You said you wanted to go away, didn't you? Have you changed your mind?"

"Of course not," she said. "Only I'd like to know what I'm running from."

I sighed. "Must we be running from something? Can't we just take a vacation?"

She thought about it for a minute. "It would be nice," she ventured, "if we went up to Lake Champlain. You always liked it there, Barney. And you'd be near at hand in case John wanted to talk to you about the play."

"As to that," I told her, "it's out. We've already talked about it. I'm not going to do it."

She looked at me as though she thought I was crazy. Then she swung her legs out of bed and started feeling for her mules. "What are you up to?" I asked.

"I'm going to telephone John Friday before he takes you seriously. This is the greatest play you've ever had a chance at, and you're going to toss it over just like that? Not if I can help it." She started for the living room.

I reached up and caught her wrist and she swung around to face me. "How come you know it's such a swell play?" I asked. "You've never read it."

"Oh, haven't I?" She drew herself up straight. "I've been reading it for the last two hours. Jake Hershey gave me a copy at the party and I brought it home with me." She leaned over the bed and tossed the manuscript in my lap. "There."

I let go her wrist and thumbed through the pages of *Halfway House*. After a minute I said, "I didn't know you had this, darling. I must be sure to give it back to

Jake before we leave. What do you say we drop the subject for a while? We'll have all summer to talk about it and make up our minds."

"My mind's made up now," Sheila said.

Eleven

We left town two days later and spent three months up on Lake Champlain. Sheila never let up on me once. John Friday kept after me, too, with letters and telegrams. And then there was the money angle. Vacations are expensive and I was running short; it was going to be tough to go back to New York and no money, without a job, and with a black eye from having run out on a play. The combination was too much for me, and I began to wonder if I wasn't attaching too much importance to minor details. I came home again on the last day of August fully committed to the part of Everett Stanton.

That was on a Wednesday afternoon, and, while Sheila worked around the apartment getting things in order, I decided to go up to the Cochran and report in person. I told Sheila where I was going, picked up my hat, and started out.

I went over to Sixth, intending to take the bus uptown and to stop in at the Lambs to see if there was any mail. But it was a nice August day, not too hot for a change, and I had a lot of energy left over from my vacation, so I decided to walk it off. I turned up Sixth Avenue and headed north.

As I walked along, I plotted a course for my future conduct. There were shoals ahead, but, with careful steering, I could give them a wide berth. Fern was going to be the biggest difficulty, because, in dealing with her, I also had my own very definite feelings to contend with. To save myself, I must and would put our relationship on a strictly business basis; I would never allow myself to be alone with her; never allow myself to think of her except as a fellow actor in the play. In that way, and in that way alone, I could carry on with what I had to do.

As to Jake, I didn't anticipate any great difficulty. Sheila seldom came to rehearsals and only when I asked her. It would be easy to keep them apart.

So I was dawdling along, thinking of these things and stopping to look into occasional shop windows, when I woke up and found that I had arrived at Twenty-Third Street. I started to cross over when I heard someone shout and, looking around, I saw Pete McCord running after me. He was bareheaded; evidently he'd seen me from the window of his studio and chased me just as he was.

"Wait a minute," he yelled. "I want to see you."

He caught up. "Why don't you tell a guy when you're coming back to town?" he panted. "Or when you're going away, for that matter. I've been trying to get in touch with you for weeks."

"Anything wrong?" I asked.

"Well, not exactly. But Sis—" He broke off then, and looked around him. "Can't we have a cup of coffee somewhere?"

"I can't, Pete. I'm on my way up to see John Friday."

"Well," he said, "that's what I want to see you about."

"John Friday?"

"In a way. You see, it's like this," he told me. "Sis has an idea that you can help her."

"Help her what?"

"Get a job—with Friday or any other producer. It doesn't matter which one."

"Sis wants to be an actress?"

"That's it." He was pretty glum about it.

"Good Lord, Pete," I told him. "I can't make Sis an actress. John can't use a girl with no experience. If she wants to go on the stage, why doesn't she go to some dramatic school or bluff her way into a job in a road company?"

"Well, I don't know," Pete said. "Frankly, Barney, I don't think she really wants to work. I think a couple of weeks of real work would cure her."

"So she'd quit," I interrupted. "She'd walk out on the play and leave it high and dry."

"Well," Pete said again, "I told her I'd ask you. I thought—or Sis thought—that if you could get John to give her just a walk-on—" He was embarrassed, on the defensive. "You know how it is."

"I know how it is. Tell me this," I asked him, "how do you feel about it? Do you want her on the stage?"

"Well," he said, "yes and no. I want her to do what she wants to do. I don't like the idea, but, if she's set on it, I'd rather have her playing a bit in a legitimate play than knocking off a job as a show girl somewhere. You know what I mean."

"Sure I do," I said. "You couldn't just get masterful and tell her to forget it, could you?"

He looked at the sidewalk. "I could," he said, "but the consequences would be unpleasant."

"Well, look here. We're opening October third," I told him. "Rehearsals start next Monday. You send Sis up to the Cochran and I'll see that she gets to John Friday. In the meantime I'll speak to John."

He looked up then, and smiled. "Thanks, Barney."

"Don't worry about it, Pete," I said. "John will take care of the whole thing."

He went on back to his studio then, and I continued my walk uptown. The quicker Pete gets wise to that little tramp, I told myself, the better off everybody's going to be. John Friday's the boy to handle this; there's just the right amount of finesse in his brutality.

And thinking backward—or forward, as the case may be—I remembered how Sis had once come between Pete McCord and myself. That was one thing that would never happen again, I was sure; I was proof against that sort of thing now.

Twelve

Monday, the fifth of September, was overcast and grey, heavy with impending rain. The call was for ten o'clock, but I had some business to attend to and I got uptown early. After that I dropped in at the Astor to get some cigarettes to last me through rehearsal. Queerly, my conscience bothered me somewhat about seeing Fern again, so, as a sort of reflex action, I stopped at the florist's on my way out and had some flowers sent to Sheila. I felt a little better after that.

Walking through the Shubert Alley on my way to the theatre, I ran into Dick Taylor just coming through the side door of the building. Dick was a nice kid and a good actor; I'd known him a long time.

"What are you doing at the Shubert's?" I asked. "I thought you were stage-managing that turkey at the National."

He fell in beside me. "I am. But I've got in the habit of hunting jobs and I'm tapering off gradually. These guys forget so easily; I like to remind them I'm still around just in case. Where are you headed?"

"Rehearsal," I told him. "We start this morning."

"Oh, yes," he said. "*Halfway House*. They say it's a natural. Is it?"

"It's all right."

"I'll go along with you," he decided. "Maybe Friday will offer me a job and I'll be able to say no. I like turning down jobs."

"You won't get a chance this time," I told him. "The cast is set."

"Maybe somebody will get fired." He smiled

cheerfully. "Maybe you will."

"If I am," I said, "they'll need an actor to replace me."

He laughed. "The thing I like about you, Barney, is your amiability." We came to the Cochran Theatre at this point and turned down the stage alley. Dick stopped dead and pointed to the stage door at the far end. "Now," he said, "it all becomes clear. 'Daylight and champagne could not discover more!'"

I followed his pointing finger and saw Sis McCord swishing through the stage door. She looked exactly like her native Boston's conception of an actress: a painted hussy. But even under the frills, the kid had something. The kind of something that makes an ageing man break his stride in a busy street and shake his head in not too pleasant memory.

Dick sighed. "And I thought you and Friday were legitimate," he said. "Are you giving dishes away, too?"

I took his arm. "Go home, Richard," I said. "This play is for adults only. Go home and bathe your feet in cold water."

He refused. "I'll have to grow up sometime. Why not now?" We went down the alley together.

The stage was lit only by the pilot light and the first border, and it was empty except for a few chairs with stage braces laid upon them in the outline of a room. John Friday sat at a small table down left, and Sis McCord was standing in front of him. Dick Taylor leaned against the right proscenium arch and I hovered in the shadows upstage. The rest of the cast sat around the auditorium reading their lines and discontentedly counting the number of pages in their parts.

John was giving Sis the Polite Brush-Off Formula Number 2-B, and doing it very nicely, too.

"I'm really sorry, Mrs. McCord," he said. "I'd like to

have you with us if only for your husband's sake. I like Pete. But, outside of the fact that this is a small cast and there is really no part for you, have you considered what this kind of work really means?"

"Well—" Sis began.

"It's tough," John said. "Very tough. I don't think you'd like it. I don't think anyone in his right mind would like it. I'm sure I wouldn't." He paused. "Do you really want my advice?"

"Well—" Sis started.

"I'll give it to you, anyway," John said. "Go on home and think it over for a month or two. Then, if you still want to go on the stage, come and see me."

"I will," Sis promised eagerly.

"At that time," he continued, "I'll give you the names of some people who may be able to help you. You'll study diction, dancing, fencing, stage mechanics, eurhythmics, and a lot of other things. You'll do this for a couple of years. After that, if you've made satisfactory progress and still want to continue, I'll try to get you a bit in a second road company or in stock. Is that fair?"

Sis looked like a little girl who's just been told she's too young to go, to the party. "Well—" she said.

"And now, if you'll excuse me"—John gave her the final whisk—"I must get on with the rehearsal. Jack"—he called the stage manager—"get the cast on the stage, please."

Jack started rounding them up and Sis wandered disconsolately toward the stage door. I felt that a consoling word was in order, but Dick Taylor got to her before I did.

"That certainly is tough, Mrs. McCord," he was saying as I came up. "I don't know how they expect you to get any experience if they won't give you a job. You come along with me."

"Lay off, Dick," I said. I turned to Sis. "You see how it

is. I'm afraid you'll get the same thing every place in town."

"She will like hell," Dick broke in. "We've got a whole pile of supers in what you disrespectfully call my turkey. One of them is always showing up too plastered to go on. You come along with me, sweetheart, and I'll introduce you to my assistant."

"That is sweet of you," Sis said.

"My name is Taylor. Dick Taylor."

"First act, Mr. Page!" That was Jack calling me to work.

I called back to him. Then, to the dopes, "You know best," I said. "At least, I hope so."

"Thanks." Dick slipped her arm through his and steered her off toward the stage door. I watched them go. Well, I thought, it's going to happen sooner or later, anyway. As for Dick, he knows what he's doing—or thinks he does, the sap.

There was one vacant chair left in the circle on the stage and I went over and sat down. I'd already said hello to the rest of the cast; they were waiting now to begin the preliminary reading. I settled myself comfortably, nodded to Bess Nichols sitting next to me, opened the script to the first act, took out my pencil and looked up, ready to start.

I looked straight into the eyes of Fern Costello seated opposite me. She was watching me, smiling as though she were amused by something.

"Good morning, Mr. Page," she said.

"Good morning, Miss Costello."

John Friday rapped with his pencil on the little table. "Miss Nichols, you have the first line. Will you begin?"

When I got home that night the flowers I'd sent Sheila in the morning were in a vase on the living-room table. They looked very pretty. Sheila thanked me politely and said it was sweet of me to think about her when I was so busy. That was all. She didn't ask how the rehearsal went or anything, and that griped me because I was only doing the play because she liked it so much. I sat around and threw out a couple of leaders, but she didn't follow them up; she went on about her business, humming to herself and wearing a bright, preoccupied look. So finally I gave up and went to bed early. She came to bed, too, but she didn't read as she usually did. She went straight to sleep, and, after a while, I got tired of sitting up with myself and I switched off the bed light and tried to go to sleep too. But it was some time before I managed it, what with thinking and things like that.

There's no drearier time during a rehearsal period than the end of the second week. Before then, the novelty of the new play and the new people keeps you interested. And during the third week you begin to look forward to the opening night. But the end of the second week is the low point; that's when tempers begin to fray and temperament to flower.

I sat in the front row of the auditorium watching John trying to whip some life into a couple of actors who looked as if they'd been up all night. It was dispiriting. Bess Nichols, the ingénue, sat next to me, and I suppose she felt the strain as much as I did because she'd been commenting rather freely on the personal appearance, habits, and immediate ancestry of the other members of the cast. I knew how she felt, all right, but her conversation was getting on my nerves, so I tried to think of some way to change the subject.

"At least," I said, "we have an ideal author. He stays where all playwrights should stay during rehearsal— far away."

"That's true," Bess said, "thanks to you."

"Why me? What have I got to do with it?"

Bess gave me a peculiar glance. "I thought you'd arranged it," she said. "Fern Costello and I both thought so when we saw them together."

"Saw who together?"

"Why," she said, "Sheila and Mr. Hershey, of course. Shouldn't I have told you that?"

"Why not?" I asked her. "Why shouldn't you have told me?" Then I got mad. "Where do you get that stuff? What business is it of yours, anyway?"

She looked pained. "You've got me wrong, Barney. I only thought—"

"The hell you did." I turned away from her. "You're just trying to stir up trouble."

She jumped to her feet. "Now look here—" she began. She was pretty indignant, and I saw that maybe I'd made a mistake. So I didn't give her a chance to go on.

"I don't want to talk about it," I said. "I'm sorry, but you shouldn't talk about things you don't understand."

I got up and walked away from her. All the way down the aisle I could feel her glare on the back of my neck like an icicle.

I went backstage and into my dressing room, closed the door and sat down. I reminded myself that Bess Nichols was a natural troublemaker, a person who created situations for the pleasure of making other people squirm. The chances were that she was lying. If she wasn't, the chances were still that Sheila's meeting Jake had been an accident, just one of those things. Anyway, it would be easy to get the straight dope. Fern's dressing room was right next door to mine.

I knocked on the wall. "Fern?" Using her first name meant nothing; formality is so much excess baggage during rehearsals.

"Yes?" Her voice was muffled. "What is it?"

"It's Barney Page. May I see you for a minute?"

"Of course. Come in."

I got up and walked next door. There was nothing to get jittery about. All this required was tact and a businesslike reserve. I could handle Fern without getting involved with her. Her door was ajar and I pushed it open and went in.

She had been reading her lines. She held the script in her hand and her eyes were closed in concentration. Her head was bare. Her longish black hair brushed against the open collar of the blue silk blouse she wore under her brown suit. I remembered that suit. She'd bought it at Bonwit Teller's. I remembered the perfume that rose from her black hair. It was Guerlain's *Liu*. I'd given her a bottle of it once. She opened her eyes and saw me studying her and laid the script on her dressing table and smiled at me.

"I've just been going over our second act scene," she said. "I'm glad you came in. We haven't got the hang of it yet."

"It'll come in time."

"It won't unless we make it. And we can't do it here with people building sets all around us."

"Well," I said, "sets have to be built. Fern—"

All of a sudden it wasn't as easy as I thought. I leaned against the wall and felt in my pocket for a cigarette. I couldn't find one and I pulled my hand out again; it felt cumbersome. "I've been talking to Bess Nichols," I said at last. "I understand you two ran into my wife with Jake Hershey."

She looked up at me, puzzled. "Yes?"

"Did you?"

"Well, yes," she said. "Purely by accident. I can't imagine why Bess should mention it. I'd already forgotten."

"Bess doesn't forget things like that. When was it, Fern?"

"Yesterday," she said. "Or maybe it was the day

before. On top of a Fifth Avenue bus." Her eyes widened and she rose from her chair. "You're not attaching importance to anything Bess tells you? You should know better than that."

I stretched my face in a smile. "It's ridiculous, isn't it? I was afraid, from what she said, that you might have the wrong idea."

Fern shook her head. "Bess has been an ingénue too many years. It's warped her." She smiled back at me. "Pay no attention to her, Barney. She should have been liquidated long ago."

Her eyes were friendly and her smile gentle. "I shan't forget about that scene," I promised. "We'll run over it a few times."

"I wish we could," she said, "but not here. John suggested that we get together by ourselves. Couldn't you come up to my place after rehearsal?"

I stiffened all over. After a moment I said, "I couldn't do that without consulting Sheila. She may have made other plans. I'll see. Can I call you?"

"Not very well," she said. "I've just taken a new apartment. The telephone isn't in yet."

"Then you call me," I told her. "I'd better get out on the stage. John will be looking for me."

I backed out of the dressing room. I stood behind John's little table and watched the rehearsal. But it seemed as though Fern were still close beside me. The odor of Guerlain's *Liu* was all around.

That night when I got home for dinner there wasn't any dinner. There wasn't any Sheila either. I sat down and waited for a while and then I went into the bathroom and washed my face and hands. After that I got a pack of cards and started playing solitaire. I made a lot of misplays and I didn't have much luck, so, when I lost four or five straight games, I threw the cards down and went to the telephone to call Pete's number. But I hung up before I got an answer; there was no reason to think Sheila would be there more than any other place. I wasn't worried about her, anyway; I was just provoked. I went downstairs, out of the apartment house, and looked up and down Tenth Street. I stood there for a while and then I went back into the apartment and picked up the cards again. I laid them out carefully in a neat game of solitaire and, while I fiddled with the cards, I told myself a few things:

Take it easy, I said. For Christ's sake, hang on to yourself. This is the sort of thing that got you down before, just little things like this. They don't amount to anything, but look what they lead to. I played a black deuce on an equally black three and I slammed the deck of cards down on the floor.

Sheila's key grated in the lock. I got up and tried to retrieve the scattered cards.

She came in hurriedly and seemed surprised to see me. "I didn't know it was so late," she said.

"That's okay," I told her. "We'll go out for dinner." I moved to kiss her and she turned her head quickly, but not before I caught the liquor on her breath.

"Hello. I thought you were on the wagon," I said.

"Did you?" she asked. "I am—practically."

"It's your own business," I assured her. "But after what happened the last time, I should think you'd be cured."

She looked at me. "Are you being unpleasant on purpose?" She kept on looking and a little smile came on her face. "After all, we only had one cocktail apiece."

"We?"

"Jake Hershey and I. We ran into each other uptown." She kept on smiling. "You don't mind, do you?"

"Mind? Have I said anything?"

"Well, no—"

"Have I ever asked you to account for how you spend your time? Have I ever checked up on your alibis?"

She didn't say anything.

"Jesus Christ Almighty!" I said. "You're a free agent, aren't you? You're supposed to be old enough to take care of yourself. If you're not, I don't know what you can expect me to do about it."

The telephone rang, but neither of us made a motion to answer it. We just stood there. When it rang the third time, Sheila said quietly, "I'll get ready for dinner. It won't take me long," and went past me into the bedroom without raising her eyes.

The telephone bell continued to ring. "God damn it," I said, and went over and answered it. "Hello."

The cool voice of Fern Costello answered me. "Mr. Page, please."

It was a second or two before I could control my voice. "Yes, Fern."

"Barney? You told me to call you."

"Yes," I said. "I can't make it tonight, Fern. I'm sorry. We'll talk about it tomorrow."

She started to say something and then changed her mind. "All right, Barney. Goodbye."

"Goodbye."

In a few minutes Sheila came out of the bedroom buttoning her gloves. She didn't ask who had telephoned. She didn't even look at me.

Finally, I asked, "Ready?"

She finished with the last button. "Yes."

"That was Fern Costello on the phone," I said. "Just some business about the play."

"Did I ask you anything?" she said.

We walked west on Tenth Street and I wrestled with myself. I had to crawl. There wasn't any alternative.

"Sheila," I said, but she acted as if she hadn't heard me. I had to repeat myself. "Sheila—"

"Yes?"

"Look, kid," I said. "I'm sorry I lost my temper. I didn't mean anything by it. Will you forgive me?"

"Of course." Her voice was brightly impersonal.

"The play's going along very nicely now," I told her. "Why don't you come up tomorrow and look us over?"

"Tomorrow?" she said. "I don't see how I can. I have an engagement with the hairdresser in the morning and I was going to see about that new chair for the living room in the afternoon. I don't see how—"

"Oh, for Christ's sake," I said. "For Christ's sake, can't you come off it? What do you want me to do? Kneel down and beg your forgiveness? I told you I'm sorry. I can't do more than that."

We walked along in silence for a while, and then, "I'll see if I can manage it," she said. "I might be able to drop in for a minute tomorrow afternoon."

I let it go at that.

Thirteen

Bess Nichols stalked up to where I was sitting in the corner by the switchboard.

"Mr. Page—" she said. She'd called me Mister ever since I'd sat on her the other day. "Your wife's out front. She asked me to tell you."

"Thanks." I got up. "I'll go out right away."

She gave me a nasty smile. "There's no hurry. Mr. Hershey is with her."

I looked her over carefully and then I turned away. There was no use saying anything. I went through the side door and down into the boxes on the left side of the auditorium. It was dark there, and I had to feel my way through the heavy velvet curtains and into the left aisle. Then my eyes became accustomed to the gloom and I walked back to the rear of the house where a few members of the cast were sitting. But Sheila and Jake were not there, so I went around to the center aisle to look for them.

They were sitting about four rows from where I stood in the rear of the house. Their heads were close together and they were whispering to each other. I waited a minute, and then I walked quietly down the aisle and dropped into a seat behind them.

Jake knew that I was there instantly. I could tell by the way his shoulders stiffened: they became alert and wary. But he didn't look around. And Sheila hadn't heard me. She glanced at Jake, puzzled by his silence.

She asked, "What's the matter?"

He didn't answer and everything was quiet for a moment. Then I coughed. "It's only me," I apologized ungrammatically. "Do you mind?"

At the sound of my voice Sheila turned. She hesitated and then she laughed. "What are you trying to do? Scare me to death?" Jake turned around slowly and looked at me over the tops of his glasses very mildly. There was an inquiring smile on his lips.

"Hello, Jake," I said.

"Hello, Barney."

Then there was silence again. We all sat and waited for someone to speak the first word.

It was Jake who broke. "This is the first time I've come to rehearsal," he offered. "I stayed away on purpose. I've always heard that authors are inclined to make nuisances of themselves."

"You heard correctly," I told him.

"Why, Barney—!" That was Sheila.

"I was speaking generally, darling," I assured her. "Jake understands me, don't you, Jake?"

"Of course," he said.

Our voices—or my voice—must have carried to the stage. John Friday jumped up from his little table, shielded his eyes from the glare of the footlights, and peered out at us.

"Can't we have a little quiet out there?" he complained. "How am I supposed to hold a rehearsal with a bunch of actors jabbering away like a God damned convention?"

"Sorry, John," I called back. "I was just welcoming our lost author."

John was partly placated. "So he finally decided to show up, did he? Send him up here. I want to talk to him."

I smiled at Jake. "Tough, isn't it? They bawl you out for staying away and if you're here you get picked on. There's no pleasing everybody."

He nodded seriously. "That's right," he said. "And yet I keep on trying."

He walked down the aisle, stumbled over the unaccustomed ladder that led to the footlights, and finally sat down with John at the little table.

Sheila asked, "Why did you do that?"

"Do what?"

"Treat Jake like that."

"Like what?"

Her eyes snapped. "You know perfectly well what I'm talking about. You ought to be ashamed of yourself. You're ridiculously jealous."

I mulled that over, and then I asked, "Have I any reason to be jealous?"

She raised her head and looked at me. "You haven't the slightest cause in the world to be jealous, and you know it. I like Jake and I feel sorry for him. That's all."

"You feel sorry for Jake?"

"Yes, I do. I think it's a shame the way you pick on him."

There wasn't much I could say to that. Fortunately I didn't have to try. A couple of cast members came over then and they took charge of the conversation. I was just as glad they did.

I left them alone after a few minutes and went backstage to get hold of Jake when John Friday should have finished with him. It was time, I figured, for a showdown.

"Well," Jake said, "it's marvelous. It's simply marvelous. I know that I'm supposed to rave and stamp and tear my hair and swear that my brain child is being butchered, but I just can't do it. It's shaped up so much better than I ever thought it would. There's real life in it. I think you people have done a marvelous job. Simply marvelous."

"Thanks," I said. "Are you in love with Sheila, Jake?"

He looked at me as though the question hadn't registered, so I had to repeat. "Are you in love with Sheila?"

His eyes began to pop a little behind his glasses; he looked at me, and then he cleared his throat and looked away.

"Well?" I prompted.

"That's a funny thing to ask—"

"Now look, Jake," I said. "I'm not carrying any concealed weapons, and I wouldn't use them if I were. I have to open in this play in a few days and I can't take time off to go to jail. So just answer the question one way or the other and we'll forget all about it."

"Forget about it?"

"Naturally. What do you expect me to do? Bring suit for alienation of affections? That's already out of the question. I've asked Sheila."

"You did? What did she say?"

"I'm sorry to disappoint you," I told him, "but she said that her affections were still unalienated."

"Oh." His face became very long.

"So," I said, "let's have your side of the story and then we'll have the record straight. It will be out in the open and we'll all know where we stand. Don't you think that's a good idea?"

"Yes," he said suddenly, "I do. I don't like this business any more than you do. Okay, I'll tell you. I am in love with Sheila. What are you going to do about it?"

"Nothing," I told him. "I'm sorry for you, of course, but that's all. I don't feel called upon to do anything."

"You understand," he assured me, "I've never said a word to her. Not a word."

"That's nice," I said, "but immaterial."

"And I never will," he went on heroically. "You don't know how I feel about Sheila. I couldn't help falling in love with her. It was something bigger than I was. It—"

"Save it, Jake," I told him. "You don't have to describe your sensations. I know what the biological urge feels like. All I'm asking you to do is to keep the act clean. Do that and you can suffer in silence to your heart's content. Is that okay?"

He studied the floor for a minute and then he nodded. "That's okay," he said quietly. He didn't look up.

They called me back to rehearsal then, and I left him standing there. I thought, as I walked to the center of the stage, that there *was* something a little tragic about Jake, something a little tragic and a little absurd. And I remembered what Sheila had told me: that she felt sorry for him. Jake invites abuse on purpose, I thought. Mix a little tragedy and a little absurdity and what does it add up to? Romance. He's got it all figured out.

But there's one angle he forgot to figure out, I thought. Me. Jake never imagined I'd be so unethical as to call his hand before he had a chance to play it. The only thing left for him to do now was to throw in his cards.

The scene didn't go well. It was the one we had spoken about the day before. It wasn't our fault; Fern and I worked together all right, and Margaret Lester, who did the maid bit, certainly wasn't to blame. The trouble was in the writing.

John saw this after a while. He called Jake Hershey up from the auditorium and told him what he wanted done. It was just a question of shifting entrances around. Then, while Jake went to work with his pencil, he called a half-hour recess. "Come on, you two," he said to Fern and myself. "We'll get a cup of coffee. Margaret, you'd better come, too."

We went over to Sardi's, and while we drank our coffee John talked to us about the scene. He told us what we had done and what we hadn't done, and then he told us what he wanted us to do.

"Time's getting short," he wound up. "I don't want to start calling night rehearsals unless it's absolutely necessary. I wish that you people would get together on these individual scenes. I spoke to you about it several days ago, Fern."

Fern looked at John and then she glanced at me. She was silent.

"Yes," I admitted, "it's my fault we haven't done it before. Fern offered the use of her apartment, but I was busy. Sheila—"

"I'll explain it to Sheila," John interrupted. "This is important. Can you get up there tonight?" He turned to Margaret Lester. "I'd like to have you there, too, Margaret."

I watched Margaret. When she nodded, it was as though a weight had been taken off my shoulders. "I don't know any reason why I couldn't make it tonight, John," I said. "I'll tell Sheila and—"

"Stop worrying about your wife," he broke in impatiently. "You've got work to do."

We went back to the rehearsal then, and John

worked me steadily the rest of the afternoon. I didn't have a chance to get out front, but that was all right. I felt that I'd disposed of the Jake Hershey menace very neatly and that, from this point on, things would be back on their old footing between Sheila and myself.

John took us straight through the play from start to finish, and, when we got to my final exit in the third act, I went out into the auditorium. It was after six o'clock, and I knew John wouldn't be going back over any of my business. So I thought I'd just wait around until the call was given for the following day. Then Sheila and I could go home for dinner and I'd be able to explain about my going up to Fern's that night.

My hands were grimy from fooling around backstage and I decided to slick myself up a bit before joining her. The washroom was on the balcony floor and all the lights were turned off, but the Cochran was my second home and I knew every foot of it. I climbed the thickly carpeted stairs and felt along the right wall of the smoking room until I came to the door, opened it, and went inside. The door closed with automatic softness and I switched on the light.

When I had washed and dried my hands, I turned the light off again, opened the door, and stepped out into the darkness. Only a faint glow was visible coming up the stairs from the orchestra floor, and I waited for a few moments until my eyes should accustom themselves to the dark.

It was then I became aware that I was not alone in the smoking room. Two other people were there; they were sitting close together in a big couch at the other end of the room and their whispered conversation was so low, and so intimately absorbing, that they were entirely oblivious of me.

I don't know how I knew who they were, but I did. I sensed it. And all of a sudden I felt weak. I had to lean against the wall.

Then Sheila laughed softly at something Jake said and I turned to the stairs and stumbled down them. I went across the foyer and sank down in a seat in the last row of the auditorium where no one could see me.

"Is that you, Barney?" Fern Costello paused in the aisle beside me.

"Yes."

"Sheila left a message for you. She went home about an hour ago."

"Did she?"

"Yes. You were busy on the stage, so I said I'd tell you."

I moved over, but she didn't sit down. "John gave her a couple of tickets to a play," she said, "and she went home early to change her clothes and have some dinner."

I didn't make any comment, so, after a minute, she asked, "Shall I expect you tonight?"

"Why not?" I said.

"Margaret Lester isn't sure she can make it. But I don't think that makes any difference, do you?"

"No," I said. "It doesn't make any difference."

She opened her purse. "I'll write my address for you."

"Never mind," I told her. "I know where you live as well as you do. I'll be there."

Fourteen

So here I was inside the ivory-colored door again and there was a fire in the fireplace and Fern stood before it, dark and lovely-looking as always. I felt at home with her and in this place, and I knew that I had no business to feel that way. I thought of all my well-laid plans and I couldn't help wondering why they hadn't worked out as I expected them to.

Our conversation was casual and there were long friendly silences. Fern had set its tone from the first and led me along devious ways to the point where we were now. There was a faint warming glow behind her eyes, and, when her attention was diverted from me, to the fire or to a cigarette, I missed their enveloping warmth.

It was all wrong, I knew. But I was tired. I hadn't realized how tired I was. My conscious mind—what was left of it—warned me: Barney, be careful. There's trouble for you here and plenty of it. But that all seemed remote and unimportant. The important, tangible present was here before me, next to me. Fern was tangible and so was the fire, and a cigarette, and the deep soft couch on which I was sitting.

"You don't drink," she said. "I've noticed that. I wonder why."

I told her. I made quite a story of it, long and rambling. "My parents were the good, religious type you run into in the theatre sometimes," I said. "I've been told they were good actors too, but I don't remember that. They died when I was too young, before my critical sense had fully developed. They were caught in a theatre fire in Dallas and burned to death. I was in the hotel room when it happened."

She didn't gush sympathy the way people do. She just nodded her understanding, and I went on:

"I suppose they brought me up pretty religiously; I don't really remember. But I do remember, I remember very distinctly, a scapular I always wore around my neck. That was my shield against harm. Nothing could really hurt me as long as I wore that scapular. One night I woke up to find the lights all lit and the room filled with strange people standing around my bed. One of them was the manager of the hotel. He pointed me out to a policeman and told him who I was. The cop scribbled in a notebook and said I'd be taken care of in the morning. That was all. They all went out and turned the lights out again and left me alone in the dark. Nobody told me what had happened. But I knew. My mother and father didn't come home and I had nothing left to hang on to but my scapular. That was enough. I couldn't be hurt —not badly, anyway— as long as I had that."

Fern nodded. "Go on."

"Well," I told her, "I grew up. Gradually, of course, and in fits and starts, and never quite completely, just the way everyone does. I grew out of some things and into others. One of the things I grew out of was my scapular. I lost it, I guess, or maybe it just wore out; I don't know. But after it had gone, things began to happen to me. And they kept on happening. Not very nice things; you wouldn't like me to tell you about them."

"You don't have to," Fern said.

"Anyway," I went on, "I found another scapular at last. And it works just as well. It's a sort of final ditch, a last defense a guy throws up to protect himself against the world. Things can get tough for me; they often do. But they can't lick me. Not as long as I don't drink. That's my scapular now, the only one I have. Understand?"

She looked at me and into me. "I understand," she said, "but I think you're wrong."

I shrugged. "It works."

"It's worked so far, you mean. That's the trouble with you mystics: you attach too much importance to symbols. Why must you think of your particular scapular as a last defense? If that's taken, your battle is lost. Why don't you think of it as one in a long series of defenses? Then, if you lose a skirmish, what of it? You say, All right, and you move back a little. Maybe the next day you win a small fight. And you move up. Symbols are all right; for some people they're necessary. But after all, the only importance a symbol has is the importance you give to it yourself. It seems foolish to me to attach too much importance to any one thing. You make yourself vulnerable."

"We're all vulnerable," I said, "but a fellow learns by experience what his best weapons are and he uses them accordingly."

"I don't know why weapons—defenses—are necessary at all," she said. "Defenses are stiff, and we should be pliable." She moved to the couch and sat beside me. "Why must you put yourself in a position to be hurt," she asked, "the way you were hurt by Sheila this afternoon? Why do you do it, Barney?"

"I don't know what you mean," I said.

"Don't you?" And for a while neither of us said anything. We stared into the fire and gradually the small rupture which had started between us was healed over and forgotten.

"What happened after that?" she asked. "After your parents died?"

"That's when John Friday came into the picture," I said. "I don't remember when I first knew John; he seems to have been always around. A friend of my father's. I'm afraid I've taken him pretty much for granted."

"John's always around." Fern nodded her head in thoughtful agreement. "I've come to think of him more as a primal force than as a person."

I threw her a quick look, but she was absorbed in her own thoughts. "He farmed me out with friends until I was old enough to go to school," I went on. "Then he saw that I gathered all the education I was able to hold. After that came stock—two bills a week and promises for salary—Number Six road companies, and all the rest."

"I've had my share of it," Fern said.

"And finally," I wound up, "New York."

"And Sheila."

"Yes," I said, "and Sheila."

She turned away from the fire and drew her knees up on the couch. Her arm lay along the back and she dropped her head to rest upon her arm. She sat like that for several minutes just quietly thinking.

"What's it all about, Barney?" she asked.

"What?"

"I feel there's something between us, something you're afraid of and won't talk about. Damn it!" she said suddenly, "I don't understand it and I want to understand it."

I turned around and faced her. She was very lovely, and I felt that she was aware of it and of the way I was feeling. I said, "Fern, I warn you. Take my advice and lay off."

She laughed. "Your defenses! You can't spend your life hiding in a hole with the hole pulled in after you. Come on out in the open; we're supposed to be rational human beings." She put her hand on mine. "Listen, Barney," she told me, "I'll say this: whatever it is, it's nothing to be afraid of. It's all right."

I don't know how it happened. I swear I don't. One minute we were like that and the next I had her in my arms. Her body was soft. I kissed her and our mouths met as long-parted friends hungry for each other. My hand, at her back, travelled familiarly upward over the slope of her shoulder. It felt her neck.

I was suddenly sick. My hands clenched on her arms and pushed her slowly, remorselessly away. I stared at her, at her neck. A picture welled up in my mind, horribly plain, etched indelibly in my memory. I felt that I was going to vomit.

She cried, "What's the matter? What is it?"

I slammed her away. "Shut up!" Then I held my head in my hands and tried to pull my sanity back to me.

Eventually, I got up and without looking at her went

across the room for my hat and coat. I put on the coat and fumbled in the pockets for my gloves. They were there and I nervously fitted them on my fingers.

Then I went back to the fire. She still sat in the position in which I had left her. Her face was drained white except for a red mark across one check. I wasn't sorry about that: only for the thing which had made it necessary.

"You see how it is, Fern," I said.

She kept on looking into the fire. She didn't answer at all.

"I'm sorry."

She stirred then and shook her head a little. "It's too bad, Barney. Why do you have to be such a fool?"

There was nothing I could say and, after a minute, she moved again. This time she looked at me.

"Why don't you let me help you?" she asked. "We weren't meant for this, you know. We were meant to be friends. If only you weren't afraid; if only you'd accept things ..." Her voice was very low, so low that I could hardly hear her. She turned back to the fire.

I waited a few minutes, but she was silent. So I said, "Good night, Fern," and crossed the apartment again and let myself out the ivory-colored door.

Better to be going out this way, I thought, than with the whole Homicide Division on my tail. I've definitely gained something tonight, I thought. I've won a battle.

Then why do I feel as though I've lost one? I wondered.

The Fifth Avenue bus stopped at Tenth Street to let me off, and there was Doc Birnbaum leaning against the railing of the corner church staring up at the moon. I said nothing, and he didn't seem to notice me as I slipped past.

I was glad of that because, somehow, the thought of talking to him tonight didn't appeal to me. My key was soft in the lock and I tiptoed into the apartment, not knowing whether Sheila would be there or not, and telling myself that it didn't make any difference, anyway. But when I heard her regular breathing from the bedroom, I knew that it did make a difference; I felt infinitely relieved.

When, at last, I was quiet in bed and Sheila undisturbed, my mind turned back to Doc Birnbaum standing on the corner staring at the moon.

Well, I told myself, maybe I haven't been exactly tolerant and understanding. Maybe I haven't leaned over backward. The strain of rehearsals has been tough on me; it's hard to do ten things at once. But tomorrow it'll be different, I thought. Tomorrow we'll start all over again.

Fifteen

"The ridiculosity of it," William and Mary said. "The sheer, asinine ridiculosity!"

I munched my supper of scrambled eggs, toast, and coffee. "That's a pretty word, William," I said. "Does it mean anything?"

He eyed me aloofly. "As a professional exponent of the *mot juste*," he said, "I assure you that ridiculosity is the only word which expresses my contempt for the particular brand of charlatanistic charades by which you earn a living."

"Not a living," I corrected him. "Merely a pittance."

"You lie," he insisted. "You're grossly overpaid. John Friday is running a private charity for his friends as well as a sucker trap for tourists."

"You disapprove?"

"No," he said. "Not if you can get away with it. The end always justifies the means when the end is the noble one of separating the bourgeoisie from its cash. Sock the merchants, my lad, and you can't go wrong.

You'll land in heaven though your sins be black as the clientele of a Harlem lunch wagon and thick as a Union Square orator's dialect."

"Then what are you kicking about?" I wanted to know. Sheila came out of the kitchen, poured me another cup of coffee, and waited to hear his answer. She was wearing an evening gown and looked very pretty.

"I'm not kicking," he said. "I'm merely registering a protest against the absurdity of your profession. For the past four weeks you have sweat blood in great quantities, you have been a mighty laborer in the Thespian vineyard, critically essaying this gesture and that gesture, discarding one and adopting the other; you have listened attentively to the sound of your own voice as you repeated lines written by someone else; you have looked into the mirror and contorted your face into strange grimaces. All that in preparation."

"Well?"

"Tonight," he continued, "the great moment is upon us. You dine frugally at five-thirty in the afternoon so you will not be tempted to belch in the middle of a love scene. Very soon now you will take a subway to your current house of prostitution, you will change your clothes and paint your face like any other harlot going to work. When the customers arrive at eight-thirty, you will be summoned from your cubicle and go into the bedroom—I beg your pardon, the stage—and do your stuff. Now I ask you. Is that a life work for an able-bodied, presumably intelligent man?"

"Listen, William," I said. "If a wing collar irks you that much, why in hell don't you go sit in the gallery? You'd feel more at home there, anyway."

"My friend," he admitted, "with your usual acumen you have driven straight to the heart of the matter. This collar does irk me, and so do these satin lapels and the shiny stripe down my pants. God damn it," he complained, "I feel respectable and I'm not used to it."

"William," Sheila said, "stop acting like a spoiled child. Those evening clothes are very becoming."

"Becoming, by God!"

"And," she continued, "Mr. Roberts is going to be impressed."

"I sincerely hope so," William said.

I looked at the two of them. "Roberts? The guy Fritz gave a Mickey Finn?"

William had the grace to appear a little embarrassed, but Sheila went on unabashed. "We've found a backer for William at last, thank goodness. We hope so, anyway. He's got a lot of money and he seems impressed by William's poetry. So you'll have to be nice to him. We'll bring him backstage after the play."

I looked at William and William cleared his throat and looked at the ceiling. "A guy has to live," he murmured.

Yes, you damned fool, I wanted to say. But you won't call it living in the place where your friend, Mr. Roberts, is going to put you unless I can stop him. Why, I wondered, do these damned things always have to turn up just when I'm the busiest?

I got up and put on my coat. "I'll have to leave now. Bring your sucker back to my dressing room and I'll try to refrain from spitting in his eye."

Sheila ran into the bedroom and came out wrapped in a long cape. "I'm going with you."

"But—"

"William and Mr. Roberts are going with the McCords. I have a seat alongside. I'll stay with you until they call the half-hour."

"It'll be a long wait," I warned her.

"I won't mind. Come on."

So we left William and Mary in the apartment and took a taxi uptown to the theatre. I was glad to have her with me because, to tell the truth, I was a little jittery. An opening night always got me that way.

My letter-box by the call board was stuffed with telegrams and I crammed them into my pocket. "Hello, Pop," I saluted the doorman, and he wished me, "Good luck, Mr. Page." There was a bright tension in the backstage air; even the voices of the stage hands had a staccato briskness to them.

I said, "Come on, darling," and we wound our way between the stage braces and canvas flats across the stage to my dressing room. The asbestos curtain was already down and all sounds were slightly muffled. The nostalgic odor of grease paint and moist rouge was in the air.

I opened my dressing room and switched on the light and put my coat on a hanger. Sheila sat down in the one extra chair. Dressing rooms are like that, not on the same plane with the gorgeous affairs which exist in the minds of Hollywood producers. Mine had a dressing table with adequate mirrors and lights, two chairs, a row of hooks and hangers on the wall, and a small and extremely uncomfortable couch which I had wangled out of the property room.

With a layer of newspaper neatly spread over the top of the dressing table, I turned, at last, to my telegrams. I read them all, smiling—from Pete, Hilda, Bob Evans, everyone I knew—and then stuck them in the frames of the mirrors. All but one, which I tried to pocket unseen.

But Sheila's eye was on me. She put her hand out firmly and I gave it to her. It was from Dick Taylor, the boy who had taken Sis McCord in charge, and I watched her while she read:

GOOD LUCK STOP IF YOU HAVE ANY
MORE SURPLUS INGENUES SEND THEM
OVER HERE STOP THERES ALWAYS ROOM
AT THE NATIONAL

Sheila looked up with inquiry back of her smile.
"What does he mean?"

"He's kidding," I told her. "Dick's sense of humor is
strictly slap-stick."

"Wait a minute," she said. "Didn't you tell me he
went out with Sis McCord the day you started
rehearsals?"

"He was only trying to get her a job."

"She's a fool." She handed me the telegram. "Sis
ought to know Dick can only waste her time. You'd
better tear that telegram up before Pete sees it."

I tore it up. Then I stripped to my underwear and
put on a dressing gown. I took off my shoes, too.

"You're not going to make up already, are you?"
Sheila protested. "It's not more than seven o'clock."

"I am not," I told her. "I'm going to stretch out on
that couch there and try to get a little sleep. I warned
you this would be a long wait for you."

"I don't mind," she assured me. "Isn't there something
you'd like me to do?"

"Two things," I said. "Tell Eddie—he's the property
man—that he has a standing order for coffee every
night at eight, starting tonight. Then stand by the
door with a club and, if anyone tries to come in, use
it."

"All right," she said, and I rolled over with my face
to the wall and closed my eyes. Immediately my mind
began to busy itself with a thousand little details
concerning the play. Was that letter in the breast
pocket of my second act suit? I must see that the door
down left actually works and doesn't stick as it did in
the dress rehearsal. Where did I leave the—? My God!

What was my first line? I'd forgotten my first line! Oh, hell, I told myself. Calm down and get some sleep. You've never blown up yet, have you? Take it easy.

There was a knock on the door that sounded like a cannon going off. I sat bolt upright on the couch.

"What was that?" I yelled. "Who's there?"

Sheila jumped and the door opened and Jake Hershey timidly stuck his head in. He seemed a little embarrassed to find Sheila there. "I just wanted to see how you were," he murmured.

"I'm all right," I told him, "and I'll stay all right as long as I'm let alone."

"Of course," he soothed. "Of course. Is there anything I can do for you?"

"Yes," I said. "Let me sleep."

Sheila reproved me with a look and, "After all, Barney, Jake's as nervous as you are."

That was unfair. "Jake's work is finished," I reminded her. "Mine's just beginning. Besides, I'm not nervous. I'm sleepy. All I want to do is get some sleep. Is that asking too much?"

She jumped up and went to the door without looking at me. "Come on, Jake," she said. "We'll leave him alone." They went out the door and closed it softly behind them.

I lay back on the couch again and tried to compose myself. God damn it, I thought. I'll never get any rest now.

When the stage manager knocked at the door and called, "Five minutes, please," I gave a final pat to my makeup, switched off the light, and went out on the stage. Everything seemed to be in order, the doors all working and the properties in place. The asbestos was up and, through the curtain, the deep, avid hum of the audience was audible. It was a packed house and sounded like it. Bess Nichols was already in place, absolutely motionless on the couch down right. The only sign of strain she showed was in her tightly clenched fists, and I knew that, when the curtain rose, those fingers would unflex, relax. Whatever you might think of her as a person, Bess Nichols was an actress. As I passed the couch, I touched her on the shoulder and murmured, "Good luck." She didn't look around, but her head jerked stiffly up and down in acknowledgement and she said, "Thanks. Same to you."

Jack called, "Places, please. Places for the first act. We're going up now. Places, please"—and I gave a final look around and went off left into the backstage world of muffled whispers, darkness pierced by sudden shafts of light, stage braces, and the bare canvas backs of flats. A utilitarian world of tension and strange acute angles. The hum from the audience grew louder and hungrier.

There was a quick rustle from behind, and I turned to see Fern coming from her dressing room. She came straight toward me and put out her hand. "Good luck, Barney," she said and, "Good luck," I wished her. She went on past me toward her entrance, a lonely figure somehow, but with power in her.

Jack's voice came from the other side of the stage now, and it sounded a little ragged and worn. "Stand by," he called; and, in a lower voice to the electrician, "Give us the foots and kill the house lights. Easy, now—easy." There was a pause. The audience's expectant drone mounted higher, then stiffened and died. There was absolute quiet. Then Jack said, "Take her up," and the curtain rose with a swish, and all the concentrated attention from out front rolled over the footlights and engulfed the stage.

Two hours and fifteen minutes later we were taking our curtain calls. As the curtain rose and fell, and rose and fell again, the anxiety and fatigue ebbed away.

When it went up for the fifth time, I caught sight of the gang grouped together in the third row center. They were pounding their hands together enthusiastically. Sheila was sitting on the edge of her seat and William and Mary's broad face was creased in a delighted grin. It looked as though they liked it.

Then some fool in the audience—probably one of Jake's relatives—began to yell, "Author! Author!" and the others took it up until it just couldn't be ignored. Not that I wanted to ignore it, of course, but Jake's attitude gave me a pain. Throughout the entire last act he had been getting in the way backstage, trotting back and forth to primp before the mirror in my dressing room. Now he was standing in the wings fiddling with his hair and adjusting his glasses, but when I motioned him on stage he pretended to be completely astonished. He forced me to pull the corniest gag in the world; I had to walk off stage and drag a presumably protesting playwright before the footlights. As though he could have been torn away from them.

But the audience loved him for it and he did his shy little speech very well; I give him credit for that. He assured the audience that he loved them in return, that he loved the cast, he loved John Friday, and that everyone in the world deserved credit for the play's success except himself. And when he finished, you could feel the audience smirking, "Isn't he sweet? So unassuming!" It was nauseating.

But that ended the curtain calls and, in the final analysis, the opening night was a personal triumph for Jake. I looked at Fern and Fern looked at me, and we both looked at the rest of the cast. They looked back at us. One more grudge had been chalked up against authors.

Fern and I walked to our dressing rooms together.

"Nice work," she said, and I thanked her and returned the compliment. I meant it, too. She was a pleasure to work with.

Then Jake caught up with us. His face was red and his eyes were shining from behind his glasses. I examined him closely as he talked. "Barney!" He grabbed my arm. "And Fern! Thanks! You were marvelous, both of you!"

"You weren't so bad yourself," I told him, and Fern murmured politely.

"Oh, but Barney!" he protested. "You shouldn't have dragged me out on the stage like that. I didn't know what to say."

"I thought that for an unprepared speech you did very well." That was Fern.

He changed the subject quickly. "Listen," he said. "I want to do something to show my appreciation. How about the whole gang of us going to the Stork Club?"

I stepped on that flatly. "That's all right for you, Jake. From now on all you have to do is collect royalties. But I'm still a working man. Tonight was just the opening. We have to do the same thing six nights a week."

"And two matinees," Fern added. "My speed is a sandwich and a glass of milk."

"All right," he took her up. "We'll go to the Chop House. We'll all go to the Chop House."

Fern said that would be fine, and, because I knew I'd have to go anyway, I said it would be fine, too.

Jake beamed at the amicable and inexpensive settlement. "Swell," he enthused. "That'll be marvelous. I'll have a chance to talk to you, Barney. I haven't finished with you yet for the dirty trick you played me."

"What dirty trick?"

"Dragging me out on the stage like that when I was completely unprepared." He shook his head ruefully.

"I haven't got over the shock yet. I was never so embarrassed in my life."

"You're right," I apologized. "That was a dirty trick and I'm sorry. But I'll make up for it now. You go right into my dressing room and use some of my cold cream."

"Cold cream?" he asked. "What for?"

"To take your makeup off," I told him. "You'll be even more embarrassed if you show up in the Chop House with grease paint on your face."

That'll hold him for a while, I thought.

Sixteen

By the time we were gathered around the big table, it was pretty apparent that Sheila was off to the races again. There was a bar just down the street from the Cochran Theatre and she evidently had spent the intermissions there. She wasn't tight—only entering upon her preliminary, dreamy stage—but I made up my mind to get her home as soon as I decently could.

But that wasn't going to be easy. Sheila wasn't the only one who had spent their between-acts in a bar; it was a lively crowd and, since the Chop House didn't sell liquor, someone had had the foresight to bring a bottle along. Mr. Roberts, on my left, passed it to me and I sent it on to Pete McCord, who poured himself a drink. When it got around to Sheila, sitting across from me, I tried to pantomime a warning, but it didn't register. Jake Hershey took the bottle from her, poured her a drink, another for Hilda Fleming, and passed the bottle on. I couldn't help noticing that he hadn't taken anything himself. The more I saw of Jake, the more I realized how I had underrated him in the past.

Pete McCord was next to me on my right and he looked as gloomy as I felt. He sipped at his glass and pretended an interest in the conversation that batted back and forth around him, but saw his eyes constantly revert to where, at the end of the table, Sis was holding forth between Jock McIntyre and Bob Evans.

"How goes it, Pete?" I asked.

He hesitated a moment. "Fine, Barney. Just fine. I haven't had the chance to see much of you lately, but I want to thank you for what you did for Sis."

"What did I do?"

He looked surprised. "Why," he said, "you introduced her to Richard Taylor, the producer, didn't you?"

"Oh," I said, "that. Yes, I introduced her to Dick Taylor." When, I wondered, did Dick promote himself to a producer's rank? Or was that just Sis's version for home consumption?

"Of course," he went on, "Taylor hasn't been able to do very much for her personally, but he's taken her around to meet a lot of people and she expects to get a job almost any time."

"Well," I said, "that's fine, isn't it?"

"Yes, that's fine." He nodded glumly. "She's enjoying herself and that's the important thing."

There was a pull at my sleeve and I turned to find Mr. Roberts blinking at me from under white eyebrows. I brushed my coat off where he had plucked it, but he didn't seem to notice.

"Mr. Page," he said, "I want to tell you how much I enjoyed your performance tonight. I enjoyed every minute, and I count it a privilege to meet you and talk to you, as it were, in a private capacity." He spoke English as though it were some rare language, savoring every word.

I watched him cautiously and wondered what he was leading up to. "You wouldn't believe me, Mr. Page, but I've been a pretty lonely man."

I grinned my sympathy and looked receptive.

"I've always wanted to lead this kind of life, the kind of life you people lead. But I haven't been able to. I've been too busy making a living."

Well, that certainly is tough, I thought. You million-aires rate a hell of a lot of sympathy from guys like me; I ought to turn Hilda Fleming loose on you.

He took a drink and pondered his unhappy lot. "And now," he said, "it's too late. I can't start over again. The best I can do is to help someone else—some deserving artist—to lead the kind of life I would like to have led, and to do the things I would like to have done." He blinked at me for approval.

"Very kind of you, I'm sure," I told him, and realized that this was the time to do something about William and Mary. But I couldn't. I was watching Sheila.

"Not at all," he assured me. "It's really a form of selfishness. If I can relieve a man—like your friend William, say—from material want, then I will be able to feel that I have in some measure contributed toward whatever success he may achieve. Do you see?"

I saw that it was up to me to put an end to his misdirected philanthropy before it got out of control. But Sheila was whispering to Jake now, and it was hard to concentrate.

"I must confess," Mr. Roberts said, "that until tonight I was somewhat doubtful as to whether William's character—his moral fiber—was of sufficient strength to warrant such an investment. Because, Mr. Page, after all, I am a business man, and I don't like to sink money in a losing venture. The possession of wealth is a great responsibility. Don't you agree?"

"I—" I began, and stopped. Jake had poured Sheila another drink—a big drink—and, as she sipped it, she was looking up at him and smiling. She had moved closer to him. And, which was worse, Bess Nichols had seen the whole act and my reaction to it. She gave me one of her dirty slow smiles that made me want to throw a coffee cup at her. I was sore and she knew it and was laughing at me.

"I have always contended," Mr. Roberts pronounced carefully, "that a man is best known by the company he keeps. Some of William's company I have not always approved of, but you and Mr. Hershey are his best friends, and I must say that I am most pleasantly impressed. Mr. Hershey has written an excellent play, and I have already told you how much I enjoyed your performance. Furthermore, I notice that neither of you drink. It seems to me—"

I rose abruptly. "You'll pardon me," I said to Mr. Roberts. "Sheila"—I attracted her attention—"it's getting late and I'm very tired. If you don't mind, we'll go home now."

Everyone protested that I was breaking up the party and that I could sleep all day tomorrow. Everyone but Sheila. She didn't say anything. She turned slowly away from Jake and looked at me. There was a stubborn, dangerous light in her eyes and a slow flush mounted on her face.

I continued to stand there waiting. The clamor died down and there was an embarrassing silence. Sheila didn't move. She sat still and looked at me.

Then Bess Nichols's voice cut drily through the silence. "Maybe Sheila doesn't want to go." There was a nervous, quickly suppressed giggle from someone. I felt my face getting hot.

Pete McCord saved the situation. "Come on, Sis. It's after midnight," he said, and stood up. "We've got to go, too."

And John Friday, bless him, backed him up. "It's all right for the idle rich to sit up all night, but we have work to do. Can I give you a lift, Barney?"

"No, thanks," I told him. "We'll take a cab. Let's go, darling."

So I got away with it that time, but only by the skin of my teeth.

We rode downtown in the same cab, Sheila and I, but we might as well have been strangers on opposite sides of the island. I tried to make conversation. I talked about the performance, but she was silent; and I tried a few conjectures about how long we should run, but she didn't answer. So I broke down completely and apologized.

"I'm sorry to drag you from the party," I said, "but the opening wore me out. I'm really tired."

But she had nothing to say to that either. She just sat on her side of the taxi looking out at the lights of Seventh Avenue as they went by. So I folded up too. When we get home, I thought, I'll make her a cup of hot chocolate and things will loosen up.

But they didn't. I started to help Sheila off with her wrap, but she walked into the bedroom without giving me a chance.

So I went into the kitchen and got my utensils together, meanwhile keeping an ear cocked for a movement in the other part of the apartment. There was none.

I got very fussy about the making of the chocolate. Since I'd laid off liquor, I'd got to like the stuff, and tonight I took even greater pains than usual. It was an outlet for me. I made some whipped cream and set it to one side first, then I mixed the chocolate in a little bit of boiling water, and, when it was all dissolved, I put in three cups of milk. Sheila took only one cup, but I had no mental hazard concerning my weight. Just at the critical moment I added a little vanilla, and then I poured the hot chocolate into the cups and put them on a tray. I decorated the tops with whipped cream and carried the tray into the living room and put it on the table by the couch. I was surprised at the way the cups rattled; I hadn't realized that I was nervous.

I went into the bedroom and called her. "I've made

some chocolate," I said. "It's in the living room. Would you rather I brought it in here?"

She didn't answer me. She was sitting in the chair under the reading lamp, but the lamp wasn't turned on. The only light in the room came through the open door behind me and it didn't seem to relieve the gloom any. I could dimly see that Sheila hadn't removed her wrap, and I was suddenly uneasy.

"I've made some chocolate; Sheila," I repeated. "Don't you want any?"

She raised her head then, and looked at me. I could feel her looking at me, although I couldn't see her eyes. "No," she said. "I don't want any."

Then she turned away again. So, after a minute, I said, "Okay, but it's here if you want it," and went back into the living room.

I sat down out there and stared at the God damned chocolate and wondered what I was going to do next.

The whipped cream dissolved and a thick congealing scum formed on the stuff as it grew cold. But for fifteen or twenty minutes nothing happened and there was not a sound from the bedroom.

The next thing I knew Sheila was walking past me and out the front door. She didn't say anything; she just walked out, and I was left sitting on the couch wondering what it was all about.

I waited awhile and she didn't come back, so I went over to the window and looked up and down Tenth Street. There was no sign of her either way. So I shut the window again and thought it over, and then I went out the apartment door and down into the foyer. She wasn't there either.

While I stood undecided, the street door opened and Doc Birnbaum came in. He nodded to me in his disjointed way. "Hello, Barney," he said.

"Hello, Doc."

Instead of going on up the stairs, he paused to peer

at me with that omniscient, all-seeing manner which doctors affect. "You're up late."

"I'm not up any later than you are."

"That's right." He nodded sagely. "But a doctor keeps late hours sometimes."

"Well," I said, "an actor's job is to entertain people. We stay up to amuse the doctors."

He pondered that awhile. "That may be true," he said at last. "Fifty per cent true, anyway. I just thought you might be worried about Sheila."

"Have you seen her?"

"I passed her just now on the corner of Sixth Avenue," he said. "Is anything the matter?"

"Not a thing," I told him. "She's just taking a walk before turning in."

He didn't believe me, but he said, "Good night," and went on up the steps. I watched him climb and listened to his footsteps die away as he reached the fifth floor, and I wondered why in hell he didn't move to a lower floor or to an apartment house that had an elevator.

Then I hurried back for my hat.

The corner of Sixth Avenue, Doc Birnbaum had said. There was a drugstore there, but it was closed. It was pretty late now and, if Sheila had stayed in the neighborhood, there were only a few places she could go. Madame Céleste's and Fritz's were the likely ones, so I started walking west.

I went to Christopher Street first and met Henri on the sidewalk as he was closing up. He passed the time of night with me and I left him without having to ask any questions.

So that left Fritz's, and I turned toward Waverly Place wondering what I'd do if she were actually there. By the time I reached Gay Street, I wasn't sure if I wanted to find her or not.

She wasn't in Fritz's, but William and Mary was. So were Jake Hershey and Bess Nichols; the trio, resplendent in evening clothes, stood at the bar surrounded by an admiring proletarian group. I put my head in the front door and pulled it out again before they could see me, and then I went around to the family entrance and looked in there. There was no sign of Sheila in either place.

So I walked slowly back to Tenth Street again, telling myself that it was just as well. She was probably at home by this time and I was lucky not to have found her at Fritz's. But when I got back to the apartment and it was still empty, I knew that I wasn't lucky; I knew that I'd be glad to find her any place, in any condition.

Then I did what I'd been afraid to do before. I went into the bathroom and forced myself to look in the medicine closet. Only the usual miscellaneous collection was there, but I wasn't satisfied until I'd gone through all of her things in the bedroom as well. I thanked God when I found nothing; there was no trace of sodium amytal or a sedative of any kind. I picked up what was left of the hot chocolate then, carried it into the kitchen and poured it into the sink. I washed the cups and saucers and put them away in the cupboard.

There was a quart bottle of Scotch in there, one that we kept for guests, and it was almost full. I took it out and held it in my hand and read the label. For the first time in all these months, I found myself wanting a drink.

I got out a siphon of soda and put it down on the shelf under the cupboard. I poured a stiff jolt—about three fingers—into a water glass and filled the rest of the glass with soda. I picked it up.

Then I hesitated and looked around the room and came to a decision. I went over to the sink and carefully poured the drink after the chocolate, and turned around and started to walk out of the kitchen.

The bottle of Scotch standing on the shelf caught my eye and I acted without thinking. I picked it up and threw it across the room at the sink. My aim was good; it hit the right place and smashed just under the water tap. There was a crash that sounded loud enough to wake everyone in the house, and the Scotch gurgled down the drain.

I felt better after that. I went into the living room, picked up my hat, put on my coat again, and went out.

This time I had no idea where to look. I walked around aimlessly for half an hour or so, and then I sat down on a bench in Washington Square and stared at the statue of Garibaldi. Garibaldi stared just as fixedly in another direction; maybe he had troubles of his own.

The dawn woke me up. I was shivering with the cold, but I must have slept for several hours in spite of it. I got up and stretched the cramp from my legs and started to walk uptown.

On Twenty-Third Street I went into a little restaurant and had some coffee. There was a morning paper on the counter and I stared at the headlines, but I didn't turn to the theatrical page; the play and the notices it might have received seemed very far away.

Around eight o'clock I decided I might as well get it over with. There was a performance to give that night and I'd have to sleep some time. So I paid my check and started out, the newspaper under my arm.

The subway got me downtown with a rush, and when I turned into Tenth Street the sun was shining brightly. It was a lovely day. At the apartment house, I didn't hesitate; I just went in and climbed the stairs and opened the front door of the apartment and went on in.

Sheila was there, but it didn't surprise me. I was too tired to feel much of anything. She had set the breakfast table in the living room and was in the kitchen dishing out bacon and eggs.

"Breakfast is ready," she called. "I saw you coming from the window."

Her voice was sweet; too sweet. She was covering something up. But I didn't care. I sat down at the table and poured myself a cup of coffee from the percolator and opened my purloined newspaper to the theatrical page.

Sheila came in with a plate of toast and put it in front of me. I said, "Thanks," but I didn't look up. All this attention must have a meaning behind it. I waited for her next move and wished it would come quickly so I could get it over with and go to bed.

She stood behind me without saying anything for a minute or two, and then she suddenly put her arms around my head and pressed herself against my face. "I'm sorry, darling," she said. "Let's forget about it, shall we?"

"Sure," I told her. "We'll forget about it."

I managed to eat some breakfast, but I couldn't read the review. My eyes were blurred. Sheila picked it up and read it, though, and carried it into the bedroom when she followed me there. After I had undressed and got into bed, she handed it to me. She sat down then on the other bed.

After a moment, "I've told you I'm sorry, Barney," she said.

"I heard you."

"Aren't you going to tell me anything?"

I was pretty sick of all this. "What do you want me to tell you? That I'm sorry, too? Okay, I'm sorry."

"Is that all?"

"I thought we were going to forget about it," I said. "I thought that was what you wanted."

She stood up quickly. "You can't just forget about things like that. Things aren't as easy as all that."

"No," I agreed. "And, if they were, you'd find some way to make them harder."

She sat down as quickly as she had risen. "Where did you go last night? Where did you sleep?"

I put the paper aside. There was no use trying to pretend I was reading.

"Last night," I told her, "I went out looking for you. You may remember that you left here without telling me where you were going. As for sleeping, I was entirely alone—if that's what's worrying you."

"You know it isn't."

"I don't know anything," I said. "I'm beginning to find that out."

There were traces of tears in her voice now. "I just went out for a little walk," she said. "And when I came home and you weren't here, I didn't know what to do. I was frantic. I haven't had a wink of sleep all night."

"You look very well, considering," I told her.

She took hold of my hand. "We can't go on like this, Barney. Something's got to be done."

"Okay," I told her. "Do it."

"But what? I try my best, and it doesn't seem to do any good. I don't know what you want me to do."

"Don't you?" I raised myself on one elbow. "All right, I'll tell you. It won't make the slightest bit of difference to you, but I'll tell you, anyway. Stay away from Jake Hershey. He's not doing you a bit of good and he's doing me a lot of harm. So stay away from him."

"That's absurd." A little color came into her cheeks. "There's nothing between Jake and myself. How could you imagine such a thing?"

"I don't imagine anything," I told her. "Put it, if you like, that I'm jealous. But, just the same, you'll be doing me a great favor if you do what I tell you to. To use a homely expression," I said, "the bastard gets in my hair."

She picked a piece of lint from the bedspread and then she examined her fingernails. "I suppose," she said at last, "that what you're asking is reasonable—from your point of view. I'll do it, of course. But I can't very well help being decent to him when we meet."

"That's entirely up to you," I assured her. "I know I'm at least fifty per cent wrong about this, and I'm willing to make allowances."

"All right," she said again. "I'll do it."

She looked at her fingernails and I looked at her, wishing I knew what she was really thinking. "Listen, Sheila," I said. "As long as we're on this subject, there's something I'd like you to do for yourself alone. It's not a favor to me or anyone else but yourself."

She raised her eyes quickly. "Yes?"

"Lay off the liquor entirely."

She blushed. "If you're suggesting that I was drunk last night—"

"Last night is wiped off the record," I said. "It's forgotten. I'm talking about the future—your future. You're not the type who can drink. You can't even take one drink. Some people are like that, you know. I am, myself. That's why I stopped. Do you see?"

"Is that why you broke the Scotch last night?" she asked. "So I couldn't have it?"

I'd forgotten that. "No," I told her. "That Scotch had nothing to do with you. That was broken for another reason. You haven't answered my question. I want to be sure you understand what I'm trying to tell you."

"Well, yes," she said. "If you really feel like that, I don't mind going on the wagon. I think you're making a fuss about nothing, but I don't mind. It'll be easy enough, God knows; I never did really like the nasty stuff."

"Okay," I said. "Now, it seems like you're making all the concessions. I know there are a lot of things you don't like about me. I'm sorry I was rude to you in the dressing room last night. It was the strain of the opening and it won't happen again. I'm sorry about a lot of other things, too, and I'll do my best about them. Is that fair?"

She smiled. "Darling," she said. She leaned over and kissed me. Then she rose, picked up the paper and handed it to me. "Have you seen the notices? No? Well, read this and tell me what you think about it. It's a peach. Then you can go to sleep."

I turned the paper over and located the column entitled FIRST NIGHTS. Sheila stood watching me as I lay back on the pillow and read it myself. This is what it said:

FIRST NIGHTS

A Newcomer

Halfway House, a play in three acts
by J. J. Hershey, staged and produced by
John Friday at the Cochran Theatre.

Betty Prone	Elizabeth Nichols
Magda Prone	Fern Costello
Everett Stanton	Bernard Page
Vincent Thompson	Arthur Grainger
John	Thomas Barnette
Eddie Hill	Paul Glasset
Nora	Margaret Lester

Although J. J. Hershey, hitherto unknown to this reviewer, puts a heavy strain upon his actors in *Halfway House*, they are more than a match for him. In this play which opened last night at the Cochran, a young playwright has, with his first venture, come into his own. There are times, we freely admit, when Mr. Hershey has written haltingly; the play is, like the minstrel, "A thing of shreds and patches." But Bernard Page as the young publisher with a streak of genius and a run of bad luck, and Fern Costello as the extremely attractive source of most of the latter, both play magnificently.

As a playwright Mr. Hershey excels both in the sweep of his story and the authenticity of his characterization. For the sharp etching of the above two parts is not solely the achievement of John Friday's splendid casting....

There was a lot more like that and it was all about Jake. Neither Fern nor I was mentioned after the first paragraphs and the supporting cast was lumped together in one sentence and patted on its collective shoulder. I put the paper down and found that Sheila was still looking at me with a peculiar light in her eyes.

"What do you think?" she asked. "Isn't it simply grand?"

"You seem to think so," I said, and rolled over on my side and closed my eyes. I heard her rustling the paper as she left the room.

That son of a bitch, Jake, I thought. The guy has a perfect genius for crossing me up. Now he's even stolen the notices.

But I was too tired to care very much anymore. In a few minutes I was asleep.

Seventeen

I bought a car. One Sunday morning I went up to Columbus Circle and drove home in a second-hand Buick coupé. There were only eight thousand miles on it and it still had its original paint job, a dark red. From then on we spent our weekends in the country. Sheila would call for me at the stage door every Saturday night at eleven; the suitcases would be packed and in the car, and by midnight we'd be out on a country road.

The treatment worked well. Sheila enjoyed the trips, and as long as the good weather lasted, we were happier together than we had been for some time. All the unpleasant things were forced into the background and we managed to keep them there fairly well.

Thanksgiving of that year fell on Sheila's birthday, and we had a little party after the show. John was there, and Pete McCord and Sis, and William and Mary. Hilda Fleming and Ruth Goldberg came, too. We had some liquor, but nobody got tight, and Sheila did a very pretty bit of faking with straight orange juice. Neither Fern Costello nor Jake Hershey was invited. Everyone had a nice peaceful evening and went home early. They left early, anyway, although I heard later that they all went over to Madame Céleste's and stayed there until Henri kicked them out. But I didn't tell that to Sheila.

And Christmas week was pretty much the same. It was a little difficult with our friends celebrating all around us; there were times when I caught a discontented shadow on Sheila's face. So I decided that, after all, I had no right to expect her to behave like a nun or a girl scout, and when plans were being made for New Year's Eve I said, okay, we'd go along too.

It started out as a gala evening even before I left the theatre. When the curtain came down and the cast lined up for their calls, someone started humming "Auld Lang Syne." The audience heard it and caught it up and, in a couple of seconds, we were all singing on both sides of the footlights. I caught a glimpse of Eddie, the property man, waving to the guy on the curtain to hold it up, and the next thing I knew the stage hands had come out and they were singing too. There's something about that song on New Year's Eve. It got me. When the curtain finally came down and the noise died away, I was feeling very mellow.

Fern walked with me toward the dressing rooms. "Going out?"

"Yes," I told her. "There's a gang of us. Aren't you coming?"

She shook her head. "I was going to, but—"

"Why 'but'? Come on." On New Year's Eve I was the friend of all the world.

She turned into her dressing room and I went next door to mine. Sheila was there already and Pete McCord and William and Mary were with her. Pete had a bottle and there were a couple of glasses on the washstand.

"It's a hell of a note," William and Mary said. "You out there carousing around the stage and your poor wife in here dying of thirst. For God's sake, tell the girl she can have a drink."

I winked at Sheila. "I'm sure I have nothing to say about it," I told him, and then I turned to Pete. "Where's Sis?"

He didn't look at me. "She's working tonight," he explained. "She's got a job in a floor show. It's only a temporary job."

"That's fine," I said. I didn't ask him what club she was working at. He looked burnt up already.

Bess Nichols put her head in the door and called, "I'll be ready in fifteen minutes. Just give me time to take my makeup off," and ran out again.

"Your doing?" I asked William and Mary.

He handed Sheila a glass. "Mine," he admitted. "Do you mind?"

I watched Sheila. "Not at all," I told him. "Not a bit. Fern's coming along too."

"Good," he said. "Well, Happy Days."

"Happy Days," Sheila repeated, and raised her glass and drank from it. She glanced at me over the rim and, when she saw that I was watching her, she turned away.

Midnight. New Year's Eve on Times Square. Snow settling in little flurries and people in the snow having a hell of a time.

A blare of noise, a shrieking of whistles, and an exultant yelling as though all the condemned souls in hell and the suffering ones in purgatory suddenly had been granted a free and unconditional pardon. People jumped up and down, throwing confetti and braying their triumph at having survived another year. They embraced each other with enthusiasm; tomorrow they'd go back to cutting each other's throats, but tonight, for one night only, they were comrades and brothers. It was a lovely feeling of release.

I felt it myself. With one hand I held tightly to Sheila and with the other I spun a wooden rattle around and around. This is a new year, I kept saying to myself. This is a new and different year. This year it's going to be different.

I looked down at Sheila and found her looking at me. A clock tolled somewhere and the noise swelled. We kissed quietly and completely. For a moment we were quite alone while the noise surged around us.

"Barney," she whispered. "Let's be happy, shall we?"

There was snow in her hair and on her shoulders, and a few crystals had fallen, melting, on her upturned face. I pressed her close. "We'll show 'em, kid," I told her. "We'll show 'em." There was liquor on her breath, but not too much; it was easy to ignore. I kissed her again.

Somebody said, "What are we waiting for?" And somebody else said, "Let's go." We fought our way through the crowd toward the subway entrance.

We went to the Village Mill where some people were holding places for us. They were there when we arrived, at a long table in the center of the room, and they shouted a welcome over the music of the orchestra. Then they immediately forgot us to pick up an argument we had interrupted.

"It's three per cent hydrogen dioxide, that's what it is, and ninety-seven per cent hydrogen and oxygen. Okay. So water is two per cent hydrogen and one part oxygen. Water like you drink. So you take an extra part of oxygen and then you put in three per cent hydrogen dioxide and you've got it. See?"

"Not on my hair."

"Okay. So you keep on going to a drugstore and paying fancy prices for peroxide. When all you have to do is take an extra part of oxygen and mix it up in a glass of water. You don't make sense."

We distributed ourselves around the table wherever there were chairs. Bess Nichols and I slipped into two places between Jake Hershey and Hilda Fleming. Fern Costello found a chair across the table. Hilda nodded to me as I sat down.

"Not on my hair," she repeated.

Jake looked up shyly over his glasses and said, "Hi, Barney. Welcome to Freshman Chemistry."

"Hi, Jake. Catch the show tonight?"

"Not tonight," he said. "I haven't been around lately."

"I've noticed that. What's up? Working?"

"I'm doing a new play," he admitted. "I'd like to talk to you about it. I'm not sure whether it will stack up with *Halfway House* or not."

"It will," I said. "You're going places, Jake. Nothing can stop you. Not even yourself."

"Why, thanks, Barney. But if I am, you're going right along with me."

I smiled and shook my head. "No," I said. "That's not in the script. I'm not going with you, Jake."

"But—"

"Forget it."

Bess Nichols was tugging at my arm. "What is it?" I asked.

She was staring across the dance floor at a table in the far corner. "Didn't Pete McCord say his wife was working tonight?"

"Yes. In a floor show some place. Why?"

"Take a look," she said. "Is that the kind of floor show he meant?"

It wasn't. Sis was with a party of two other girls—tramps, by the look of them—and three men. I knew one of the men: Dick Taylor, the self-appointed producer.

"The damned little fool," I said. "How'm I going to keep Pete from seeing that?"

Bess shrugged. She wasn't interested in saving anyone else's feelings. I floundered around trying to dope some way out, but it looked like a blind alley. Even if I managed to get word to Dick Taylor, he'd never be able to smuggle Sis out unseen. She was tight and he didn't look any too sober himself. Their table was squarely on the most direct route to the men's room, and, at the rate Pete was downing highballs, it was only a question of minutes before he'd pass right by them. I didn't know what to do.

I found myself looking across the table at Fern Costello. She must have seen the same thing I had, because she nodded reassuringly to me. I felt easier then; there wasn't any reason why I should, but I did. She seemed very competent, very sure of herself. And women are better at handling things like that than men are.

I took a card from my pocket and scribbled a note. Then I excused myself and left the table. As I passed Dick, I dropped the card in front of him and went on into the men's room, straightened my tie, lit a cigarette, and fooled around for a minute before going out again.

Sis had her head lowered when I repassed her table, but she glanced up quickly and gave me a slight nod. She looked frightened. Dick winked at me; he wasn't so tight that he hadn't shifted his chair around to block any possible view from our table.

When I got back, Fern caught hold of my hand. "Here's Barney," she announced. "I'll leave it up to Barney."

Everybody quieted down and focused on me.

"You'll leave what up to me?" I asked.

"I've asked everyone up to my apartment," Fern said. "I want to give a party. A big party."

That sounded like a solution. "At least we can be alone," I said. "We can raise hell in peace."

Fern jumped up as though it were all settled. As a matter of fact, it was. We won our point by not listening to other opinions, which is as good a method as any.

Four of us got in one taxi: Jake Hershey, Bess Nichols, Sheila, and myself. Bess was sulking in her corner all the way uptown, and I suspected that she was disappointed because Pete hadn't seen Sis. Sheila was quiet, too, and I hoped she wasn't going into her dreamy state. So far she had shown no sign of it, although I'd seen her take three more drinks since the one she had in the theatre. Anyway, she and Bess were sitting this one out and the social responsibilities of the little group fell on Jake and myself. Which made it ever so cheerful. We were all glad when the cab pulled up at Fern's address on Park Avenue and we found the rest of the bunch waiting on the sidewalk.

Fern and a couple of others who had taken a taxi together hadn't shown up yet, but, after a few minutes, they came along too. Fern explained that she had stopped to get some liquor in case we ran out. There was half a case of rum on the floor of the cab, so I shouldered it and carried it into the apartment house.

Sheila and I took the elevator together; the others had gone ahead while she waited for me. My hands were occupied with the case of rum, so, when we got out of the elevator, I let her close the door.

"Be sure you shut it," I told her. "It has a way of sticking." I heard it slam as I entered the apartment.

Fern saw me as I came in. "Put it right in the kitchen, Barney," she said.

I carried the case into the kitchen, opened one of the bottles, and set it in readiness until there was a call for it. Then I got a tray of glasses and carried it into the living room. Fern was already dealing out drinks. "I opened a bottle for you," I told her. But she gestured toward the liquor cabinet. "I'd forgotten how much I had," she said. "I think there's plenty right here." She handed me a Scotch-and-soda and I looked around for a place to put it.

Pete McCord was sitting by himself over on the window-seat. He was staring out into Park Avenue, looking pretty low. So I pushed my way across the room—they were dancing now—and put my glass in his hand and sat down beside him.

He nodded his thanks. He poured the drink down his throat and, with his left hand, made a nervous gesture of feeling his face. I looked at him more attentively; I hadn't noticed before that he was badly shaven, if he had shaved that day at all. There were little red bristles all over his chin which passed unnoticed at a distance. One more thing became very apparent close up. He was drunk. He didn't stagger and his speech was only a little thick, but you could see it in his eyes.

He noticed my empty hands. "You're not drinking."

"No, Pete. I don't drink anymore."

"You don't drink anymore," he said. "You're a very funny fellow. You know that."

"No. I don't know that."

"Well," he told me, "you are, anyway." He handed me his empty glass. "Get me another drink, will you? I don't like to move."

"Sure," I said, and went over to the liquor cabinet and mixed him a stiff one. I took it back to him and sat down beside him again. He kept looking at me.

"You're a funny fellow," he repeated. "Thanks."

"Thanks for what?"

His tongue got a little twisted. "For"—he said at last—"for getting—for trying to get me out of there without seeing her. I did see her, you know."

"No," I said. "I didn't know. That's too bad."

"It's not too bad. Not at all," he came back. "What the hell? Everybody knows about it. Everybody knows I sprouted horns. See?" He put his fists to his forehead and wiggled his forefingers at me. Trying to hold his glass upright at the same time was too much for him and the drink spilled on his trousers. I took the glass and put it on the window-sill.

"You're tight, Pete," I told him. "I'm taking you home pretty soon."

He shook his head. "No, you're not. I may be drunk, but I'm not that drunk. Not drunk enough to want to go home."

I looked at his eyes with their dilated, wavering pupils, at his drawn face with the red bristles sticking unevenly out of the skin. He was in a bad way. "You're as drunk as you can get without passing out. And I don't want you to pass out. You're enough of a mess as it is. I'll bet you haven't had a good night's sleep for weeks."

"Months," he said. "Ha!"

"You're a mess. You need sleep and you need a shave. A Turkish bath is the place for you. I'll drop you at the Luxor on Forty-Sixth."

He felt his face. Rubbed his hand over the little red bristles. "No," he said. "I don't want a shave. I've been thinking about it for a long time. I'm going to raise a beard."

I stood up.

A memory jolted vividly through my mind: *Madame Céleste's joint and Pete, with a red beard on him, looking up at me from the table. "It's been a long time, Pete," and, "Not long enough, Barney. Not nearly long enough."*

I felt sick.

Fern came up and stood by my side. "Dance, Barney?" She slipped her arm through mine.

"Sure," I told her. "Sure." I put my arm around her and we circled off into the center of the room.

I felt like a fellow in a picture show who sees the film rolling around to the point where he came in. And this was one show I didn't want to sit through twice.

Eighteen

"Masculine will only be
Things that you can touch and see."

So much for education.

I felt an intense need for facts, hard masculine facts. I asked myself a favor: Please, Barney, I asked, don't get fanciful on me. Get the facts; hold on to the facts.

Okay. It was the first of January, maybe two, maybe two-thirty, in the morning. William and Mary was feeding dance records into the machine. Sheila was sitting on the couch talking to Bess Nichols. She had a drink in her hand and looked mad about something. People were dancing, drinking, talking. Pete McCord was passing out on the window-seat. He was growing a beard.

That was bad, all right, but what the hell could I do about it? Something, maybe; I'd try, anyway. How about Sheila—why was she mad? I'd learn that sooner or later; I always did. And William. Where is Mr. Roberts, William? I'd have to find out about that. It was certainly time to do something, but what? Take it easy, hang on to the facts, start at the beginning.

It was the first of January, New Year's Eve, and I was dancing with Fern Costello.

"Why?" I asked her. "Why am I dancing with you?"

She didn't move her dark head from where it was pressed against my chest. Seen from above, her neck fell away in a softly obtuse angle into her white shoulder. Her lips moved against the lapel of my coat.

"Because I asked you to."

"Why?"

"Because I was watching you and, all of a sudden, you looked scared to death. What scared you?"

The record scratched to an end. William and Mary put on another.

I didn't know what to tell her and the music started again before I had to try. It was a number which had been popular a couple of years before and we went on dancing. Fern hummed, *I'll never smile again* ...

"We shouldn't be doing this, Fern," I said.

"... *until I smile at you* ... You can't stop things from happening."

"Why can't you? Why are you dancing with me? Why

don't you leave me alone?"

"Would it make any difference?"

"I don't think so. I'm afraid not."

"... the tears would fill my eyes—my heart would realize ..."

We danced. I said, "You've never forgotten that night up here in the apartment, have you?"

"No."

"You hate my guts, don't you?"

"I love you."

We kept on dancing. After a minute, I asked her, "What are you going to do about it?"

"Nothing. Nothing can be done. It's too late."

"Well, then—?"

"Don't worry," she said. And, by mutual consent, we stopped. She went into the bedroom, passing behind the couch where Bess Nichols and Sheila sat. She was still humming *I'll never smile again* as she went into the bedroom.

I walked over to William and Mary. "Where's Mr. Roberts, William?" I asked.

His face screwed itself up as though he were in pain. "You do ask the God damnedest, most depressing questions," he complained. "Just when I'm enjoying myself."

"You don't have to tell me," I said. "I was only being polite."

He had a half-dozen records in his hands trying to read the titles on them. I doubt if he could even see the labels. "Beautiful, beautiful music," he crooned. "Lovely, marvelous music." He selected one at random and started it on the machine. "I don't mind telling you, Barney," he said above the music. "I'd tell you anything."

"That's nice."

"It certainly is," he agreed. "About Mr. Roberts. Friends and well-wishers will be gratified to learn that that prince of merchants is spending the holidays in the bosom of his family. Back in Wyoming or Nebraska, I believe; I'm not sure which."

"If he'd only stay there."

"He won't," William assured me. "He'll be back. He's taken an apartment, a marvelous apartment, by the year. I'm living in it now."

"Well," I said, "you're that much ahead, anyway."

"If you look at it from that angle," he agreed. "I'm eating regularly, too. He's guaranteed all my bills at Madame Céleste's. Come and have dinner with me. Bring your creditors."

"No, thanks. Listen, William," I told him, "if it's only a question of money, you've managed to get along pretty well so far. There's no reason for you to stick your neck out the way you're doing. You've never asked me; you've never asked any of your friends, but you know damned well—"

He smiled and shook his head. "That would be breaking with tradition," he said. "I couldn't do that. We geniuses—as differentiated from genii—have always been supported by the moneyed classes and, by God, they owe it to us. It isn't too much to ask for one compensating gesture from the merchants, is it? Life was swell before the bourgeoisie took it over; they're the boys who made it the nasty thing it is, aren't they? Then let the sons of bitches pay for it."

He was serious. I think it was the first time I had ever seen him dead in earnest. I didn't like it. "But William," I protested, "if you feel that way, why do you put up with it? Break with the old bastard. You don't owe him anything. You're not married to him, you know."

He smiled. When he answered, his voice was back to normal. "That's what you think," he said.

Someone had lured Bess Nichols from Sheila's side

and was prancing around the room with her. So that left Sheila alone on the couch and I went over and sat down beside her. I was a little groggy and confused, the way a slow, heavy fighter is confused by a lighter but faster opponent. Lightning-like taps that come from nowhere and don't seem to hurt much at the time, but, after ten rounds of them, the big guy starts feeling for his corner.

Sheila looked safe; she seemed stable. I thought of her face looking up at me from among the flurrying snowflakes, and remembered, *"Let's be happy, Barney, shall we?"* That had been earlier this evening, this very same New Year's Eve.

Her right hand held a glass, her left one lay neglected in her lap. I appropriated it as I sat down. "Happy New Year," I said.

She didn't bother to turn to me. After a chilling moment, she asked, "Is it?" and finished her drink. She let her hand stay where it was, but it lay impersonally in mine as though she didn't know I held it.

That wasn't encouraging. I tried thinking back to what I could have done, but, as far as I could remember, my record was clear. So I blamed it on the liquor.

"Darling," I said, "I don't want to spoil your fun, but I wish you'd go a little easy. You said you would, you know."

She turned then and gave me a curious, detached look. She looked me up and down as though she were mildly surprised that I could speak English and then turned away again.

"Well, what is it?" I asked at last. "What have I done now?"

"Have you done something?"

That griped me. "Oh, for Christ's sake," I told her, "come off it. If you're peeved about something, tell me what it is. If it's only the liquor, then lay off. You've had plenty now; you know what it does to you."

She didn't answer, so "I don't want to spend New Year's Eve taking care of an hysterical female," I said.

That snapped her out of it. I knew it would, and that's the only reason I said it, so help me God.

She was so furious that her face got set and hard, and ugly lines showed up in it. "You—!" she started, and had to stop and get her breath before she went on. "God damn you!" she said. "Isn't it enough that you've tricked me into coming to this place, without insulting me now that I'm here?"

I was really surprised. More at the extent of her anger, I think, than at what she said. "Nobody tricked you into coming here, Sheila. If you didn't want to you had plenty of chance to say so. We were alone together downstairs. Why didn't you tell me then, or when we came up together in the elevator?"

"The elevator!" She jerked her hand out of mine and jumped to her feet. Her glass fell to the floor and rolled under the couch while she stood tensely glaring at me. Then, without another word, she snapped away. She walked over to the corner where the liquor cabinet was and I saw her take another glass from one of the gang hovering around there.

I was stumped. The whole thing was so completely beyond me that I just sat there wondering what in hell had got into her. After a few minutes Bess Nichols came back and sat beside me. She said something, but I didn't catch what it was.

"What did you say?" I asked.

"I said, what's the matter with Sheila? You two fighting?"

"Of course not," I assured her. "What gave you that idea?"

Bess was right in her element. "Well," she said, "when I was talking to her, she didn't seem to fancy the idea of your being so much at home in Fern's apartment. That was rather stupid of you, Barney, you know."

"Stupid?" I didn't get it. "I just carried some rum into the kitchen for her. Anybody would have done that."

"Sure," Bess agreed. "But would anyone have known where the kitchen was? And where the corkscrew was kept? A man has to be pretty much of a dope, Barney, to take his wife to another woman's apartment, warn her to be careful shutting the elevator door—that it has a way of sticking—and not expect her to get a little suspicious."

So that was it. "Well, I'll be damned," I said. "If that isn't the silliest thing. If I were trying to keep something under cover, do you suppose I'd have come here in the first place?"

"It's not me that's supposing," Bess reminded me. "It's Sheila."

"Oh, nuts," I said. "Of course I've been here before. Once. Fern and I ran over a few scenes together. Once."

"Then I'd tell her that, if I were you. You should have told her when it happened."

"I did tell her," I said. And then I remembered that I hadn't. The reason I hadn't was because that was the night Sheila had gone off with Jake Hershey to the theatre and I had been pretty peeved about it. "Good Lord," I said, "what an asinine thing to fight about."

"Isn't it?" Bess agreed, and we both looked over at Sheila. She was leaning against the wall by the liquor cabinet and she held a glass in her hand. William and Mary was talking to her, but she didn't seem to be paying any attention to him. I didn't like the way she looked; I didn't even like the way she held her glass. She looked surly and flushed, and her glass was at an angle that was a menace to the rug. I knew it was time to be getting her home, but I couldn't figure how to go about it.

Bess piped up again. She had been talking for some time, but I had been too engrossed with my own problems to hear more than a vague droning at my side. I tuned in on her now, though, and caught, "— not so very important. These things are always happening in married life."

"What do you know about married life? You've never been married."

"No," she said, "but I've played brides so often that I'm able to think like one when I like. Which isn't often. I'd rather take my wedded bliss vicariously."

"That's all right with me," I told her.

Jake Hershey had moved into the picture. He was talking to Sheila. William and Mary went off somewhere and Sheila brightened up. She listened to Jake and he talked to her intently. He was on the other side of the cabinet and leaned across it, resting his elbows on the top. He was damned near breathing down her neck and she was paying bright attention to everything he said.

Bess kept droning on beside me. "What's that?" I asked her.

"What happened to you that night?" she repeated. "Where did you go?"

"What night?"

"You are worked up, aren't you? You haven't heard a word I said. The night of the opening. After you left us at the Chop House. We missed you when you didn't show up at Fritz's Place. I suppose Sheila told us what happened, but I've forgotten. We had a lot of fun."

Smack. Right on the button. That one dazed me a little; it hurt. It had come so fast I hadn't even seen it start.

"The night of the opening? Lord, Bess, I don't remember. It's too long ago. We left you uptown, didn't we? Sheila and I?"

That long, cold ride downtown in a taxi. Sheila and

I in our separate solitary confinement cells, not speaking to each other.

"—and then, later," Bess was saying, "Sheila came over and joined us at Fritz's. Jake Hershey and William and myself. I was so tight by that time that I can't remember what she said happened to you."

"I had some business to attend to," I told her. "But, as a matter of fact, I did come looking for you later. I saw you in the bar, but Sheila wasn't with you, so I didn't go in."

"Did you look in the back room?" she asked.

"I did."

She laughed. "Well, in that case there's only one other place she could have been. I'm sure you didn't look in the little girls' room."

"No," I said. "I didn't look there. Excuse me, will you, Bess? I want to get a drink of water."

I got up and walked away without waiting for an answer. I went on out in the kitchen and closed the door and leaned against the sink. I knew that I'd better be by myself for a little while.

I was mad. It's funny. I'd thought I was all over being peeved about that night Sheila had walked out and not come home. Now, finding that she had been with Jake Hershey, it started all over again. I was so God damned mad I wanted to kick things, but I held myself in and tried to rationalize the situation.

I stayed out in the kitchen five minutes or so, and then I went back into the living room. It was in my mind to quietly tell Sheila to get her things and come on home.

The party looked about the same; the same people were talking and laughing and dancing. The same record I had danced to with Fern was on the Victrola again. Sheila was standing by the liquor cabinet and Jake was still leaning intimately across and talking to her.

He saw me coming, whispered something, straightened up, felt his glasses, and moved away. Sheila gave me a quick glance and then turned her back on me. She drained her glass, picked up a bottle of Scotch and poured another slug into it. She was holding a seltzer bottle in her hand when I came up to her.

I took the seltzer bottle and the glass firmly away from her and set them down on the cabinet. "Sheila," I said, "if you don't mind, you've had enough to drink. Get your things, now. We're going home." I was surprised to hear my voice shaking.

She didn't answer. Her face set in a nasty, hard pattern and she picked up another glass and reached for the bottle of Scotch. My hand beat hers to the bottle. I jerked it away, set it down abruptly on the far side of the cabinet, and tried to take the glass away from her.

She held on to it and, just like that, something snapped. I put my left hand on her arm for leverage and, with my right hand, I pried the glass away from her and slammed it down on the floor. It broke with a small crash and, for a moment, the noise of the party hushed itself curiously. Her elbow recoiled against the cabinet with a knock that must have hurt her and, given another instant, I would have been filled with contrition and sympathy. But she didn't give me that instant.

She hauled off and slammed me on the cheek with her closed fist.

The surprise and the shock of it dazed me. All my mind could think was: Jesus Christ, this shouldn't have been allowed to happen.

But it had happened. And Sheila had turned and walked away from me. She went through the door into the kitchen and the door swung to behind her.

I stood there rubbing my hand over my cheek and

the room was very quiet, waiting. I didn't know what to do; I only knew I had to do something and do it immediately. The kitchen door was still swinging back and forth from the momentum Sheila's passage had given it and, still in a kind of daze, I went over and pushed it open and followed her inside.

She was standing by the sink with the bottle of rum in her hand. She had the cork out and was pouring the stuff down her throat. I lunged for the bottle and pulled it away from her.

"Jesus!" I said. "What are you trying to do—kill yourself?"

She backed away slightly and then made a quick run around me for the door. But I caught her arm. "Listen—!"

"Take your hands off me!" she said.

I held on. "Don't go out there, Sheila," I told her. "No one will give you anything more to drink; they all saw what happened. Don't make a fool of yourself. Get your stuff and let me take you home."

"Take your hands off me!" she screamed.

I released her. She stood looking at me for a second and then deliberately walked over to the sink where I had put the bottle of rum. She picked up the bottle and, still looking at me, started to walk out of the kitchen. I grabbed her arm again and, this time, I was rough. I jerked the bottle away from her.

"You damned little fool," I said, "I guess I can't stop you from making an ass out of yourself, but there's one thing I can do. I can see that you don't get any more liquor. Now, go on out there if you want to, but if you'll take my advice you won't try to get another drink. I'll take it away from you just as fast as you can get it."

She kept on looking at me with that funny light in her eyes, and, after a minute, she turned around and went out through the swinging door. I set the rum back on the sink and followed her, but, when I got to the living room, I was just in time to see her disappear into Fern's bedroom and slam the door behind her. Well, I thought, she's safe there, anyway; I'll let her cool off for a while before I take her home.

Everyone was trying to act as though they hadn't noticed anything, but there's a malicious curiosity in people that's hard to disguise. I walked over to where Pete McCord was sleeping on the window-seat and sat down beside him. People went on talking and laughing, but I could feel the little side glances that were shot in my direction, and I could hear the artificially brightened tone of the conversation after that momentary lull. Pete McCord snored gently when I sat down, and that was the only really friendly sound in the room.

William and Mary ambled over and squatted beside me. "Well, you big bully," he asked, "why don't you pick on someone your size?"

"It's not funny, William," I told him.

"Of course it's not," he agreed. "That's why you have to kid about it. Do you want to tell me what it's all about?"

"I don't know, myself," I said. "One thing you can tell me, though: the night *Halfway House* opened and Sheila and I left you at the Chop House, remember? And she met you later at Fritz's?"

He looked at me out of the corner of his eyes. "Yes," he admitted. "Is that it?"

"What happened?"

"Nothing."

"Nothing?"

"Not a thing. Fritz closed up at four and I took Sheila home myself. Is that all you wanted to know?"

"I guess so," I said. "You wouldn't lie to me, would you?"

"Of course I would," he told me. "But it just happens

that this time I'm telling the truth."

Pete snored again. William and Mary put a friendly hand on his shoulder and shook him gently. He gave a little snort.

"I guess I'm a little crazy," I said.

"Sure," William agreed. "Who isn't? Anything I can do for you? Want me to talk to Sheila?"

"Not yet," I decided. "Maybe in a little while. Then I'll take her home."

Fern came over to us and William and Mary rose. He nodded to Fern. "I'll leave him to you, comrade," he said, and walked away. Fern took his place by my side.

She didn't talk or ask any questions; she just sat there and I was grateful for her company. After a little while I began to feel better. Pete rolled over in his sleep and we both looked down at him. We smiled at each other.

"I don't know," I said doubtfully. "I was going to take him home, but I don't know now if I'll be able to."

"That's all right. If anyone's going his way they can take him along. If not, he's comfortable where he is. I'll put a blanket over him and take his shoes off."

"It's tough," I said. "Pete's really a swell guy when you get to know him."

"He's a swell guy, anyway. People aren't always responsible for the things that happen to them. You ought to know that."

"Maybe that's so." I thought it over. "Maybe certain things—the major things—are going to happen, regardless. But you've got to keep fighting; you owe it to yourself to keep fighting. And if you can't help the things, maybe you can help what the things do to you."

"Maybe," she admitted. "But it doesn't sound very important, does it?"

"No," I said. "Not when you boil it down."

We sat there quite a while after that—maybe fifteen or twenty minutes—without talking. Jake Hershey got his hat and coat and slipped out of the apartment without saying goodbye to anyone, and neither of us moved. Bess Nichols, tight and happy now, insisted on giving her imitation of Allyn Joslyn's *Arsenic and Old Lace* pantomime when he discovers the corpse in the window-seat, and they let her do it because they couldn't help themselves. But no one watched her, and she got mad and went over in a corner and sulked, and eventually she jumped up and grabbed her wrap and flounced out of the apartment.

William and Mary looked at me from across the room and, when I nodded, he went to the bedroom door, eased it open, and went inside. After a few minutes he came out again and walked slowly across the room toward us. He stood in front of me with his head a little bowed as though he were embarrassed.

"Has Sheila slipped out the back way?" I asked him. I rather expected that she had.

He shook his head. "She's there, all right, but I think you'd better go into the bedroom. You too, Fern. I'll come along and help."

I looked at him, and then I got up. Fern came right behind me and William and Mary followed Fern. We went through the door in that order, and William and Mary closed it carefully behind him.

The reading lamp over the bed was lit and everything in the room, though shadowy, was perfectly visible. There was a heavy, sweet odor in the place, an odor I couldn't identify. But Sheila was not there.

A shaft of bright light came through the open door of the bathroom. William nodded to me, and we all went over together and looked in.

Sheila was slumped untidily on the floor. She was breathing hard and her face was very flushed. The water tap was running.

We all stood around and looked down at her. "Well," I said at last—"well, Fern, maybe you'd better call a cab and have the driver wait by the side door. When you come back, bring Sheila's things with you."

She went quickly out of the bedroom. I got some water from the running tap and bathed Sheila's face, but it didn't do any good. She was completely passed out. When I let go of her head, it wobbled uncontrollably on her shoulders.

Fern came back almost immediately with the wrap. "The taxi will be downstairs by the time you get there," she said.

I picked Sheila up and, with William's help, managed to wrap her coat around her.

"Do you want me to help carry her?" William asked.

"No." I thanked him. "I think I can manage, but if you'll come along to open doors—?"

He said, "Sure," and went on ahead of me.

"Thanks, Fern," I said. "Sorry to have been so much trouble."

Her eyes were wide and very serious. "Call me tomorrow, Barney, will you? Just as soon as you can?"

"Sure."

"Promise?"

"Yes, I promise. I'll call you tomorrow. Good night."

"Good night."

William and Mary held the elevator door for me and we went down to the ground floor and out into the street. It was very dark and cold and the snow was coming down thickly. The cab was waiting and, together, we got Sheila inside. I thanked William and gave the driver my address.

I said, "Good night, William," and he said, "Good night, Barney," and the driver walked around to the front and got into his seat and we started off at last.

Nineteen

The apartment house lobby was empty when we got home, so, with the driver's help, I smuggled Sheila into our living room without being seen. The cabby was sympathetic, but casual. He accepted his tip with a "Thanks, Buddy. Happy New Year," and went out whistling.

I locked the door and carried Sheila into the bedroom. She didn't come to once, not even when I undressed her and got her into bed. A nightgown was more than I could manage, but I got her blue dressing gown from the closet, pushed her arms into the sleeves, tied the cord loosely around her middle and pulled the bedclothes up to her chin. I was as gentle as I possibly could be, but it's hard to handle a dead weight like that without using some force, and every time I had to be a little rough my conscience or something hurt me. I felt like I was taking it out on her when she couldn't protect herself. And then I'd get mad at myself for feeling that way. I was glad when the job was finished and I could turn out the light and go back into the living room.

To make the situation worse, there had been a nasty odor in the bedroom. A sweet odor; I couldn't have slept there. I removed my shoes and pulled my overcoat over me and stretched out on the couch just as I was.

Sleep came intermittently. Once or twice I started wide awake to hear Sheila stirring and muttering to herself, but, sometime before morning, I must have given way to an utter weariness because the next thing I knew the apartment was bright with sun.

When I opened my eyes the first thing I thought was, "Special matinee today. Oh God!" Then I remembered what had happened the night before and that this was the first day of the new year, and that made me feel even worse. But I got up anyway and went out into the kitchen and started the coffee.

The alarm clock in the kitchen said that it was a little after eleven-thirty, so I didn't have a lot of time to fool around. While the coffee was getting ready to percolate, I peeked into the bedroom. Sheila was lying on her right side, facing away from me toward the window. I didn't call her; I knew she'd be needing all the sleep she could get.

I took a shower and got dressed again and, by the time the coffee was ready, I felt better. I fixed a tray and carried it into the living room and set it down on the table. Then I looked into the bedroom, but Sheila hadn't moved.

"There's some breakfast out here," I told her. "I think you'd feel better if you got up and tried to eat a little." I waited a minute or two, but she didn't answer, so I said, "Well, it's here when you want it," and went back to my own toast and coffee.

I munched on my toast and thought, It's too bad she has to sulk like that. It puts me on the defensive whether it's my fault or not. I don't know why I always have to make the conciliatory gestures.

Then I shrugged. I got up and washed the dishes and stacked them to dry and started for the living room. But I stopped and went back. I dried the dishes and carefully put them away. Leaving things around was one of my little domestic habits to which Sheila objected, and I figured the best way to get cooperation from her was to do some cooperating myself.

But when I came to the bedroom door with my overcoat on ready to leave, she still refused to speak. She had turned over on her back, but her eyes were closed and she wouldn't answer me.

"I'll have to go," I said at last. "It's New Year's and I

have to do two shows. After I've gone you might try taking a hot bath and eating something. It'll make you feel better." I waited, but she didn't say anything. "I'll call you after the matinee," I told her.

She mumbled something and turned over on her side again, facing the window. "What did you say?" I asked, but she didn't answer. I felt rotten. Try as I would to be hard-boiled about it, I still felt rotten. "I'm sorry, darling," I said. "I'm really awfully sorry. You take it easy and I'll call you after the matinee." I waited a second more, and then I said, "So long," and went on out.

It was early when I got to the theatre and I didn't run into anyone. It was dim and cool in my dressing room; a wan daylight found its way down the air shaft and filtered through the frosted window. It lit my makeup table and the couch and showed up little eddies of gathered dust that were never noticed at night. I hung up my things and put on my dressing gown and lay down on the couch, grateful for my aloneness and for the comfortable, familiar smell of greasepaint and blending powder.

I was half asleep when there was a knock at the door. "Are you decent?" I recognized Fern's voice.

"Come in," I told her and, when she had opened the door, I motioned her to a chair by the makeup table. "Sit down and pardon me for not standing up. I'm tired."

She sat on the edge of the chair. Sort of tentatively. "I saw that your key wasn't on the rack. I was worried about Sheila. You didn't call me."

"I didn't get a chance," I said. "She's all right, though. Sleeping when I left."

She looked relieved. She sat on the edge of the chair for a few moments more and then rose abruptly. "That's good," she said. "Well, I was just worried. You can go back to sleep now."

I swung my feet to the floor. "Don't go. It's time for me to get ready, anyway." But she opened the door.

"No," she said. "I have some things to do, too. I'll see you after the show."

"All right," I said, and she hesitated a little and then went out and closed the door after her. I took off my shirt, switched the light on, and started to work on my face. I heard her open her own door and, a couple of seconds later, I heard the scrape of a chair on the floor of her dressing room.

"Barney—" Coming through the wall, her call was muffled. I took my grease-covered hand off my mouth. "Yup?"

"Pete McCord—remember?"

I remembered. "Yup."

"I don't know what to do with him." Her voice was worried.

"Why?"

"He—well, he doesn't want to go home."

I called, "Wait a minute," and wound my dressing robe around me and went out of my room and into hers. I closed the door. "What happened?"

She was sitting at the table in a dressing gown and it had slipped down over her shoulders. The suggested intimacy of the situation disturbed me. I had to force myself to concentrate on what she was saying. "Well," she told me, "nothing, really. He woke up this morning pretty sick, of course—"

I sat down where I wouldn't have to face her. "Of course."

"And he didn't want to go home. Sis, you know. He wanted to go to a hotel. I think that's foolish. I promised that we'd have dinner together and you'd come along. Can you?"

"I don't know," I said. "I can try. Where is he?"

"I left him at the Dutchman's down the street."

"Drinking?"

"Yes—no. So-so. Not much."

"That's all right. I'll see what I can do." I got up and went to the door.

"Will you have dinner with us?"

"If I can."

"I'm sorry," she said. "I didn't like to ask because of Sheila. But I've been worried."

"Don't be," I told her. "I'll make some calls now. I'll dope something out."

"I knew you would," she said, and smiled. "Thanks."

I looked back at her and thought what a really swell person she was. After all, Pete was my friend rather than hers, and I was grateful for her unselfish interest in him. I started to tell her so. I stepped toward her— and then I put my hand under her chin, tilted her head back and kissed her. It was meant to be just a friendly kiss, I believe. "Thanks for taking care of him," I said.

She didn't answer, but she put her hand back of my head and drew my mouth down to hers again. She kissed me, and I knew then that it wasn't just a friendly kiss and I got frightened.

I mumbled, "I'll phone somebody," and backed out the door and closed it after me. I went over to a stage brace that was holding up a canvas flat and leaned against it and let it hold me up, too.

"Jesus Christ!" I said to myself. Then I pulled myself together and crossed over to the right side of the stage where the phone was.

I called William and Mary at his new apartment. He'd given me his number and for some reason it had stuck in my head, but I always distrust my memory in these things and I was pleasantly surprised when his voice answered. I told him the situation and he said he'd go right down to the Dutchman's and wait for us. He hesitated a little, so I asked him if he had made any other plans.

"Nothing I can't unmake," he said. "Just a little business deal I'll have to postpone. Don't worry about Pete. I'll take care of him."

"Swell," I said, and hung up.

Then I called Sheila. I let the phone buzz ten times and on the eleventh buzz I hung up and called again, but she obviously wasn't there. Either that or she wasn't answering the phone, which was unlikely. I reckoned the time that had passed since I left the apartment and I realized that she must have got up immediately after I left, and dressed herself and gone out. She had just stayed in bed so she wouldn't be forced to talk to me.

Well, there was nothing I could do about it; I'd call her from the Dutchman's after the matinee. I went on back to my dressing room and finished putting on my makeup.

When the final curtain came down, we did a quick degreasing job, Fern and I, and hurried over to the Dutchman's. Pete and William were sitting at a table waiting for us. Pete looked terrible; his red whiskers had sprouted overnight and there were hollows under his eyes you could have rolled a marble around in. William and Mary seemed as blithe as ever, but there was a warning gleam in his eyes when he greeted us. I noted it and sat down and spoke casually to Pete.

"Well, stinker," I asked him, "when are you going to shave?"

He gave me a sickly grin and shook his head. He was uncommunicative, but perfectly sober; I knew I'd be able to handle him.

William and Mary said, "We were just ordering dinner. What'll you have?"

"You get something for me," I told him. "Sauerbraten and potato pancakes. I have a call to make. Get some red cabbage, too."

I got up and went into the phone booth and closed the door. I dialed my own number and, waiting for Sheila to answer, I figured out what I'd tell her; I knew I could square things somehow. If necessary, she could come uptown and join us.

After the phone rang ten times, I hung up and got my nickel back and dialed the number again. Still no answer, and I began to get sore. After all, I'd said I'd call her; she might at least have had the courtesy to come home long enough to answer the phone. I got a little unnecessarily rough with the receiver when I returned it to its hook.

Then I dialed Pete's studio, an Endicott number. Sheila's absence gave me liberty to make my plans without consulting her, and I was going ahead. Sis answered the phone on the first buzz; she had probably been waiting right next to it.

I said, "Hello, Sis?"

"Pete?"

"No," I said, "it's not Pete. It's Barney Page. Now listen—"

I gave her a full nickel's worth of my undiluted opinion of her and, when the operator told me my time was up, I put in a dime and told her some more. She took it without a peep.

"What can I do?" she wanted to know. "What do you want me to do?"

"Stay right where you are," I told her. "I'll keep Pete with me until after my performance tonight. Then I'll come down and talk to you. You stay put until I get there."

"All right, Barney," she said. "I do appreciate your doing this for me."

"Nuts," I said, and hung up. The damned woman had me feeling almost sorry for her, for a second. Even her voice was a mild aphrodisiac.

We all had dinner together without further mention

of Pete's troubles. Fern asked me how Sheila was and, when I told her that she'd gone out, she seemed relieved. I asked William and Mary about the business deal he'd mentioned, and he told me, after some prying, that he was making pocket money by renting the apartment to a club one night a week.

"I'll clear them out before Brother Roberts gets back," he assured me.

"You'd better," I said.

Ordinarily I dislike having people backstage during a performance, but this was something special. So I asked—or, rather, told—Pete and William to spend the evening in my dressing room. They said okay and, walking back to the theatre, I took Pete's arm and let the others go ahead. He plodded along in the same daze he had been in throughout dinner.

"I called Sis," I told him.

Automatically, he said, "I don't want to go home." Then he took a few more steps and asked, in a less robot-like tone, "How is she? Is she all right?" You could tell that the poor cluck had been worrying about her in spite of everything.

"She's all right," I said. "She wants you to come home."

"Yeah."

"Pete, you're in lousy condition. You know that, don't you?"

"Sure."

"Suppose you let me handle this. You do just as I say, will you?"

He thought about it all the rest of the way to the stage door, and I let him think. I knew he'd dope it the right way eventually. Just as we were about to go into the theatre, he said, "Maybe you're right. I'm not thinking very straight. I'll do whatever you say."

I've never known Pete when he wasn't reasonable. A thoroughly good sort of a guy.

As soon as the night's work was finished, we got out of the theatre and the three of us, William, Pete, and myself, walked over to Times Square and caught a downtown local. We got off at Twenty-Third, and I left them in the little restaurant where I had spent such a miserable morning not long before, and went on down to the studio by myself.

Sis answered my knock immediately and seemed both disappointed and relieved when she saw that I was alone.

"Come in," she said. "Where is he? What's happened?"

I took off my hat and closed the door and went over to the corner where the piscatorial statue was, and sat down in a chair. I took plenty of time. Sis was worried and nervous, but she had managed to get herself up very fetchingly nevertheless. Her hair circled down around her shoulders in seeming casualness, but I knew enough about women's hair to tell that she had gone to a lot of trouble to achieve that exact intimate effect. She pulled a chair up close to mine and sat down on it and took my hand.

"Tell me, Barney," she said. "Please. I'm all upset."

I removed my hand carefully and lit a cigarette without offering her one, and then I said:

"He's up on Twenty-Third Street having a cup of coffee."

"Is he coming home?"

"Well," I asked her, "do you think he ought to?"

She got up and went over to the model's stand where there was a pack of cigarettes. She extracted one and lit it, but it wasn't meant as a rebuke to me. She wasn't conscious of any slight.

She took a couple of puffs and blew out a long inhalation of smoke, nervously, as though she wanted to be rid of it. Then she turned around to face me. "Well, what do you want me to say?"

When you came right down to it, I knew there wasn't anything I wanted her to say; nothing she could say would do any good. I told her that.

"So all you want to do is bawl me out," she said. "Well, you've got me down. Go ahead and get it out of your system."

I looked her over. "You take that attitude," I told her, "and I'll do more than bawl you out. I'll slap hell out of you."

I meant it, too, and she saw that I did. "I'm sorry," she apologized. "I'm all worked up. I know you're trying to do your best. But what can I do?"

"Well," I said, "I don't know. I think—I believe—that I can smooth it over this time. Pete's in love with you and he'll overlook almost anything. But that won't prevent the same damned thing from happening again. Pete's a friend of mine. I hate to see him hurt; I'd hate worse to see him go on being hurt indefinitely."

"I know," she said. "And I don't want to hurt him either. I'm telling you the truth."

I liked her better then. "Sure," I told her. "I believe you. Nobody'd hurt Pete intentionally."

I got up and walked over to the fireplace and got rid of my partly smoked cigarette. I thought it over, and then I went back to where she was standing.

"Listen, Sis," I said. "Let me put it to you in my own language. You and I are pretty much alike in a lot of ways. I've got a hunch we can understand each other."

She looked up, and there was a flicker of interest in her face. "Go on," she said.

"You and I don't amount to a hell of a lot," I said. "In the general scheme of things we're a couple of parasites; you because of your sex—the way you misuse it—and I because of my profession, which is, when you look at it one way, a pretty socially unprofitable way of making a living. We're not work-ers, creators. We're entertainers; our job is to keep the workers amused. And it's a pretty good job, too—if we do it well and don't get above ourselves. But Pete's different. Pete's a worker. He's worth a dozen of us put together. Look around—" I indicated the furniture, the statues, the paintings. "Pete did that. He made that furniture, every damned stick of it. I can sit in that chair and tell a funny story, but I have to remember that Pete made the chair. You can lie in that bed and be damned entertaining; but you mustn't forget that if it weren't for Pete you'd be lying on the floor. Now, I couldn't make those things. And you couldn't."

"I could create," Sis said quietly.

"Yeah. But will you?"

"Well—"

"That's what I thought," I said. "So, until you're ready to take a step up in society and to assume the responsibilities that go with that step, you'll have to do your second-rate job as well as you can. Catch on?"

"But what can I do?" she asked again.

"God damn it," I said, "you can do what you were made to do. You can have a baby or a whole litter of babies if you want to. But if you don't want to, the least you can do is keep your legs crossed, when Pete's not doing the uncrossing. Is that plain?"

She stood perfectly still. The only thing that moved was the blood that surged up from her shoulders and into her face. It was the most complete blush I'd ever seen; I thought she was going to swing on me.

But she didn't. She stood like that for a moment and then she slowly lowered her head. "Yes, that's plain," she said softly. "Please don't say any more. Just tell Pete to come home, will you?"

I felt a little sorry for her and I liked her better than I ever had before. "Okay, Sis," I said. "I'm afraid you're going to hold this against me."

"No, I won't," she said. "You don't know me yet. But

you will."

She smiled and I smiled and I put my hand out and she took it. Then I said goodbye and went out of the studio, down the stairs to the street, and back to the restaurant.

I got Pete started home without any trouble, and I said good night to William and Mary and went down the subway steps and took a local to Christopher Street, feeling pretty much like a disreputable boy scout. Maybe the scoutmaster wouldn't exactly approve of my methods, but he couldn't deny that I was an indefatigable good-deed-doer.

When I got off at Sheridan Square, it was snowing again, and I hurried over to Sixth Avenue and walked east toward Fifth. Pete's problems had temporarily pushed my own into the background, but now they all surged back and took over again. I'd forgotten to call Sheila before going to the studio. Maybe she was worried because I was late. Maybe she'd come home and found I wasn't there, and got huffy and walked out again.

Then, too, there was the possibility—probability— that she hadn't come home at all. That wouldn't be so good.

It wasn't so good. I opened the front door and let myself in quietly, but the apartment was dark and there was no sound in it at all. I switched on the lights and stood in the open doorway and called, "Sheila!" but there was no answer.

So I closed the door and took my coat off and dropped it on the couch. The breakfast tray was still on the table where I had left it. It hadn't been touched. I didn't know what to do. This, it seemed to me, was about as far as I could go.

Well, I said to myself after a while, to hell with it; I might as well go to bed. So I went into the bedroom and turned on the lights.

Sheila's bed was empty, and it was still unmade. The bedclothes were trailing to the floor as if they had been jerked off. I saw the blue of her dressing gown on the floor between the two beds, but there was an appreciable fraction of a second before I realized that it was lying unnaturally humped up.

And then my heart started pounding like a triphammer. The reason it was humped up like that was because Sheila was lying under it.

I swerved around the end of the nearer bed and bent over her. She was lying on her face, breathing but completely unconscious, and her hair was spread out over the floor, sticky in a little pool of drying vomit.

I sat down on the bed. For a moment or so I couldn't think at all. I didn't know what to do first, and I was so weak I couldn't stand up.

Then I heard her draw a rasping breath and that galvanized me into action. I ran out of the bedroom and threw open the living-room door and pounded up the stairs. All the way up to the fifth floor I heard myself calling, "Birnbaum! Doctor Birnbaum!"

Twenty

The air in the closed living room was stagnant; my mouth and throat were thick from breathing it. Birnbaum had been in the bedroom for what seemed like a long time and, when at last he came out, he didn't look at me. He ran his fingers through his hair in a nervous gesture and went quickly over to the telephone. He called a hospital, gave the address of the apartment and its number, and told them to send an ambulance. I sank down on the couch and put my arms around my knees. That way I could keep myself from shaking.

He hung up the receiver and turned to me. "When

did this happen?"

"Last night," I said. "I brought her home and—"

"Why didn't you call me then?"

"Call you?" I asked. "I didn't know. How could I tell—?"

"Christ!" he said. "You didn't know! You could smell, couldn't you?"

"Smell?"

"The wood alcohol. The whole room stinks of it."

I got up slowly and stared at him. I knew that my mouth was hanging open, but I couldn't help it. "Wood—?"

"Where did she get it?"

"I—I don't know. We were at a party." Then I remembered that I'd seen Fern and Pete McCord. "She couldn't have got it there. Nobody else got sick."

He indicated the telephone. "Call up and make sure." I didn't move immediately, and he rasped, "Hurry up, damn it! The ambulance will be here in a minute."

I took the phone and dialed Fern's number. While it rang I asked, "Is she—? Will she—?"

He shook his head. "I can't tell. From what you say it may be too late for a stomach pump. But I'll try. I'll know more after I get her to a hospital."

"Yes," I said, and just then Fern answered the phone. "Hello," she said.

"Fern"—I could hear my voice shaking; I cleared my throat, "This is Barney."

"What's happened?" She was alarmed. My voice had alarmed her.

"Fern, has anyone—do you know if anyone else at the party got sick? Got sick—sick like—?" I couldn't say any more.

"What's the matter?" she asked. "What is the matter?"

"Sheila," I said, "the Doctor's here now. He says it's wood alcohol. Do you know if anyone else—?"

She broke in jerkily. "It couldn't be. We all drank the

same stuff. I drank it. I—"

She broke off, and there was a dead silence at her end of the wire. I waited for her to continue, but there was no sound. I thought maybe we'd been disconnected, but, just as I was about to call her again, her voice came through,

"Oh God," she said, just like that. Flatly with no emotion. "Oh God," she said, "listen. I've just thought. After you'd gone last night I found my bottle of cologne under the bed. A big bottle. It was nearly empty. It was lying on its side with the top missing, but it hadn't run out on the rug. I could tell."

That's the answer, I thought to myself. That's the missing link. Cologne has a wood-alcohol base. That's the answer. My thoughts marched ponderously around in a circle. That's the answer. That's the missing link.

Her voice went on relentlessly. "It was nearly empty," she repeated. "I found the top in the bathroom. Where Sheila had been lying. I never realized—I never thought—"

Doc Birnbaum eased the telephone away from me and held one of his arms around my shoulders. He nodded toward the couch, but I disregarded the gesture. I just let him take the phone and stood still where I was.

"This is Doctor Birnbaum," he began into the telephone. I didn't hear the rest of what he said. When he finished, he hung up the receiver and led me over to the couch. "Sit down," he said, and I sat down. "You're going to have to take it, Barney," he went on. "I know it's tough, but you're going to have to pull yourself together. Can you do it?"

I said, "Yes," and hoped I meant it. He nodded briefly. "I'll get her ready," he said. "You stay here and open the door."

I didn't answer, and he went into the bedroom, and, not long after that, there was a knock on the front door and I got up and opened it and a man in a white uniform and a funny-looking cap, like the ones they used to call forage caps, came in and went into the bedroom. Two policemen followed him and stood in the living room waiting; one of them carried a stretcher. The man in the funny hat put his head in at the door and motioned to the waiting cops and they went into the bedroom, too. There was some subdued noise in there, and then they all came out. The two policemen came first; they were carrying the stretcher between them, and on it was a quiet form under some bedclothes, and I knew that that was Sheila. They went out the front door. Then the man in the white uniform and the funny hat came out talking to Birnbaum, and the two of them shook hands in the middle of the living room, and the man looked at me curiously and then he went out, too.

Doc Birnbaum put his hand on my shoulder. "Get your coat, Barney," he said. "We'll follow them over."

"I've got a car," I said. "A red Buick. I bought it secondhand. It's parked in the garage down the street. It's a red Buick."

The doctor nodded. "Good," he said. "We'll make better time that way. But I'll drive."

I handed him the keys to the car. "It's a red Buick," I told him. And we went out together, the doctor holding me by the arm.

Far away down at the other end of the hospital waiting room, Doc Birnbaum came in at the door. I saw him the way a marijuana smoker sees things. Out of focus, funnily. One instant he came in at the door and he was just a little animated pin-point in the distance. Then he took two monstrous, impossible strides and loomed over me, pendulous and gigantic.

"Barney," he said, and touched me with a hand the size of Saint Patrick's Cathedral. But the hand was very light. "Hi," I said. "Hi, Doc."

He shook me gently and I began to respond to his shaking and stood up, and things were in focus again.

"Well?" I asked, not hoping. And he said, "I'd rather you didn't see her now."

"She's dead."

"No," he said. "I think—I can't promise, but I think—we'll save her. But her sight—it's too late for that."

"Her what?"

"Her sight. I called in a specialist; I knew you'd want me to."

"Yes."

"The optic nerve—paralyzed. It's too bad, Barney."

"You mean—never—?"

He shook his head and, taking my arm, steered me toward the door. "I'm afraid not," he said. "But, of course, we won't tell her that."

I shook off his hand. "Blind," I said.

"I'm afraid so. We'd better go home now."

I didn't say anything more; he took my arm and we went out into the street together. The sun was shining; it was morning now, and the air was fresh and very cold. The red Buick was parked in the snow at the curb. He led me toward it and opened the door, but I drew back.

"No," I told him. "I don't want to go home."

"Barney—" he began, but I said, "No, no, no," and turned from him and walked rapidly up the street. I don't think he followed me after the first couple of steps. I walked quickly around the corner and then I walked a block and turned another corner and, when I looked back at last, there was no one on the street but myself and, far down at the other end, a milkman climbing into his wagon.

I dug my hands deep into my overcoat pockets and lowered my head and started walking again.

There were so many things I had to do that I didn't know where to start. I walked around and around Bryant Park behind the Library, and every once in a while, when I got tired, I'd sit down on one of the stone benches and think. I'd think about all the things I had to do, and all the things I hadn't done that were the cause of the things I had to do, and then I'd get up and walk some more.

The doctor would have to be called; I knew that. Now that I was rational again, or nearly rational, I'd have to find out definitely about Sheila. That was my first obligation and I'd attend to it very shortly now; just as soon as I could bring myself to go through the mechanics of making a telephone call.

And I'd have to talk to John Friday. Over the phone. I didn't want to see him or anybody else. I'd have to tell him to notify my understudy that he was going on tonight. And tomorrow night and all the rest of the nights. I'd have to tell John that I was through, washed up, finished.

Sheila needed me now. She'd needed me all along, but I hadn't seen it. Birnbaum had warned me and I'd disregarded the warning. Well, it still wasn't too late—maybe. The thing to do now was to get some rest. I'd have to go some place where I wouldn't be disturbed by doorbells or telephone calls or pounding, pounding thoughts. I'd have to go somewhere and rest.

And I remembered my dressing room at the Cochran, its dusty daylight quiet, and I left the Park and walked west toward the theatre.

There was a low rap at the door and I flicked my eyes in that direction. I didn't move. But when the knock came a second and then a third time, I called out, "Yes?"

John Friday's voice asked, "May I come in, Barney?"

"Yes," I told him, and he opened the door and came

in quietly and sat down in the chair by the makeup table. In the half-light of the dressing room his face and figure were indistinct, merging with the gloom.

He said, "I'm sorry, Barney. How do you feel?"

So he's heard already, I thought. It's wonderful how news gets around. "You'll have to call my understudy," I told him. I told him this definitely, flatly, to abort any Pagliacci, Sonny Boy sentimentalism.

But he acted as though that were understood. "I called him as soon as I saw you come in," he said. "He's on his way over now."

I thought about that. "Do I look that bad?" I asked.

"You don't look very well," he said. "What are you going to do?"

That was a question. That *was* a question. "What would you do?" I asked him.

He said, "I don't know."

We let a few minutes go by, and then I pulled my thoughts together. "John," I said, "would you mind calling the doctor for me? Doctor Birnbaum; he's in the book, the same address as mine. Ask him how she is; find out things for me; you understand."

He got up slowly and went to the door. "Sure," he said. "I know what to do. Take it easy; I'll be right back." And he went out.

I lay there and let things trickle through my mind and gradually an idea assumed shape, became a determination. When John Friday came back, I was ready for him.

He entered quietly and closed the door and sat down. "I called the hospital, too," he said. "They gave me the usual 'well as can be expected' line. But Birnbaum says she's all right. You'll be able to see her before long. I liked Birnbaum; he sounded intelligent. Worried about you."

"She's blind," I told him. "She'll never be able to see again. You realize that?"

"Yes," he said, "but—" He spread his hands in a vague gesture. "The thing for you to do is take a rest. Let your understudy play out the week. You can come back on Monday. Sheila will be home in ten days or so. You can get a nurse to take care of her. You'll have to learn to readjust your life."

I swung my feet to the floor and sat up. "Listen, John," I said. "I don't want it. I don't want any part of it. You don't seem to realize that Sheila will never be able to see again, and that I'm the cause of it. Me. Do you think I'll be able to readjust my life to that?"

He made that futile gesture with his hands again. "You'll have to. You're wrong when you say it was your fault, but, even if it were, what else is there to do?"

I stood up. "I can get out of it," I told him. I realized that my voice was unnecessarily loud, but I made no attempt to check it. "I can go back. Anything is better than this. I can go back."

He looked up at me from the chair and his eyes were kindly but puzzled. "How?" he asked.

"For Christ's sake," I said. "You ask me how. Suppose you tell me. You started this. You tell me how."

"I don't know what you're talking about," he said.

I stopped pacing and looked at him, and then I sat down. I put my elbows on my knees and leaned forward and looked into his eyes. "John," I said, "don't give me that stuff. Not now. This is no time to be holding out on me. I'm asking you, John; I'm pleading with you. Tell me the truth."

"So help me God, Barney," he said, "I don't know what you're talking about."

I lowered my head. "You're going to let me down," I said. "I didn't think you'd do that, John."

He rose from his chair, and I looked up again and saw that the shaft of bleak daylight from the window flooded his face. It was filled with troubled concern. "I've never let you down in my life," he said quietly.

"I've always thought of you as if you were my own son. If it was a question of money, I'd give you anything I had. If you were in a jam of some kind—by God, if you'd even committed murder—I'd try to get you out of it. But can't help you in this, Barney. I guess you'll just have to work it out yourself."

I turned away from him at last. "Okay, John," I told him. "I'll work it out. Now where's that understudy?"

John walked to the door with a show of briskness. "That's better," he said. "I'll send him in. You take it easy until Monday, and remember I'll do anything I possibly can."

"Goodbye, John," I said. "And thanks for everything. But you won't see me Monday."

"Maybe not," he said. "Maybe not. You can't tell about these things. I'll send in the understudy. Goodbye."

"Goodbye," I said.

Twenty-One

It was five minutes to eleven that same night and I was alone in the Grand Central Station. The place was crowded with people catching trains, waiting for friends, hurrying here and there, but I was alone.

This, I thought, is where I started, and this, please God, is where I'm going to finish. On the platform at Times Square there are two cops and a detective waiting for me; I should never have run away from them. What they will do to me will be unpleasant, but it will be normal.

There was a great yearning in me for normality. In five minutes, I told myself, the shuttle I want will leave. I'd better get started.

I found the stairs to the shuttle and walked down them. The train was there just as if it were waiting for me, and I went in and sat down. After a minute the compressed air hissed, the doors slid shut, the car jerked a couple of times, and got under way.

It picked up speed and went *clatter clatter bang bang bang*, just as it always did, but something was missing; I don't know what. Maybe it was something in me. I pushed it, the lack of whatever it was, out of my mind and sent my thoughts ahead of the train.

It's almost over now, I told myself. I hope they haven't taken William and Mary away. It will be nice to have him with me if only for a little while. Maybe they'll put us in a cell together and it'll be nice and friendly and homelike.

The shuttle jerked and began to slow down. I stood up and, holding to the uprights, swung myself into position by the door. When it stops, I thought, there won't be any trouble. I'll just walk out and say, "Here I am," and they'll take me away. I won't make any trouble.

The train jerked again and then it stopped. The doors hissed and slid open. I stepped out on the platform and looked around.

There was no one there. Just the usual mob of hurrying people. No cops, no William and Mary dripping quarters on the platform. It didn't seem fair; I'd nerved myself up to this thing and now I was being let down.

A guard strolled up to me. "What's the matter, buddy? Lost?"

I considered the question. "In a way," I admitted. "Can you tell me what the date is?"

He looked at me and then he began to laugh. "You've been on a beauty, haven't you? New Year's Eve was night before last."

"Thank you," I said.

"Don't mention it. Anything else you want to know?"

"Not a thing," I told him. "Thanks." And started off.

I crossed over to the west side and climbed down

the steps, hanging on to the handrail. When the downtown local came by, I got on it and slumped down on a seat. That's the last I remember.

"I come," William and Mary said, "like April bearing gifts."

He had an apron wrapped around his waist and he carried a tray which he set down on the table by my bed. His round face was twisted into a happy smile and I looked at him curiously.

"How come?" I asked, and was surprised by the weakness of my voice. "How did I get here?"

He handed me a plate of soup from the tray. "Drink this," he said. "Or, if you prefer, eat it. And don't ask questions. You're supposed to be sick."

That seemed improbable. I felt light-headed, certainly, and very weak, and I had no recollection of how I had gotten into bed or of anything that had happened since I got on the downtown subway. But I wasn't sick. Actually, I felt better than I had in a long time.

I tasted the soup. It was very good and I was hungry. "Suppose," I suggested, "that you save a lot of time by just telling me what happened."

He sat down on the other bed, my bed, and nodded. "Okay. What do you want to know?"

"How is Sheila?" I asked. "And what am I doing in her bed?"

The smile momentarily flicked off his face. "Sheila's all right," he told me. "By the time you're up and around they'll be sending her home. You have nothing to worry about there."

But, by the tone of his voice, I knew that I did have something to worry about. Plenty. Only, it didn't seem to bother me anymore. My blank spell seemed to have changed my outlook on things.

His smile crept back. "As to your being in the wrong

bed, who are Pete and I to know about your sleeping arrangements? We just dumped you."

"You found me?"

"No," he said. "The Doctor did that, I think. He called John Friday and Friday called Pete and Pete called me. Very complicated, but it worked out all right. I've been staying here ever since."

"Since?" I asked. "When did this happen?"

"Three days ago," he said. "Or, rather, nights. You were a mess. I wanted to trade you in on a new model, but they talked me out of it."

"Thanks," I said. "It's been nice of you."

"On the contrary," he told me, "you've been a God-send. You've furnished me with a place to hide."

I looked at him inquiringly. "The new apartment?"

He shook his head. "Is not for me. It was all very tragic."

"What was?"

"You're talking too much," William and Mary said. "The Doctor said you weren't to talk."

"Go to hell," I told him. "I want to hear what happened."

He smiled again. "That sounds more natural. Well—Mr. Roberts returned from the bosom of his family. In Nebraska or Wyoming. I think they spewed him forth, but I have no way of proving it. Anyway, he came back mad. And he got madder still when he walked into his marvelous new apartment."

"Why?"

"There was a club meeting going on."

"Oh God," I said. "I warned you about that."

"Sure," William agreed, "but how was I to know he'd appear so abruptly? Anyway, he walked in on the club meeting."

"What kind of a club meeting?"

"Well, they were pansies."

"A drag."

"No," William said, "I don't think he'd have minded a drag so much. I might have talked him out of that. But these pansies were perverted."

"Really," I said.

"Yes," he said, "really. They were perverted pansies. They were celebrating a Black Mass. It seems that the head priest, or priestess, was using Mr. Roberts's favorite chiffonier for an altar and he'd got blood all over it. And the others were sitting around in a circle wearing horns and tails and things. It was all very upsetting because Mr. Roberts is fundamentally a religious man and the whole thing smacked of heresy."

"Go on," I said.

"That's about all. He made a scene and these perverted pansies got mad and put a hex on him. They gave him the Fairies' Curse, and then they got him down and yanked out some of his hair and said they were going to make a wax figure with his hair inside it and stick pins in the wax figure. It will be interesting," William said, "to see if it works."

"Oh God," I said again. "Get me a cigarette."

He got one and lit it and handed it to me. Then he sat down again and said, "Of course Mr. Roberts was provoked. And maybe he was a little worried about the wax figure business. Anyway, he started looking for me and the first place he went was Madame Céleste's. She gave him my bill and, from what I understand, it was a little exorbitant."

"How much?"

"Four hundred and some odd dollars, I believe. I had a lot of social obligations I had to pay off."

"And now?" I asked.

"Now," he said, "I'm hiding out. To put it vulgarly, I'm on the lam until they turn the heat off. It won't be long; he'll calm down in a few days."

I knew better, but there was no use saying anything. William and Mary got up and took my empty plate and started out. "Where are you going?" I asked.

"To spread the glad news," he said. "This damned telephone has been ringing for three days. I'll have to call John Friday and Pete and Fern Costello and fifty others and tell them that you're back among us again. Incidentally, I'm very glad that you are."

He smiled at me and went out and, a few minutes later, I heard him at the telephone. His voice was very happy.

This happened on a Sunday, and I lay in bed all that day and all day Monday and Tuesday. I took things easy and gradually my strength came back to me. And with the return of my physical strength came a certain resilient quality I'd never had before. A moral and psychic toughness. I don't mean to say that I got hard-boiled; I don't believe any outer change was noticeable. But things didn't affect me the way they had before.

There was the question of money, for instance. I'd always made a good salary, but I'd spent it as fast as it came in. Now, looking over my bank book, I found that I had less than fifteen hundred dollars, and I knew that Sheila's hospital and doctor bills would take the major part of that. Then, too, the lease on the apartment would be up on the first of March. Ordinarily I would have thrown a wingding at the prospect of being broke at such a critical time. But now I merely told myself that something was sure to happen. So many things happened whether I wanted them to or not that it seemed foolish to worry about it.

Wednesday afternoon Jake Hershey came to see me; Pete McCord and Sis brought him. They'd all gone over to the hospital together and Jake seemed pretty cut up. A lot more cut up than I was, I couldn't help thinking; I'd gone through all that and it didn't bother me anymore. All the emotion had been drained out of me like the core from a boil, and now the place where the boil had been was covered with a tough scar tissue. He sat on my bed—I was still using Sheila's because it was nearer the window—and talked about how sorry he was and how devoted he was to Sheila and myself, and he wanted to know what he could do.

I looked at him and wondered why he didn't annoy me the way he used to, and I told him there was nothing he could do and thanks just the same.

He talked about a house he was buying out in Westchester; he'd got an F.H.A. loan and made a down payment already.

"It's just a small place," he said, "and very rustic. But it's quiet and it will be swell for working. I'll move in about the end of this month."

"How's the new play coming?" I asked. I didn't care much about Jake's domestic arrangements.

"Almost finished," he said. "There are a few changes to be made in the third act. That's all."

"Has Friday seen it?"

"Yes. And he likes it. He says it's better than *Halfway House*. But he hasn't committed himself."

"No?"

"He says he doesn't know what he's going to do next season. He says his plans are indefinite. When can you read the script?"

"Any time."

"I'll bring it in. If you want any changes made, let me know and I'll stick them in before I make the final draft."

"That's very accommodating of you," I told him. "But why should I make any changes?"

"Why," he said, surprised, "I've written the lead for you. You knew that."

I shook my head. "This is all new to me. You'd better make that part pretty elastic."

"You mean you don't want to play it?" He seemed really hurt and disappointed; he was a funny guy to figure out.

"No," I told him, "I'm like John Friday. My plans for next season are indefinite."

He looked at me, and then he shrugged his shoulders and stood up. He smiled. "You're still not up to par," he said. "You'll change your mind before it's time to start rehearsals. Is there anything you want?"

"Not a thing," I told him.

He looked around. Pete and Sis were in the living room with William and Mary; we were alone. "Look," he said. "I don't know exactly how to say this, but, if you don't want me seeing Sheila, all you have to do is say so."

I reached for a cigarette and took my time lighting it. "Jake," I told him, "your seeing Sheila can't make a bit of difference anymore one way or the other. The point is that Sheila can't see you. She can't *see* you, understand? Don't start something you can't finish."

He stood by the bed with his head drooped, pondering what I had said. "You and I," he remarked quietly, at last, "we'll never be able to understand each other. Not really." Then he brightened up: "How about medicine?" he asked. "Up in Westchester I can get practically anything without a prescription; it's cheaper that way."

"Such as sodium amytal?" I asked.

"Why, yes," he said. "I can get you sodium amytal if you like. As much as you want. How much do you need?"

"Not a bit," I told him. "I was just wondering."

Pete and Sis came in then, and he picked up his hat and got ready to go.

"Wait a minute," Pete stopped him. "I'll go along with you. Sis is going to stay with Barney."

"That's not necessary," I said. "I'm not sick."

"But I want to," Sis said.

She looked very fetching in a cool linen house dress and her hair falling down almost to her shoulders. I was a little tired of exclusively male society. "In that case," I said, "that's swell. Kick 'em all out."

She went to the front door with them and I lay back on the pillow and wondered about the change in myself. Things didn't matter the way they once had. I'd stopped fighting for a while and I just didn't give a damn.

Twenty-Two

The next morning I awoke early and got out of bed and went into the bathroom and ran the tub full of hot water. I lay in it for over half an hour, letting out a little water as it grew colder and running in more of the hot to take its place. I lay at full length almost completely submerged and let my thoughts float away. It was almost a religious state, where all existence could be regarded in its true transitory form, a bubble riding the flow of the infinite. But after a while, William and Mary pounded on the door and wanted to know what in hell I was doing so long, and I got out of the tub and dried myself and shaved, and went back into the bedroom.

He had breakfast ready for me there, and I picked up the tray and carried it into the kitchen where his own breakfast was laid. He said, "Good God, man, you're supposed to be sick. Go back to bed and get into character." And I told him, "I can't be sick forever. I'll have to get up some time."

We compromised. I was to have breakfast, and then, or shortly after, I was to go back to bed.

"And I want to see you there before I leave," he said.

"Where are you going?"

"Pete," he said, "is going to take me to see a merchant who's leaving town for a few months. I may be able to get his apartment for, let us say, reduced rates."

"That's nice. In that case I'll be left alone. It will be a pleasant change."

"You will not. Sis will be here almost immediately. She'll take over until either Pete or I relieve her."

"That's even nicer," I said. "I'll find a clean suit of pajamas and put on my dressing gown."

"No. I mean it. You're supposed to be in bed and I'm not going to leave until you get there."

"Oh, all right. All right," I said.

"And promise to stay."

"All right."

I got up and went into the bedroom, peeved at the way I was being ordered around. But when I got there, I saw that William and Mary had changed my bedclothes and remade the bed; he'd done it while I was taking a bath and I hadn't noticed when I got my breakfast tray. You can't stay mad at a guy like that. I called my thanks to him, found a fresh suit of pajamas in the dresser, put them on and climbed in between the clean sheets. It was very luxurious. I lit a cigarette, picked up a copy of the *New Yorker* and settled down content.

William and Mary came in twenty minutes or so later. He had his hat and coat on. "I don't know what's keeping Sis," he said. "But if you're all right, I think I'll go on. We want to catch this fellow before he goes to work."

"Go ahead," I told him. "Nothing can happen to me. Leave the door on the latch and I won't have to get up."

"You'll stay in bed?"

"Listen," I said. "Stop worrying. You're turning into an old Mother Superior. Of course I'll stay in bed. But if I don't, there won't be any harm done. I'm as well as

I've ever been."

He looked at me doubtfully. "Well," he said, "maybe you are. Anyway, I'll be back this afternoon." He started for the door.

I called, "Look out for Mr. Roberts," and he smiled and shrugged goodbye and went on out.

I snubbed the fire from my cigarette and picked up the *New Yorker* again and tried to read.

But there was a restlessness and a vague excitement in me that I couldn't place. I couldn't concentrate on the magazine; I kept listening to the sounds in the apartment house, trying to place each individual sound and to associate it with its cause. That is what I told myself I was doing. But I was really listening for something else, and I didn't know what it was until I heard it.

In the silence of the apartment the click of the front door as it opened, and the soft shutting of it, were perfectly audible. I felt my body tense under the bedclothes and I wondered at it and then lost my wonder waiting for the next development.

Sis peeked in the door and, seeing that I was awake, she walked in, taking off her hat as she came. "Hello," she said—"sorry I'm late," and came over to the bed and put the back of her hand against my cheek. "You're well again," she said. "There's not a sign of temperature."

I took her hand. "I've been well all the time," I said. "This was just a put-up job."

She smiled and let her hand stay where it was for a moment. Then she withdrew it. "Let me get my hat and coat off," she said, and went into the living room.

I waited for her to come back and, as I waited, I wondered at myself again.

She came in the door and, without pausing, went over to the dresser and started combing her hair. It had become disarranged in taking off her hat, and she picked up one of Sheila's combs and started using it. She had her back turned to me, but I could see her in the mirror and I kept watching her.

"Is there anything you'd like me to do?" she asked.

"Yes," I said. "Come over here and talk to me."

She turned lightly and smiled at me through the tangle of her hair. "Just a minute," she said, "till I"— for a fraction of a second the comb halted in its downward stroke and I saw the expression in her eyes change as they met my own, then the comb continued downward, more slowly, and she turned gravely toward the mirror and finished her sentence—"till I fix my hair." The last part of the sentence was in different tempo from the first part, and I knew that in that fraction of a second she had seen and understood and made up her mind. But there were still certain amenities which must be observed; they make life, such as it is, supportable, and as human beings we owe them to each other.

She bent her head forward, and then, with a swoop, she threw it back and her hair fell in place and she ran the comb through it and, with another twist, the job was done. It was a delicate operation professionally performed and a delight to watch. She turned around and paused and seemed to consider. Then she came over and sat on the edge of the bed.

"May I have a cigarette?" she asked. She took one from the package on the little table without waiting for my reply, and lit it and inhaled deeply. She held the smoke in her lungs and let it come out slowly. She was thinking, and I let her think; I didn't try to rush her.

"I'm so tired," she said. "People kept dropping in last night and they stayed till nearly dawn. And I had to get up early."

I said, "That's what I keep the extra bed for. Go

ahead and stretch out. No one will bother you."

"Oh," she said, "if I only could. But that wouldn't look right, would it?"

Small talk.

"You'll find a dressing gown in the closet," I told her. "Don't use the blue one; it's—it's dirty. There's a white silk one there."

"Well," she said, "if you're sure you wouldn't mind—"

"I don't mind."

"I'll go in the living room and slip my dress off."

"Don't be silly," I said. "I'm an actor, and, furthermore, I'm married. But if it will make you feel any happier, I'll turn my back." I rolled over on my right side and faced the window.

What am I so mad about? I wondered. I'd diagnosed my restlessness at last: it was anger. God knows what I was angry at; it was all very complicated. Birnbaum would call it a masculine protest or something, I thought. The ego hitting back. But why should it hit back this way? Well, why not? The best people do it and you can call it a protest, or you can call it what you like, but the point is, it works. Like kicking a kitchen chair works. You may hurt your foot, but, for the time being, it cures what ails you.

She came back from the living room wearing the white silk dressing gown and a pair of mules she'd found that fit her. Her face was flushed and she seemed nervous and uncertain.

"Hello," I said. "Back again?"

She lowered her eyes and busied herself with the spread on the other bed.

"Come here," I said.

She straightened up and came over to my bed slowly, still a little uncertain. I took her hand.

She didn't protest much. "Barney," she said, "we

shouldn't. After all you said the other night. We shouldn't."

That was about all.

I had fallen asleep. I awoke gradually, and the first thing I saw was the back of her head. It was lying on my left shoulder. She was facing me and her forehead was pressed against my chest; she was sound asleep, breathing softly.

My mind began to race at top speed, frantically seeking a way out. Jesus Christ, it clamored, now you've done it; you've screwed yourself up properly this time; what in the hell made you do it? All of my anger and my newfound detachment had fled; I was back in the middle of things again, panicky and vulnerable as ever.

I'll have to get her out of here, I thought. I'll have to impress it upon her that this was a mistake, that it won't happen again, and that the best thing to do is to forget it quickly. I'll have to get her dressed and out of here right away.

And, while I thought all this, I became gradually aware that someone was watching me. I got scared, not physically scared but spiritually, which is worse, and I tried to keep my eyes from turning, but, in spite of myself, they turned toward the door, and I stared at what I saw there.

Pete McCord stood in the center of the doorway, and now I remembered too late that the front door had been left on the latch. A shaft of sunlight from the window shone directly on his face and lit up the red stubble of beard which he hadn't shaved since New Year's. I looked at him and he looked at me, and I knew what he was thinking, and I knew there wasn't anything I could do or say.

If he'd only kill me, I thought. That would make it easier all around. But he won't. Pete isn't built that way; Pete was built to be hurt.

And that's the way it turned out. We looked at each other for a full thirty seconds, and then he turned around and went out of the room and I heard the front door close very softly and I knew I'd never see him again. Sis snored gently, and I looked at her with distaste and carefully withdrew my arm without disturbing her. There was no hurry now. I got up quietly and went into the living room and began to dress.

Twenty-Three

Tuesday was the day Sheila was coming home. On Tuesday morning I took up the business of living again. I got my overcoat out of the hall closet and put it on. I took a last hasty once-over to see that everything was in order—the beds neat, the flowers arranged in the bedroom—picked up my hat, and went out.

Birnbaum had returned the keys to my car and I walked down the street toward the garage. The snow was slushy, melting on the sidewalk; it was unseasonably warm with the oppressive warmth of a January thaw. I squished along the pavement with my head lowered, watching the slush spurt out from beneath my shoes as I put my feet down. I was engrossed in my own thoughts and only gradually became aware that someone was walking directly behind me. Then I turned quickly without breaking my stride and saw that it was William and Mary. He was looking at me anxiously.

"Well?" It was the first time I'd seen him since the Sis episode, and I wasn't cordial. "What's the idea?"

"I'm going to the hospital with you," he told me simply. He hurried his steps and came up abreast of me and we walked along together for a few paces.

"Did it ever occur to you," I said, "that there are times when a guy wants to be alone, and that this might be one of the times?"

"Did it ever occur to you," he countered, "that I know you as well as, or better than, you know yourself? And that, consequently, I know you're lying?"

We trudged along in silence for a few minutes. Finally, "William," I said, "please go away. There are people who are definitely bad luck, and I'm one of those people. Go away."

He smiled. "I'm in no danger from you," he said. "I've got no wife."

Someone—Pete of Sis, herself—had talked. "So you know about that already. I'm sorry."

"Don't get yourself stewed up," William said. "It's the best thing that could have happened. She's gone back to Boston and Pete can pick up where he left off. He should be grateful to you."

"Don't joke about it," I said. "It's not funny."

"All right," he agreed. "I'll be more serious if you'll be less tragic. Between us we'll hit a happy medium. Why," he wondered, "are happy mediums always being hit, and never unhappy ones? It must be tough to have to go around with a scowl on your face just because you happen to be a medium."

I let that pass, and after a moment William looked at me from the corner of his eyes. "Well," he murmured, "it was funny once, anyway."

We came to the garage and I turned in. He turned in with me. "Now, look—" I started to say.

"I'm going with you," William repeated, and we went on down to the far end where the Buick was parked and climbed in.

Birnbaum met us in the waiting room where I had spent the night only a little over a week before. It seemed infinitely longer than that, now. He looked at William and Mary and then at me.

"She's ready," he said. "Perhaps you'd rather come up alone?"

I said, "All right," and William and Mary nodded. "It's warm outside," he said. "I'll wait in the car."

I reached in my pocket and took out the keys. "You'd better take these," I said. "You can drive on the way home." He took the keys and tried to wish me luck with his eyes. "Don't worry," he said, and went out the door and down the corridor. Birnbaum said, "The elevator's this way."

The elevator ascended to the third floor in that hush-hush manner peculiar to hospital elevators, the operator reverently opened the door, and we stepped out into a long corridor. That insidious odor which is so disturbing to laymen was very strong up here.

The elevator door closed softly behind us, and Birnbaum, who had turned to the left, halted. He came back to me. "Barney—"

"Yes, Doc?" My voice was a little weak, and I resented its getting like that.

"This isn't going to be pleasant for you. Sheila's condition isn't—hasn't improved as much as I should like. You're going to have to show some guts."

"Okay." I cleared my throat. "That's okay. I can do anything I have to; just tell me what I'm to expect. But if she's still sick, why let her leave the hospital?"

"Because," he said, "we've done all we can for her here. It's up to you now. And time. We have every reason to hope that the shock will wear off and in time she'll get better."

"Her eyes will get better?"

"Not her eyes."

"Oh," I said. "I see. She knows about her eyes?"

"No. We wouldn't tell her that. Not yet, anyway."

"Then what's this shock you're talking about?"

"Well," he said, "we're not sure. It's hard to be sure in a case like this."

"Oh, for God's sake, Birnbaum," I said. "Come on. I can take it. What do I have to expect?"

"Frankly," he said after a moment, "I don't know. If I did, I'd tell you. But it's impossible to find out anything from her. She won't talk."

"She won't talk?"

"No," he said. "The nurse tells me that if she wants anything she'll ask for it—sometimes. But that's all. She hasn't said a word to me. I'm hoping—"

"Well," I asked, "what are you hoping?"

"That she'll respond better to a different atmosphere. That's why I want her to go home. I don't think that the hospital or some kind of an institution would be as good for her as more familiar surroundings. Do you understand?"

"Why, yes," I said. "I understand. At least, I'm beginning to understand, now."

He shook his head reprovingly. "That's not the way to take it, Barney," he said. "You're going to have to be gentle. Can you do it?"

"Sure," I said. "Sure, I can. I can do anything or be anything. Only, for God's sake, let's get it over with."

"All right," he said. "Come on."

We walked down the corridor and around a bend. Birnbaum stopped at a closed door. He was about to knock when the door opened and a nurse came out. She nodded to the doctor and looked at me inquiringly.

Birnbaum asked, "Is she ready? This is Mr. Page."

"How do you do, Mr. Page." She was unbearably bright and professional. "Go right in. Mrs. Page is all ready. I dressed her an hour ago."

You dressed her, I thought. But of course that would be necessary. Just at first, anyway.

"Aren't you coming, Barney?" the doctor asked,

"Yes," I said, "I'm coming."

I followed him into the room and looked around. It was very nice; large, airy, and depressingly impersonal, polished to shuck off death and pain. Sheila was sitting in a chair by the window, over on the other side of the high, white bed. She didn't look up at our entrance and I paused just inside the door. The bright light from the window fell on her face; it was drawn and pale and there were dark circles under her eyes. It was the face of a person who was suffering and, oddly, that relieved me; I guess it was because, more than anything else, I had dreaded seeing a face that was an utter blank. When there's suffering in a face, there must be reasoning behind it.

I felt the doctor looking at me. I turned to him and he nodded. I went across the room and stood by her chair. "Hello, Sheila," I said.

She didn't look up. She didn't move or make any attempt to answer. I stood there for a minute, and then I knelt down by her and put my arms around her. "Darling," I said, "it's Barney. I've come to take you home."

Her body was yielding, but perfectly listless. She gave no sign that she understood or even heard me. I knelt there, waiting, but nothing happened. "Sheila," I said, "Sheila, baby, it's Barney." But she didn't move.

I looked up at the doctor. He came over and took Sheila's hand, and I arose and stood helplessly by. "Come on, Sheila," Birnbaum said. "We're going home, now."

She rose to her feet when he pulled on her hand; she was perfectly pliant. He motioned to her coat lying across the bed. I got it and helped her into it. Then I put my arm around her and led her toward the door. She seemed to hesitate, pull back a little, then, as I insisted, she allowed me to lead her from the room. She walked cautiously, as though she wanted to feel her way with her feet. Now, for the first time, I knew that she was blind.

"Don't be afraid, darling," I told her. "We'll be very careful."

We went slowly down the corridor, the three of us, and stopped by the elevator. Birnbaum pushed the button and we waited interminably for it to come. People passed by us in the corridor, politely curious people and people who were completely indifferent: nurses and interns and orderlies. And one patient, an old woman in a wheel chair, rolled past us and part way up the corridor and then turned and rolled past again, looking us over. The elevator came at last, and we got in.

Birnbaum left us at the waiting room on the ground floor. "Do what you can, Barney," he said, "and I'll be over to see you in an hour or so. She might be better off in bed, but, if she wants to stay up, it doesn't really matter. Do what you think best. Good luck."

"Thanks, Doctor," I said. "We'll be all right."

"Sure," he said. "I'll be over as soon as I can."

He left us then, and I put my arm around Sheila once more. "Come on, darling," I said. "This way."

She made no protest; she let me lead her wherever I wanted; to the front door and down the steps and across the pavement.

William and Mary saw us coming. He got out and opened the door of the car. Sheila's extended hand touched him and asked a question.

"It's William," I said, "William and Mary."

"Hello, Sheila," he said.

Her hand discarded him; she didn't answer. I helped her into the car and climbed in after her, and William and Mary walked around and got into the driver's seat. We started off and there wasn't anything said on the way home.

That was a grotesque homecoming. Things seemed

out of place, clashing one with another like mismated colors clash, or discordant jangles on the piano. The flowers in the bedroom looked self-conscious; bright non-essentials in a gray world. The beds seemed not so much neat as overdressed.

William and Mary caught my signal and halted in the living room. I led Sheila into the bedroom and closed the door carefully. Then I helped her off with her hat and coat. I hung them in the closet and turned back to her, rather at a loss as to what I should do next.

She stood in the position in which I had left her, as lifeless as a catatonic zombie. I shook my head, trying to rid myself of the simile, and went to her and took her hands in mine.

"Here we are, darling," I said. "Home."

She didn't move.

Then I said: "The door's closed. William's in the living room; he can't hear. Isn't there anything you want? or anything you'd like to tell me?"

She didn't answer.

"Darling," I said. "Please, Sheila, don't make it any harder than it is already. I know you've been through a tough time. I want to help you. Please, Sheila."

She gave no indication that she heard. She just stood there, waiting. After a while I let go her hands. "Well," I told her, "the doctor said you'd be better off in bed. What do you say we get you undressed?"

I led her over to the easy-chair in the corner and she came readily enough. I took off her shoes and stockings, and, when I indicated that she was to rise, she stood up and allowed me to slip the dress over her head. I got her nightgown on and led her to the bed, and she got in of her own accord. Her dressing gown I laid across the foot, and told her where she could find it.

"Is there anything you want?" I asked. "The doctor

will be here pretty soon. I could fix a cup of tea before he comes."

She sat half-propped up in bed and made no move at all. So I said, after a moment, "Well, I'll get you some tea. I think it will be good for you." And this time I didn't wait for a reply because I was sure I shouldn't get one. I went on out of the bedroom and closed the door after me.

William and Mary was sitting on the couch with his hands folded and his face a cautious blank. He glanced up inquiringly as I came in and I forestalled any questions by saying, "I don't know. I'm going to fix her something to eat." I went into the kitchen and put some water on to boil.

He followed me in. "What do you want me to do?" he asked.

I said, "Nothing. And, if you'll take my advice, you'll clear out. I don't think there's anything either of us can do, but there's no reason for you to stay here."

"I'm staying," he said.

I got the things ready, and then I began to wonder if she wouldn't like a piece of toast. It didn't occur to me that there was no way of finding out, that I couldn't just go in and say, "Sheila, would you like a piece of toast?" and get an answer. That didn't occur to me; I wasn't acclimated yet.

I told William to watch the things and went back to the bedroom and opened the door. "Sheila—" I began, and stopped. She wasn't in bed. She was sitting in the easy-chair in the corner.

"What's the matter, darling?" I asked. "Isn't the bed comfortable?"

This time I didn't wait for an answer. "Come on, Sheila," I said. "The doctor says you'd better stay in bed." And I took her hand.

She let me lead her back to the bed. I covered her up well and told her, "The tea will be ready in a minute.

I'm fixing you a piece of toast, too." And I hurried out of the room; I forced myself not to wait for the silence that would be my only reply.

Out in the kitchen, the toast was in the oven and William and Mary was mixing himself a Scotch-and-soda. "Want one?" he asked.

"No," I told him, and got the toast out and buttered it and put it on a plate. I made the tea and fixed a tray and started to carry it in to Sheila. "Why don't you take your glass into the living room?" I asked William. "You'll be more comfortable there."

"Thanks," he said, "I will. And the bottle, too." He took the things he wanted and followed me as I left the kitchen.

I pushed the tray against the bedroom door and it swung quietly open. I walked in and stopped short. Sheila was in the chair again; she must have got out of bed as soon as I had left the room. I put the tray on the dresser and got a smoking table from the living room and carried it back and set it before the chair. Then I put the tray on the table and got her dressing gown and she stood up, when I told her to, and let me put it around her. I made her as comfortable in the chair as I could, and pushed up the tray to where she could reach it easily.

"Sheila," I said, "if you don't want to get into bed, it's perfectly all right. I don't mind. All I want is for you to be happy and comfortable. If you want anything at all, you only have to tell me. I'll get it for you or do it for you, whatever it is. Don't you understand?"

It was like talking to a corpse. So, at last, I said, "Your tea and toast is right in front of you. Please eat it. Or would you rather I helped you?"

I waited, and then I turned around wearily and left the room. I closed the door from the outside and leaned heavily against it.

There was a slight sound inside the bedroom; I could

hear it through the door. Quietly, I pressed against it and it swung slightly open. Through the crack I could see Sheila; she had the toast in one hand, the cup of tea in the other; she was eating the way a blind person eats, uncertainly, but as though she relished the food.

I must have leaned too hard against the door. It squeaked and, instantly, she froze. She put the cup and the piece of toast back on the tray and relapsed into her familiar, immobile position. Waiting.

I closed the door again. Almost immediately I heard the small tinkle of the teacup against the saucer. There couldn't be any doubt about it; Sheila heard and understood; her mind was working, working furiously. She just wouldn't talk; she had severed connections with the world. Birnbaum, I thought, could probably give me a name for what's wrong with her. But what good would a name do? You can't cure a thing by putting a label on it, and there are some things nothing can cure. Birnbaum, it seemed to me, had come to the end of his usefulness in this case. And maybe I had, too.

I went into the living room and sat down by William and Mary on the couch. He indicated an empty glass standing by the bottle of Scotch.

"Pour yourself a drink," he suggested. "I think it would do you good."

"No," I said. "I don't want a drink. I'm not licked yet. Not yet."

"In that case," he said, "pour me one. I'm licked enough for both of us."

Twenty-Four

That night I found it impossible to stay in the same room with Sheila. Because Sheila didn't sleep. I don't know how I was able to tell that, but, lying awake during the night, I knew perfectly well that she, in the adjoining bed, was as wide awake as I was. It got so that I found myself straining all my senses trying to catch, to find out, what was going on in her mind; I was that close to hearing her mind working.

So I got up and bundled some bedclothes together and went into the living room and settled down on the sofa. William and Mary had at last gone home; moved into the apartment of his new friend. I stayed on the sofa half an hour or so, wrestling with my conscience, and then I got up again and tiptoed back to the bedroom to see how Sheila was doing. She was no longer in bed; she was sitting up in the chair.

I went in then, and without turning on the lights I saw to it that she was warm and shielded from draughts. Then I returned to my couch; there wasn't anything else I could do. Trying to reason with her would get me nowhere.

I didn't go back to the bedroom that night. In the morning, when I got up and went to the bathroom, the bedroom door was shut. I was suddenly panic-stricken, but, when I threw it open, she was still sitting in the chair. She hadn't moved.

But while I was in the kitchen getting breakfast I heard her in the bathroom. I purposely took a lot of time, and, when I came out with her tray, she was back again in her chair, washed and with her hair combed. I said, "Good morning," and put the tray down and tried to be cheerful, but it didn't register. She kept silent and wouldn't touch the food as long as I was in the room. So I gave up and went out to the kitchen and managed to drink a cup of coffee.

After that, I washed my dishes and went back for hers. She had eaten her breakfast, every bit of it. Well, I thought, she's healthy, anyway. She'll live a long time if she waits to die from malnutrition.

Doctor Birnbaum came in while I was still in the

kitchen. I told him everything that had happened and he looked serious and very wise and went into the bedroom. But he didn't stay long. He came back into the kitchen and put his bag down on the table and drank a cup of coffee I poured for him.

"Well," he said professionally, "things are very much as I expected."

"You didn't expect much, did you?" I asked.

He ran his hand over his freshly shaved jaw and looked at me. "To tell the truth, Barney, I didn't. But she's better off here than she was at the hospital, and I think she should stay here as long as possible."

"Where else would she go?" I asked.

He looked up at the ceiling. "Some institution or private nursing home, I suppose. There are lots of them around."

"Not for Sheila," I told him definitely.

"No," he agreed. "Not for the present, anyway. She hasn't shown any hysterical tendencies, has she?"

"No," I said. "Did she at the hospital?"

He nodded. "She had delusions of a sort, but I don't think they were very serious. It may even have been a slight attack of delirium tremens: an aftermath from the stuff she drank." He finished his coffee and stood up. "Don't worry about it," he said.

I looked at a coffee stain on the tablecloth. "He tells me not to worry about it," I said.

The telephone rang and I excused myself and went to answer it. Birnbaum followed me, putting on his hat. It was Jake calling; he wanted to know if he could see Sheila.

"Just a minute," I told him, and turned to Birnbaum. "How about visitors?"

He thought about it, and then nodded. "She can have them. But don't let her get excited or tired."

I told Jake it would be okay and hung up. Birnbaum was leaving. "I'll be at the hospital most of the day," he called back. "And when I'm not there I'll be upstairs. Let me know how she reacts to the visitors."

"All right, Doc," I said. "About your bill—"

He waved me off. "I'll talk to you later about that," he said, and went out the door.

I thought about it and thought about it and thought about it. And then I got up and took a book—it was Steinbeck's *Tortilla Flat*—from the bookcase, and went into the bedroom and sat down on the edge of the bed.

"I thought maybe you'd like me to read to you," I said.

No answer.

I opened the book to a scene which she had always loved. It was Chapter XII, "How Danny's Friends assisted the Pirate to keep a vow, and how as a reward for merit the Pirate's dogs saw an holy vision." I read how the Pirate went to Mass and how his dogs embarrassed him there, and of the kindly sermon preached by Father Ramon and of how, afterward, the Pirate took his dogs into the forest and retold the sermon to them, speaking of the love which Saint Francis bore for animals.

It was lovely. For a little while I almost forgot myself. But then, when I glanced up, not quite hoping, I saw that it was no use. She was just sitting there; it didn't mean anything. I closed the book and laid it on the bed.

"Sheila," I said, "this is pretty tough going. What can we do about it?"

Perhaps I was only talking to put myself on record. I'm not sure. I know I didn't expect an answer.

"All this—this thing between us—has happened in a few months. We were happy before then; remember? You remember last summer up on Lake Champlain? We were close to each other then; things weren't like they are now. And that day we went rowing in the

Park and I told you that foolishness about the nail in Roseland. It would be hard for two people to be closer than we were then. What's happened to all that?"

I could feel that I wasn't getting anywhere, but I kept on trying.

"Here's the way I look at it," I said. "This thing can either break us or we can break it. If we keep on the way we're going now, we're licked before we start. But if we take it the right way, it might be the saving of us. Let me help you, darling. If we work together we can lick this. And if we work together we'll grow together again. Please, Sheila."

Then I stopped, having said all that I could, and waited. And when I'd waited long enough, I rose from where I was sitting on the bed and picked up my book. I said, "Well, think it over, darling," and started to go out of the room. But just then the front doorbell rang.

I turned back to her. "That's Jake Hershey," I said. "He phoned this morning and the doctor said it would be all right for you to see him. I'll bring him in."

But when I opened the front door, I found that it wasn't Jake. It was Fern Costello. She looked at me uncertainly and hesitated on the doorstep.

"Hello." I was surprised. "I was expecting someone else."

"May I come in?"

"Why, yes. Yes, come in." I stepped aside, and she entered slowly and I closed the door. She stopped just inside the entrance and turned to me.

"Maybe I shouldn't have come like this," she said, "but I've been worried. About you, I mean. And Jake told me Sheila would be able to see people today, so—"

"Of course," I told her. "Let me take your coat." She yielded it to me and I followed her into the living room. "How's the play going?"

"Not so well." She brightened up with the switch in conversation. "Not since you left. Aren't you coming back soon?"

"I don't know," I said. "I doubt it. It's hard to make plans."

"Naturally." She hesitated, and then asked, "How is she?"

I glanced at the bedroom door; it was closed. "Not too well, Fern; you'll see. It doesn't seem to me that she should have visitors, but the doctor said—"

"I'll be very careful," she assured me. "I won't upset her. May I see her now?"

"If you like," I said. "Let me go first."

I opened the door and preceded her into the room. Sheila was as I had left her, sitting in the chair. She didn't look up. "Darling," I said, "here's Fern Costello to see you."

"Hello, Sheila," Fern said, and crossed over to her and took her hand.

Sheila didn't say anything. Fern held her hand for a moment, looking down at her, then replaced it in her lap. She knelt by the chair and looked at me. Her eyes told me to leave them alone.

There was nothing to be lost by it. I turned around and went out of the door and closed it after me. I sat down on the couch and waited.

Not for long. The door opened, and Fern came out and sat down beside me. She looked puzzled and worried.

"Well—?" I started to ask, but I was interrupted. The bell rang again. "That's Jake Hershey," I said. "Excuse me."

I opened the front door and Jake came into the living room. He was carrying some flowers which he shifted under his arm when he shook hands with Fern.

"It's luck finding you here," he said. "We can go up to the theatre together. How is she, Barney?"

The bedroom door slammed shut. It was a vicious slam; it sounded as though the person who did it was very angry. We were startled, all of us, and we looked at the blank surface of the door and then at each other. Particularly Fern and I looked at each other.

"She's not very well, Jake," I answered at last.

Jake looked at his flowers. "Couldn't I just give her these?"

"Go ahead," I shrugged. "Just knock on the door and let yourself in."

He nodded and went over to the door and knocked. "It's Jake, Sheila," he called. "May I come in?" Then he opened the door, went inside and closed it again. Fern and I turned to each other.

"I'm sorry, Fern," I said.

She got up from the couch and stood by me. It was as though she'd reached a decision about something. "Barney," she said, "this is a time for straight talking. You're in a fix and I wish there were something I could do about it. I'd do anything I could. I want you to know that. And there's something else I want to tell you. It's this: I've been an awful fool, letting you know the way I feel about you. But—"

"Listen, Fern—"

"No, you listen. This is hard to say, but I have to say it. Don't interrupt. I've been a fool, but you don't have to worry about that anymore. I won't make things difficult for you, Barney. Not any more difficult than they are. We'll forget all that. Or, at least, you can forget it. It won't come up again. And please, please let me know if there's anything I can do. I guess that's all."

She put her hand out and I took it. I was all mixed up. There was something I wanted to tell her, but I couldn't put it into words.

Maybe she understood, anyway. She went back to the couch again and sat down. "I suppose I'll have to wait for Jake." Her voice was quite casual now. "I have some shopping to do before the matinee, though."

"I'll see what's holding him," I said, and started toward the bedroom. And then I stopped because of the sound I heard coming from behind the closed door.

It was Sheila's voice, talking just as she had always talked. I couldn't distinguish the words; the words were unimportant. The important thing was that she was talking. That Jake had been able to make her talk.

I turned around slowly and looked at Fern, and I found that she was looking at me. Her eyes were wide and startled; probably mine were the same. We stayed like that, she on the couch and I standing near the door, looking at each other for what must have been a full minute. And all through that minute we heard the voices, Sheila's and then Jake's, Sheila's and then Jake's. The words were unintelligible; the meaning was very plain.

Fern got up abruptly. "I shan't wait for him," she said. "Goodbye, Barney." She walked toward the front hall.

I followed her quickly. "Fern—"

She faced me in the dim entranceway. "No," she said. "Don't say anything. Please don't say anything." She jerked open the door and backed out. And then she was gone.

I went back to the couch and sank down on it. When Jake came in a few minutes later, I had myself in hand. I looked up at him curiously.

"You got her to talk," I said.

"Yes. She was very quiet at first." He sighed deeply. "She's had a hard time. Doesn't sleep well."

"But you got her to talk."

"Yes." He looked a little worried. "This is very decent of you, Barney, letting me call on Sheila like this. You know how much she means to me. It would be awfully hard to know she was going through a thing like this and not to be able to see her."

"You can see her," I said.

"Yes. It's very decent of you."

"I'm a very decent guy," I told him.

I let him out then. But before I sat down again, I looked in the bedroom. Curiously. Sheila was sitting in her chair, just as usual. "Everything all right?" I asked. And she didn't answer, just as usual.

I went back to my station on the couch, marveling, like a disinterested spectator, at the way things were shaping up.

That was the morning, that Wednesday, that Fritz phoned me from his bar. He told me that Mr. Roberts had sworn out a complaint—or whatever it is they swear out—against William and Mary. And that William and Mary was up in the psycho ward of Bellevue Hospital for observation and would I please send him some cigarettes.

The old steam roller, I thought. Once it starts rolling it's pretty hard to stop. I was beginning to take an almost impersonal interest in its progress.

Twenty-Five

Jake came visiting again the next day. He brought another bunch of flowers and he showed up smelling extravagantly of hair tonic. When I told him about William and Mary, he shook his head sadly.

"Poor William. Yes, I'd heard about it. It's too bad."

"Have you seen him?"

He looked surprised "Seen him? Why, no. I've been awfully busy," he explained. "My new play and the house in Westchester. I don't get a lot of time."

"Do you have any time now?"

He got wary; he looked at his watch.

"Look, Jake," I told him patiently. "I don't give a

damn if you see him or not. But I want to. It's a question of Sheila; I can't leave her alone."

His watch went back into his pocket and he brightened up at once. "Why, Barney," he said, "I'd be delighted. Anything I can do. Anything at all."

"I'm sorry to have to ask you, but you know how it is. After I've arranged for a nurse, it'll be different."

"Must you have a nurse?" He looked surprised. "Sheila seems pretty well. I thought she'd be over this soon."

"She thinks so, too, I hope. But that isn't the truth."

"You mean—?" His eyes were shocked.

"It's permanent," I told him. "You might as well know. Will it be all right if I'm gone a couple of hours?"

He nodded vaguely. "Take your time, old man. As a matter of fact, I have nothing to do until late this afternoon."

Bellevue is over on First Avenue between Twenty-Sixth and Thirtieth Streets. So, when I'd bought the stuff I needed, I took a crosstown bus and then the Third Avenue El and got off and walked east on a street I knew. It would have been easier to have taken another route, but something kept pulling me that way, daring me to go take a look.

But when I came to the Highland Hotel, REAL BEDS TWENTY-FIVE CENTS, I didn't even glance in the window. What was the use? I walked around and through the little knots of listless men who stand on the sidewalk there, and I went straight down to First Avenue without looking to right or left. The sight of Bellevue was almost a relief; it was depressing, all right, but at least there was a reason for Bellevue; it served a purpose.

They let me in without any trouble, asking me only casually what my package contained. "Cigarettes," I told them; and they gave me a pass and told me that patients were not allowed to have matches or razor blades and sent me up to the second floor. I got in a large elevator with a lot of worried, self-conscious people, and, when we got out, a nurse unlocked a door and ushered us into a ward and locked the door behind us.

We all looked around nervously when the key turned in the lock, and, Jesus, I thought, how William and Mary must hate all this! Locked in, not even allowed to have matches; I suppose they even watch him when he goes to the toilet. An attendant was showing us the way, and, just then, we passed the toilet and I looked in. There was another attendant in there, sure enough. He leaned against a washstand smoking a cigarette and looking bored. He looked as if he thought he was capable of holding a better job than the one he had, and I hoped that he was capable of it and, also, that he never got it. I didn't like this joint. I didn't like the idea of a friend of mine being in it.

And of course I thought of Sheila. Well, there was no use worrying about that. She'd never land here; I'd see to that. I'd do anything before I allowed that to happen.

We went into the dining room and sat stiffly at small tables and eyed one another furtively while our passes were collected and taken away. Down at the far end of the ward, names were sung out. They were the names of patients who were not yet completely dead, who still had occasional visitors, and pretty soon the ones who had been called began to trickle in and sit at the tables and whisper to their company: to call faintly to an outside world which was doing its best to forget them. They were an ordinary-looking lot, no better or worse than you'd find on any subway car; just a cross-section. Every race and nationality and religious persuasion in the world with only one thing common to all of them: they looked beaten. They all looked as though they'd given up hope; they seemed to say, Well, here I am. This is what life has done to me. I may get out of here someday, but it won't make any difference. I'm licked, now. Once you've been licked as I am, you can't climb back on top again. The thing that puts you on top, that makes you a human being among other human beings, is all taken out of you. That's what they do here; they take it out of you.

And then William and Mary came ambling along with his fat grin and chortled at me, and I felt better. Here's one guy, I thought, that they'll never lick. William must be a problem to them; you can't lick a guy who just laughs at you.

"Hello, stinker." I rose to meet him. "So they finally got wise to you."

"Less persiflage," he said, "and more presents." He sat down and picked up the package. "What's this? A carton of cigarettes? One carton? Why so penurious?"

"I'll send you more."

"Well, I should hope so." He grinned at me. "It isn't everyone who has a friend in the booby-hatch with interesting complications like mine."

"What's the matter with you?"

"That's what puzzles them," he said. "At first they thought I was just an ordinary run-of-the-mill schizophrenic, but then another doctor came along who said he detected symptoms of manic depression or something. That got more of them interested, and they took turns poking their fingers at me and asking me foolish questions and socking me on the knee with little mallets. They've all got their pet ideas and I try to keep everybody happy. There's only one thing they're agreed on," he told me, "and that is that I'm a screwball. I'm inclined to think they're right. By the way, what did you do with the matches that came with the cigarettes?"

"They're in my pocket."

"Hand them over." He indicated an attendant

roaming around the tables. "The Cossack doesn't care."

I gave him the matches and he put them away. The attendant saw it, but made no comment; William and Mary told me that the more matches there were in the place, the fewer lights the attendants would be called upon to give out, and that the general policy of the ward was live and let live.

"With some exceptions," he amended. "When you give me that bottle, for instance, you'd better slide it under the table."

"What bottle?"

"The one in your hip pocket."

"What makes you think I have a bottle?"

"Haven't you?" He looked disappointed.

So I slipped him the bottle under the table and he put it inside his shirt. "What's the procedure from now on, William?"

"You mean about me?" I nodded, and he said, "Well, they'll keep me here for a little while yet, until everyone has had a crack at me and all my possibilities have been exhausted. Then they'll take me down before a judge and have me committed."

"You can fight that, you know. I'll get you a lawyer."

"I've thought about that." His smile was gone. "But I shan't fight it. What do I have to lose?"

"Your liberty. Doesn't that mean anything to you?"

"Not much. I've had a lot of liberty; more than most people. It hasn't done me any good. Maybe this will. I've been getting tired lately."

"If you're going to get esoteric on me—"

"How about you? Aren't you tired?"

"Tired?" I said. "Sure, I'm tired. Everybody's tired. But that's no excuse. You've got to keep fighting."

"Why?" he asked.

There wasn't any answer to that and I didn't try to make one. We talked for half an hour or so, and I told him everything that had happened as well as I could, and then I got up to go.

"I'll have to relieve Jake," I excused myself.

We shook hands, and that gesture—because I don't believe we had ever shaken hands before—seemed to put us on a different footing. It gave an added consequence to our meeting and a finality to our parting.

"Don't worry." He put his arm over my shoulder. "Cultivate an objective viewpoint and take things as they come. You'll be all right."

"Look here," I said. "You're the one who's in the hospital, not me. I'm visiting you, remember?"

"Yes." He walked with me to the door. "But don't let it upset you. These little discrepancies are always popping up. Goodbye, Barney."

The nurse unlocked the door and let me out. William stood inside the ward and smiled at me until it closed. The key turned in the lock, and he was on one side and I was on the other. The wrong side, it seemed to me, in both cases. This isn't just a discrepancy, I thought, this is criminal negligence. I'd better get out of this place before they change their minds.

So I hurried downstairs and out onto First Avenue and back the way I had come. This time, when I passed the Highland Hotel, I didn't turn away. I tipped my hat.

One of the bums standing outside saw me do it. He nudged another bum and told him, and they both looked at me and laughed.

Okay, comrades, I thought. But if you knew what I know—

I didn't want to go home yet, I dreaded the thought of returning to the apartment. What I really wanted to do—I could admit this to myself now—was to hail a cab and give the driver Fern's address and go up to her place and take her in my arms and say, Fern, I love you. I love you, Fern, and you love me. Let's hang on to each other tight and, pressing together, let's press out all remembrance and all conjecture and let's just be us and live only in us.

But I knew I couldn't do that. Not now, not ever. So I got on the El and rode downtown, and I took the crosstown bus on Ninth Street, and eventually I got to Fritz's bar and went inside.

Fritz saw me coming in and kept on polishing glasses. He was down at the far end by the cash register and he looked up and saw me, but he didn't say anything. I went down to where he was and leaned against the bar, waiting until he should decide to take notice of me. He gave the glass he was holding a few more licks and set it down carefully, and then he turned around and nodded to me.

"Ginger ale?"

I said, "Please," thinking it was funny that I, who used to be the white-haired boy in this place, was being treated as politely as a tourist. When he put the glass of ginger ale before me, I laid a dime on the bar; I did it deliberately to see what he would do. He picked it up and rang the sale on the cash register. That had never happened before.

He's heard about Pete and Sis, I thought immediately.

And then I thought, or maybe he's just peeved about something, or off his feed. And I remembered with something of a shock that naturally he would be. I looked at him closely, trying to see in his face the thing I knew must be there. It was there, all right, when you knew what to look for. Fritz was a dying man; he was dying on his feet. In another month he'd be dead, and he didn't know it.

I sipped the ginger ale, realizing that anything I could say would be useless. Then I told him about William and Mary. I knew he'd be interested, and he was.

"Look," he said, and reaching under the bar, came out with a bung-starter. "That's for Mr. Roberts next time he comes in." He sighed. "Giving that guy a Mickey don't make any impression on him; he just comes back for more."

"He thinks you're playing with him."

"He'll find out."

The telephone rang, and he put the bung-starter away and answered it. "No," he said, "he's not here. Who's calling?" Then, "Okay. I'll tell him if he comes in," and hung up.

He turned to me. "That was Jake Hershey calling you," he said. "I didn't know if you wanted to talk to him."

I set my glass down. "Thanks." I wasn't worried. I'd developed a sort of feeling about these things. When something really important happened, I felt that I'd know about it without being told. I said, "Thanks," again, and started out.

When I was halfway down the bar, the swinging doors were pushed open and Pete McCord came in. He was drunk and a mess; his clothes looked as though he hadn't had them off in a week. He saw me at the same time I saw him, and came to a halt just as I did.

Then he turned around quickly and went out again.

I said, "Well—" and looked at Fritz. Fritz looked back at me without a trace of expression on his face, and then he picked up another glass and began polishing it.

I left the bar and walked east toward the apartment, hurrying a little to see what was wrong.

At first glance nothing was. But Jake jumped up when I came in and seemed glad to see me, and that made me suspicious. And the fact that he was sitting in the living room by himself, and that the bedroom door was closed, looked funny.

I mentioned it half-jokingly. "What's up? A lovers' quarrel?"

He flushed. "I don't think Sheila's feeling well. She's not quite herself. Where have you been? I telephoned all over."

"Why? Anything happen?" It was obvious that something had.

"Not a thing. But I remembered that I'm supposed to be uptown. I was supposed to have lunch with my architect"

"You told me—"

"I know, but I forgot this. Well—" He picked up his coat, anxious to be gone. But I got very hospitable.

"You can't be in all that hurry," I protested. "You've missed your luncheon date already. Sit down. I haven't had a chance to talk to you for a long time."

"Maybe I can catch him at his office. It's important."

"An architect, you say. I thought you were buying a house."

"I'm building an addition."

"Oh," I said, "a nursery, perhaps? The patter of little footsteps?"

"That's not very funny."

"You're right. My humor has been strained lately. "Well," I insisted, "you can tell me about Sheila, anyway. What's wrong with her?"

"I don't know," he said. "I can't imagine."

"Were you talking to her? Was she talking?"

"Yes. Up to a point. And then she wouldn't talk anymore. It was as though she were mad at me. But I didn't do anything she could get mad about."

"Well, don't worry about it." I started for the kitchen. "I'm going to make a cup of coffee. Will you have one?"

He picked up his hat and followed me. "No," he said, "I really have to go."

"How about a drink? Some Scotch-and-soda?"

"No. I'm in a hurry."

I looked at him. "Why?"

"Why?"

"Yes. Why are you in such a hurry to get out of here?"

He got flustered. "I don't know what you're talking about," he said. "My God, I've told you I'm late for my date already."

"You haven't got a date."

It was as close to calling him a liar as I wanted to go just at that moment. But it was close enough; it worked.

"Look here." He seemed pretty angry. "What do you mean talking to me like that?"

"Did I say something?"

"It seems to me you're trying to start an argument."

"Why, Jake," I said. "With a guest? Under my own roof? Just because you and Sheila had a misunderstanding is no reason why you should take it out on me. It seems to me that I've been more than considerate. Now be fair. Don't you think I have been?"

This time he got really mad. "God damn it," he said, "I've stood for your insinuations long enough. You're blaming me because Sheila won't speak to you, and I won't have it. I tell you I won't have it! A man who has treated his wife as filthily as you've treated Sheila doesn't deserve much consideration. I don't blame her for not speaking to you."

That surprised me; the moral indignation in his tone was real. Maybe I was getting someplace. I kept on trying.

"I don't follow you, Jake. How have I treated her filthily?"

"What do you call sleeping with another woman?"

"Oh."

"In your own wife's bed?"

"Oh."

Then there was silence for a moment as we looked

each other over. His face was flushed and he was breathing heavily; his eyes, back of the glasses, were snapping.

"I see," I said. "There may be something in what you say. But there's just one item that puzzles me. How did Sheila find out about all this?"

That did him in. That dropped his mouth open. He stared at me like a blustering fish. "How should I know?"

"There are only three people who have talked to her," I told him. "You and William and Mary and Fern Costello. Fern didn't know about it and William didn't tell her. So that leaves you."

He sucked up his jaw and pulled himself together for a final stand. "I don't know where you get your facts and figures," he said, "and I don't give a damn. They're all wrong. And I'm not interested, anyway."

He looked very defiant standing there with his head up and his glasses gleaming. Glasses give a lot of moral courage to a man. A guy has to be awfully mad to hit a man wearing glasses.

And I wasn't mad. I laughed. "Okay, Jake. Now it's all out of our systems. Will you have a cup of coffee now?"

"No." He was still huffy. "I'm leaving. But I think you owe me an apology before I go."

"All right," I said. "I apologize. Not even a Scotch-and-soda?"

"Nothing at all." He walked out of the kitchen. "Goodbye."

"Goodbye, Jake," I said. And I heard the front door close.

I went into the bedroom. Sheila was sitting in her chair; she was bent over the little table and, on the table, was a sheet of paper on which she was making marks with a pencil. There's something very pitiful about a blind person trying to write; writing calls for the use of your eyes more than anything else.

She heard me come in and snatched up the paper and hid it in her dressing gown. Then she sat back in the chair and waited for me to leave.

"I just came in to see if there was anything you wanted," I said, and turned around and started to go out.

My foot crunched a piece of broken glass lying on the floor. I looked down and saw a vase, or what was left of a vase, lying there. So I looked over on the dresser and, sure enough, a small cut-glass gadget that usually stood there was missing. The place where it had stood was easily within reach of Sheila's hand.

Elemental, my dear Watson, I thought. Elemental. And now, Doctor Watson, if you'll just cast your eyes over at the bed—

I did, and it was rumpled. Very rumpled. Not that that proves anything, I told myself. You can twist circumstantial evidence around to prove almost anything you want it to prove.

I went out of the room and closed the door quietly after me.

About five minutes later, the front doorbell rang. I opened it and Jake was there, looking sheepish.

"Well!" I was very cordial. "Welcome home. Have you come back for a cup of coffee or another apology?"

He smiled self-consciously. "I'm sorry about that, Barney. I guess we both lost our tempers. Let's forget about it."

"Sure," I said. "The coffee will be ready in a few minutes."

"No." He shook his head. "I'm really in a hurry whether you believe it or not. I just came back to tell you about the medicine."

"Medicine?"

"Sheila asked me to bring her some yesterday. She

complained of not being able to sleep and I got her a bottle of sodium amytal. You know how to give them to her?"

"Yes," I said. "I know how."

"Well"—he was going again—"I thought I'd better tell you. That stuff can be dangerous, you know. Goodbye. I'll call you later this week. Goodbye."

"Goodbye," I said.

Sheila was working with the pencil and paper again when I came into the bedroom. I was halfway across to her before she heard me and snatched them away.

"Sheila," I said, "Jake gave you a bottle of medicine. If you don't mind, I'll keep it for you."

She didn't answer me, so, after a second, I said, "I'm sorry, but this is important. If you won't give it to me, I'll have to take it away from you." I was surprised to find that I was trembling and that my heart was beating rapidly.

She heard me, all right; a shadow flicked over her face and her jaw set defiantly.

"All right," I said. "If you insist on having it this way——"

She fought me. She fought me silently with amazing strength and ferocity. She scratched my face and her fingernails came within half an inch of my eyes. She seemed to be clawing for them particularly. And all the time she was fighting she didn't make a sound.

I found the bottle in the pocket of her dressing gown and took it away from her and put it in my own pocket. Then I stood back, panting, and wiped my face with my handkerchief. It came away with blood on it; those scratches hadn't been love-pats.

"I'm sorry," I told her. "I didn't want to do that. I simply had to."

She didn't say anything. The piece of paper she'd been writing on had fallen to the floor. I picked it up, and then an idea occurred to me and I didn't give it back to her; I kept it. After a moment more, I turned around and went out of the room. But this time I left the door open.

I sat down on the couch and wiped the blood from my face again and looked at the letter. For it was a letter. The pencil had scrawled every which way on it and most of the page was completely undecipherable, but the first couple of lines were clear enough.

They read: "Jake—After what happened today I can't go on any more. Your promise—"

Then there was a lot I couldn't read. There was another phrase that looked like "buoyed up," and halfway down the page I made out, "house in the country," and toward the end, "better for all—" The letter stopped about there; it hadn't been finished.

But I got its meaning. Its meaning slapped me right in the eye.

That night Sheila threw her first wingding. I worked with her half an hour or so, trying to stop her screaming, but at last I gave up and called Birnbaum. He wasn't at home, and it took quite some time to locate him at the hospital, and all the while I was at the phone Sheila was pounding on the bedroom door which I'd been forced to lock. When I finally got Birnbaum, he said he'd come at once, but by that time I was so worn out I didn't care much whether he came or not.

Twenty-Six

Birnbaum came out of the bedroom, putting his things in his little bag. "I think she'll be all right for the rest of the night. I've given her a hypo and she's sleeping." He put his bag down and timed my pulse.

Then he doled out a couple of yellow capsules I recognized as a sedative and put them on the table. "You'd better get some rest, yourself," he said. "You look done in. I'm leaving some medicine for you."

He lit a cigarette and walked over to the window and stared down into the night. "I'm afraid we're going to have to do something about Sheila, Barney."

"What?"

"We'll have to send her some place where she'll have proper care. Her heart's not good; it won't stand up under these hypos."

I stiffened. I remembered Bellevue and the white uniforms. "Where?"

"That depends. How do you stand—financially?"

"I don't. We never saved any money. The hospital bill played hell with my bank account. The other bills will finish it off. I've got a few things left."

"Such as—?"

"Well—the car. A little jewelry. Enough to keep us until I go back to work."

"That," he said, "may be some time."

"What do you mean?" I didn't like the way he said it.

"You're in bad condition, Barney. You'll have to take a rest and build yourself up again before you'll be able to work."

"Rest!" That was funny.

"I know it'll be hard. That's another reason why Sheila must go away."

"But where? Where would she go?"

"A State Hospital seems the only solution."

"You mean a nut-house."

He spread his hands. "It's not as bad as that."

"No," I said, "it's worse. In the old-fashioned booby-hatch they chained them to the wall and forgot about them. Now, they experiment, they keep watching them, they—"

"Really, Barney—!"

"No," I said. "I won't do it."

He accepted defeat, temporarily. "At least," he said, "you must let me send a nurse over here. Sheila needs a nurse."

How could I tell him I wouldn't trust the best nurse in the world? That I wouldn't trust anyone but myself? "Look, Doc," I said. "Let's compromise. Let's go on as we are for a week. Then, if she isn't any better, we'll do something."

"It won't do any good."

"It may."

"It will be a terrific strain on you."

"I can stand it."

"In that case," he gave in, "I suppose I must humor you. But I don't like it." His eyes considered me doubtfully. "I don't like it, Barney. If anything happens, you must get in touch with me immediately. Keep in touch with me all the time."

"I called you tonight, didn't I?"

"Yes," he conceded. "Well, I've done all I can. Take those capsules I've left and try to get some sleep. Good night."

When he had gone, I put on a dressing gown and started to lie down on the couch. Then I saw the yellow capsules and picked them up and looked around for a place to put them; I had no intention of doping myself with the stuff. I thought of the bottle of sodium amytal in my coat pocket, and I went over to where I had hung my coat on the back of a chair, took the bottle out of the pocket, added the medicine and put the bottle back in the pocket again. Then I went back to the couch and stretched out.

I was tired, dog-tired, but not a bit sleepy. I knew that sooner or later I should be, though, and perhaps the doc's suggestion of a nurse might be a good idea. Not that I'd trust Sheila alone with any nurse; I'd never let myself get outside of hearing distance again.

But a nurse could sit with her while I snatched some rest out here in the living room. Well, we'd see. Birnbaum had given me a week; I could stick it by myself for that long, and a lot can happen in a week. Jake Hershey would be back; he could relieve me for an hour or so. I'd almost rather not be relieved at all, but, with William and Mary gone, and Pete gone, I had to use what material was available. I had to talk to Jake, anyway. Oh, there was a lot that little Jake and I had to talk about; it would be very interesting.

Why had I acted the way I had about the sodium amytal? Well, the answer was obvious: automatic reflex. Say you're climbing a mountain, a steep, dangerous mountain, with some guy. You hate this guy's guts; you'd be better off—and you know you'd be better off—if his foot slipped and he fell. Maybe a part of your mind has even played with the idea of helping his foot to slip a little, accidentally of course. You're climbing along, you may be ten or fifteen feet higher than he is and nothing between the two of you but a dangling rope, and it happens. He slips. He yells, and you look down and see him falling. What do you do? Tip your hat and ask him to remember you to your uncle who died last April? Like hell you do! You grab the rope and hang on. It's automatic. And, brother, if that rope is tied around your own waist and, by falling, there's a chance he can drag you with him, you not only hang on, but you pull your heart out; you keep on pulling till he's safe again.

That was it. Well, pretty close to it, anyway. Close enough. Of course, I didn't hate Sheila; I could never hate Sheila. Not after all we'd been to each other. And her safety was linked to mine just as tangibly as the rope links one mountaineer to the other. Or wasn't it? If I'd been mistaken in that idea—and I could be mistaken—and the rope were to break—

And there was Fern. I'd made an ass of myself about

Fern. Fern and I loved each other and I'd tossed the whole thing overboard. Well, it was too late now. But was it too late? If I'd been wrong in thinking that Sheila's and my destinies were necessarily tied together, and if Sheila fell—

Stop thinking like that, I told myself. Snap out of it. Get hold of yourself. If Sheila falls, you fall; you have no reason to think otherwise. You've got a good grip on the rope; for Christ's sake, don't let go. Keep pulling. Brother, keep pulling, because that's the only thing left for you to do.

Before three days had passed, I knew I'd never be able to last out the week Birnbaum had given me. No one came to help me. Jake Hershey didn't come back as he said he would. With all there was between us, I couldn't ask Fern; I just couldn't do it. I had to stick it out alone.

Sheila's hysteria seemed to follow a pattern, varied but recognizable. A long period of sitting immobile in her chair, followed by a shorter period of intense restlessness. She would get up and feel her way around the room as if in search of something. Then would come the screams. I'd call the doctor and he would come and give her a hypo and, gradually, she would quiet down and go to sleep. Then I could relax. I'd go lie down myself, safe until she woke again.

Sometimes she had periods in which she talked very rapidly to herself. Very rapidly and with an air of sly secrecy. Hallucinations, Birnbaum said. Of course. But you can learn a lot from other people's hallucinations. I did, and it was not pleasant learning. Sometimes it got so bad I'd try to shut my ears, to force myself not to hear what she was saying. It would be a relief when her screaming started again. Then I could call the doctor.

I learned a lot of things which I would have preferred

not learning. Among them was one piece of information which gave me just a faint glimmer of hope. Only a possibility, but worth trying.

But when I attempted to get in touch with Jake, I ran into difficulties. I found that he had already moved to Westchester and his number out there was private; the operator wouldn't give it to me. So I called John Friday at the Cochran, and his secretary told me that the boss was out of town and that she didn't know Jake's new number; he hadn't given it to her. She also told me that John intended to let the Cochran go after *Halfway House* closed, that it looked as though he were shutting up shop. That was a puzzler, but I had more immediate worries. Since I couldn't do what I had to do any other way, I called Fern. She, I knew, would be able to help me.

She said, "I don't know his number, Barney, but I see him almost every day. Either at the theatre or he telephones me. I'll tell him to call you."

"Do more than that, Fern," I begged her. "See to it that he does call me. I have an idea he's giving me the brush-off, and it's necessary that I get in touch with him. It's very important."

"Nothing's happened, has it, Barney? You're not in trouble, are you?"

"No, Fern. No more trouble than usual."

"If anything happens, you'll let me know, won't you?"

"Sure. Just see that Jake calls me. I'll take care of the rest."

"I'll do it. I've been thinking. I want to see you."

"I want to see you, Fern," I said. "Maybe, in a few days—"

"All right. I'm here. I'll be waiting."

"It does me good to know that."

"Goodbye, Barney. I'll take care of Jake."

"I know you will. Goodbye."

So, the next morning when the phone rang, I knew

who it was.

"Hello."

"Hello, Barney. How are you? This is Jake."

"I know it."

"I understand you want to talk to me."

"That's perfectly correct," I told him. "But not on the phone. Come on down here."

"Yes." He was very airy. "I've been intending to do that. But I've got all tied up lately. Now, let me see. Suppose I telephone you."

"To hell with that," I said. "You're telephoning me now. I want to see you."

"Why, sure—sure. Just as soon, as I can make it."

"Listen, Jake," I told him. "Stop futzing around. I'm waiting here for you and I'm expecting you right away. See?"

"You can't order me around like that." He was quite huffy. "Who do you think you are?"

"I," I told him, "am a guy who has a note with your name on it. A suicide note, if you know what that is. It's addressed to you."

"Oh, God—" That got him. "She hasn't—?"

"Not yet," I said. "But do you understand why you'd better come down?"

Moral indignation. "What is this? Blackmail?"

"Suppose you stay away and find out."

There was a pause, and then he said, "All right," very quietly. "I'll come down."

"That's better."

"I can't get away until five o'clock. I'll come then."

"I'll give you a cup of tea," I said, and hung up.

It was nearly six o'clock when he finally showed up. He came in looking harassed and he nervously refused to take off his coat.

"I've only a minute," he said. "I'm here against my better judgment as it is."

"So?"

"This affair has distressed me very much, Barney. And I don't understand your attitude. You have no idea how your attitude has upset me."

"Me too."

"This business about a letter. That's ridiculous, you know."

"Is it?"

"Sheila and I have never had any correspondence. None whatever."

"Now, Jake, I didn't mean that you were in the habit of writing each other all the time. I only said that I had a note she wrote you just before she tried to kill herself."

"Oh, Barney!" His eyes were shocked. "I can't believe that. It's horrible."

"Isn't it?" I agreed.

"You don't think—" He was having a little difficulty. "You surely don't think—?"

I nodded. "Oh, but I do. And it's not a question of thinking, Jake. I know. I just want you to tell me one thing. Are you in love with Sheila?"

"No." There was no equivocation about that answer. "I was very fond of Sheila, of course. We were very good friends. This is terrible, Barney."

"I know you were good friends." I held him to the subject "You told me so. You told me that you were in love with her. You told Sheila that, too." He jerked his head up and stared at me. He was on the defensive now. "Take it easy, Jake. I'm not trying to start a fight. I'm just trying to see if we can't reason this thing out together. Maybe, if we put our heads together, we can find an out somewhere."

But he was suspicious. "I'd be very glad to help you if I could. That goes without saying. But I don't see where I fit into this thing at all."

He wasn't going to be helpful; that was plain. I got

up and walked over to the window and, after a minute, I turned around and faced him.

"Jake," I said, "one last time. I need your help. You're the only guy in the world who can help me. And you owe it to me."

He stood up. "I'm sorry," he said. "I should have been glad to help you if you'd been decent about it. But I don't owe you anything. And I don't like your attitude. I've heard a lot of talk about a letter, but I haven't seen any letter. I'm very busy now, and I'll have to go. If you want to see me in the future, you'd better get in touch with my lawyers."

"Sit down," I said.

"Really—"

"Sit down."

He sat down. On the edge of the couch. I stayed where I was; his eyes, back of the glasses, blinked nervously at me across the room.

"I'm going to tell you something, Jake," I said. "I don't want to, but I guess it's necessary: just to show you that I'm not talking through my hat. You made love to Sheila the very first time you met her. I know you did. I knew it at the time, but I tried to disregard it. That's why I took her away last summer. But, when we came back, you made love to her again. You told me, yourself, that you were in love with her. Now, I don't know or care how far the affair went at that time—"

"It didn't," he interrupted. "It didn't at all. You can take my word for it."

"Jake," I told him, "for Christ's sake, don't bother to lie to me. I don't give a damn. That's past; it's not important anymore. I know—I absolutely know—that on at least one occasion you slept with her. Probably more. But I don't care."

"That's not true." His face was flaming as he jumped up. "That's a lie. You can't prove it."

"Sit down." It took him a minute, but he sat down. "I'll prove it, Jake, when I get around to it. Everything in order."

He muttered something I didn't catch. I went on. "I tell you again there's no necessity for you to get upset. I'm not angry; I went through that stage a long time ago; it's all over now. You bought your house in Westchester with the idea that you and Sheila would live there after she got a divorce from me." His mouth opened, but I didn't gave him a chance to speak. "And then, unfortunately for everyone concerned, this—this tough luck happened to Sheila; and that, you reasoned, released you. It made you as free as the air. Only, it didn't release you, because Sheila didn't quite understand it that way. She thought her blindness was only temporary; she expected you to see her through it just as she would have seen you through a broken leg or something. She didn't know she'd never see again. Until you told her. Until you were forced to tell her because that was the only way you could make her understand why you were walking out. You did that the morning I left you alone with her, when I went up to see William."

"No." He was desperate. "No. No. That's not true. I—"

"And when she found that out," I said, "she naturally didn't want to live anymore. So she tried to kill herself. Now, it seems to me that Sheila has been given a pretty dirty deal. I'm trying to reason with you, Jake, not pick a fight. I'm trying to make you see that the only possible chance Sheila has is for you to go in there and make her believe that it's all been a misunderstanding. That you still love her and want to marry her. That you'll take her to Westchester with you. That's the only chance she has, and that's why I'm reasoning with you the way I am when I would infinitely prefer to be smashing your God damned supercilious nose all over your stinking face."

He jumped up from the couch. He sputtered: "You can't—you can't say those things. You've got the wrong idea about it in the first place. It never happened like that. It's a frame-up. You can't ruin my whole life just because of a little thing like that. You can't prove a word you say."

"Jake," I said, "for days I've been listening to Sheila talk. I know more than you dream. I've read the letter she wrote you. I could plot for you every move that you and Sheila made that morning from the time I left for the hospital until she threw the vase at you."

"The vase!"

"Yes. You forgot to clean up the mess it made. Just as you forgot to remake the bed. Things happened too fast for you. And that's the story, Jake. That's why I think you sort of owe it to Sheila to do something about it. Because, I tell you frankly, unless something is done immediately, it will be too late. Catch on?"

"I—"

"You're upset now, Jake. Sit down and take it easy. I'll go fix you a drink."

I went out into the kitchen without glancing at him. He looked so collapsed and pitiful that it was a little sickening to see him. I mixed a Scotch-and-soda, a strong one, and took my time doing it. Then I carried it back and gave it to him.

He drank it and put the glass to one side. His hand still trembled a little, but the recess had done him good. He seemed in command of himself again.

"Well?" I asked.

He cleared his throat. "It's this way, Barney." His voice was shaky, but getting back to normal. "I believe that, when you think over some of the accusations you've made, you'll realize how silly they are. We're neither of us at our best right now and we're apt to say things we'll both regret, so I'll just have to ask you to take my word for it. But I think that my word should stand up beside that of a girl who even you admit is—well, not quite herself. However, I'm very sorry—sorrier than I can tell you—about the way things have worked out. And if there's anything that I can do—within reason—I'll be only too glad to do it."

"I see."

"But," he pointed out, "you realize how ridiculous it would be if I were to assume any obligation, moral or otherwise, for Sheila. After all, Barney, she's your wife, not mine. I feel very sorry for her and, as a friend—as a friend to both of you—I'd do anything in my power—"

"What?"

He lifted his eyebrows.

"What would you do?"

"Well," he said, "if it's my advice you're asking, it seems to me that the proper place for Sheila is a home, a nursing home of some kind." He gave me a sidelong glance. "Now, I realize that you've been under a great strain, financially as well as every other way. Of course, things haven't been going any too well for me, either; this house has set me back considerably. But, just the same, I'm going to write you out a check. And, Barney, don't you worry about it. You can pay it back when you get on your feet again."

I looked at him wonderingly. "How large would this check be?"

"That's better," he said, and smiled. He reached inside his coat pocket and took out a check book. "Now you're yourself again. Well, as I said, there's been a lot going out and not much coming in, but I think I can let you have a hundred"—he paused, and then added, "and fifty dollars." He unscrewed his fountain pen and started to write with the book on his knee. Then he stopped, with the pen uplifted, and said, "Of course you understand that I'll want that letter. Not that you'd ever use it; I know you wouldn't. But just as a matter of business."

I kept on staring at him and he got fidgety. "What's the matter? Isn't that enough? You ought to be damn thankful you're getting that much."

"Never mind the check, Jake," I told him. "I'll take these." I walked over to him and jerked the glasses off his nose before he knew what I was doing.

"Here—!" he protested. "You can't do that! Give those back to me. I can't see without them."

"While you were running off at the mouth," I told him quietly, "I was wondering just what I could do that would really hurt a son of a bitch like you. I thought of killing you; nobody saw you come in here; I could get away with it. It's a temptation. There's an alley back of Fritz's where I could drop your body and you wouldn't be found for a week. Then I thought it would be poetic justice to knock you out, grind up these spectacles and rub the broken glass in your eyes. That would put you on Sheila's level; maybe if I did that you would understand how she feels. That's why I took your glasses."

"Barney," he said, "you wouldn't—! Give me my glasses, Barney. Please."

"No," I told him. "I won't give you your glasses. They won't be any good after this, anyway." I took them by the metal part and smashed them on the top of the table. "On the other hand," I promised, "I won't hurt you—much. Now, get out of here."

"I can't," he said. "I can't see." He stood up, faltering. "I don't know where the door is."

"Find it, you son of a bitch," I said, and kicked his ass. I put everything I had into the kick; he gave a little jump and a yelp and floundered across the room. "Find it, you bastard," I told him. "You lecherous, perverted bastard." And I kicked his ass again.

He went yelping and jumping around the room and I kept right behind him. Every time he paused or came up against a piece of furniture, I kicked him.

His ass was soft from too much sitting; my hard shoe sank into it and ground against the bone. I was sorry when, at last, he found his way into the passage that led to the front door. I gave him a kick that lifted him the length of the passage and he blundered against the knob and turned it and ran out. Tears were streaming down his face and he was whimpering with rage and mortification. I followed him into the hall and, when he tried to feel his way along the banister and down the stairs, I put my foot against his back and shoved.

He went sprawling down the steps and landed in a tangled heap at the bottom. For a moment he didn't move, then he got on his hands and knees and crawled along for several yards until he reached the wall. All the time he was sobbing and whimpering to himself. Holding on to the wall, he managed to get to his feet and, leaning against it, he slid along until he made the front door and staggered out into the street.

I went on back into the apartment and closed the door. I was tired, but my heart was racing and I felt happy and very elated.

That night I couldn't rest at all. Sleep, without a sedative, was impossible. But I knew that, if I stayed awake, I'd think, and that wouldn't do me any good. I'd go crazy if I allowed myself to think.

So I got up and tiptoed into the bedroom. Sheila seemed to be sleeping and I went to the clothes closet and stood on a chair and ran my hand over the upper shelf until I found the bottle of sodium amytal where I'd hidden it. I took it down and went silently back to the living room.

The yellow capsules which Birnbaum had given me were in the top part of the bottle. I got a glass of water from the kitchen and swallowed them. The bottle of sodium amytal I put in the pocket of my coat where it was hanging on the back of a chair in the corner.

Then I lay down on the couch again and waited for the stuff to take effect. Gradually a drowsiness crept over me and I didn't fight it; I closed my eyes and waited and, at last, I slept.

Actually, it was more like a drugged daze than sleep. I know that part of the time my eyes must have been wide open because I was conscious of the dim outline of things in the room. But, even then, I wasn't really awake; my eyes were open and I saw, but my brain slept.

So, when Sheila came fumbling her way through the door of the bedroom, my mind merely noted the fact, but did nothing about it. It didn't flash a message of warning to my body, or, if it did, the message didn't get through.

I watched her figure in the room, a white blue in the dark, feeling over the table and along the walls, her hands flickering here and there as she walked. She came to the chair where my coat was hanging, and I saw one of her hands feel and then dart into my pocket where the bottle of sodium amytal was. I saw her take the bottle and then, with that air of sly secrecy, drift back into the bedroom and softly close the door.

I saw all this, I say, but it didn't mean anything to me. Not immediately. But, a moment after her bedroom door was shut, it did mean something. A message came shouting through my whole body. My brain had got its message through at last. Get up, it commanded; get up and do something. Do something!

But I didn't get up. I was tired. I'd done all that I could do already. Now there was nothing left.

Twenty-Seven

Sheila's funeral was held four days after that. It was a clear day and the sun was shining, but it was very cold. The ground was crisp and frosty underfoot, and the cold came up through my shoes and spread numbingly over all my body.

When it was over at last and I could go away, there wasn't any place for me to go. Not home. I didn't want to go there again. But I didn't have any money; I had just enough to get back to the Village. I'd have to get a little money, anyway, and the only way I could get some was to go home.

So I did. I let myself into the apartment and went quickly through the living room and into the bedroom. I didn't look around at all, just went straight to the clothes closet and grabbed all of my clothes that were hanging there and stuffed them into a bag and went out again. When the door closed behind me, I realized that I'd left my key on the table in the living room and that I was locked out. But that didn't make any difference; I didn't intend to go back there again.

It was a long walk over to Larry's pawnshop on Hudson Street, and the bag was heavy. I could have taken a cab and had the driver wait, but it didn't occur to me. Besides, I had all the time in the world and nothing to do with it. Well, not all the time in the world, but until the end of next May, anyway. May twenty-first, to be exact. Four months.

Larry looked up from his ledgers and greeted me with a smile. I'd always thought he was a funny guy to be running a pawnshop; he wasn't the type. Maybe that was why people came for miles to deal with him when it would be easier and quicker, to go some other place.

"You've been a stranger, Barney, but I see your name in the papers; I'm glad you're getting along. Why don't you come and see me? You don't always have to come on business, you know."

I didn't want to talk. "Look, Larry. I don't feel very well. Just see what you can give me on these." I pushed the bag across the counter.

He gave me a quick glance, opened the bag and spread the clothes out on the counter. He made a pretence of looking the stuff over, but I could see that his mind was on me.

"How much would you be needing, Barney?"

"Enough to last me four months."

He smiled and swept the clothes together in a pile and then leaned over the pile toward me.

"Not drinking, are you?"

"No."

"I didn't think so. Look, Barney; take this stuff home. You need it in your business. Tell me how much you want; I'll lend it to you."

"No, thanks. Just give me what you can on the clothes."

He shrugged. "It wouldn't be much. Twenty bucks for the lot."

"Give me the twenty."

He shoved a book toward me and handed me a pencil. "Sign here." While I signed, he went to the drawer where he kept his money and came back with a couple of bills. He gave them to me.

"You don't have to leave the clothes, kid. If you need any for your business, come on back. You can have what you want."

I folded the money and put it in my pocket. "Thanks. I don't have any business." I started out.

"Come back, anyway," he called. "I've missed seeing you around."

I felt rotten when I got out on the street. I didn't

want people to be nice to me.

There were twenty dollars in my pocket and I had no place to go and nothing to do for four months. Somehow or other the time would have to be put in. Because it was cold and the nearest warm place I could think of was Fritz's, I went over there.

It was night now, and I had been sitting at the table all day since early afternoon. It was maybe six-thirty; the late afternoon crowd had thinned out and the evening rush hadn't started. It wouldn't start for another hour or so. Through the door that led from the back room into the bar, I could see Fritz polishing his glasses, getting ready for the night's business. He hadn't spoken to me since his brief nod when I came in; he had left me strictly alone, and that was what I wanted. I watched him carefully as he worked back of the bar. His movements, when he thought no one was looking, were tired and slow; the signs of death were on him very plain.

It was maybe six-thirty and I had been out of cigarettes since four o'clock. The cigarette machine was in the bar; I wanted to get up and walk in there and put my money in the machine and get a pack, but that required effort; it required sustained and directed effort. One movement, and only one movement, must follow another; it would be necessary first to stand up and then walk into the bar and then reach into my pocket for the money and then—

I wasn't up to it. I could never remember all those things at once.

Perhaps I fell asleep. I must have fallen asleep because here I was standing at the bar with a torn package of cigarettes in my hand and I was asking Fritz for something. A match. That was it: a match. I wanted one to light my cigarette.

Fritz gave me one. Rather, he found a packet of safety matches and threw them at me. "Keep those. And don't ask me for another."

That meant I must have asked him before. In fact, I remembered now that I had. Several times. I felt in my pocket and my fingers closed around matches. Five or six of them. Well—

I lit my cigarette and leaned against the bar, holding the deeply inhaled smoke in my lungs. It came seeping through my nostrils, a small gray curl at a time that rose a little and then dissolved into nothingness. The way life seeps out of the guts of a man and is whisked away in small gray curls. There wasn't much of it left in me, now. Four months? Why so much? One quick exhale, one cleansing of the lungs; that would be all that was necessary. I blew out the rest of the smoke. Why wait? There wasn't much smoke left and it was soon gone, lost in the room that had become crowded again now.

Fritz was across the bar from me, standing still and looking at me. He had his hands on his hips, a bar rag in one hand, and he was looking at me with distaste. I looked back at him; I hadn't done anything.

"Why don't you go home?"

"Why?" He wasn't quite in focus. "I'm not drunk. I haven't been drinking."

"That's got nothing to do with it," Fritz said. "Any guy that's a right guy is welcome here whether he's drunk or sober. But you ain't a right guy anymore. You'd better go away."

I felt that Fritz shouldn't talk to me like that; I hadn't hurt him. "What have I done to you?"

"Nothing. A guy like you can't do nothing to me."

"Then why—?"

"I don't like you anymore. So you'd better get out."

I thought about that. It was all right; I didn't care. "Okay," I said. "But I want to tell you something."

"There ain't anything you can tell me I want to hear."

"This is important. This is very important." I leaned across the bar so that no one else could hear. "You're going to die. In a month you'll be dead."

He didn't move; his face didn't change a bit. "Is that all?" he asked.

"Isn't it enough?"

"You can get out now," he said. "I've known about that for the last six months. It's not news to me; my doctor told me. You'd better get out."

"You can take it like that?"

"What do you want me to do? Bellyache like you're doing?" He moved closer. "Listen. I never asked for any favors, and I ain't asking any now. I done the best I know how, and if it's time for me to kick off—well, to hell with it. I'll kick off the way I am; I won't be a broken-down, whining whore like you are. Now, I've told you before, and this is the last time. I don't like your face. Get out and stay out."

I couldn't make him see. "Fritz—"

The wet bar rag smacked into my face. It stank of beer, and beer trickled down my face and on to my collar. Fritz rounded the bar and got me by the arm. He headed me for the front door and shoved. There were men standing at the bar, strange men I didn't know, and they thought it was funny. They turned around and watched and laughed. I fell against the swinging door and it opened and I went through it into the street.

There was a lamp post on the corner. I leaned against it and wiped my face with my handkerchief and stared down at the cobblestones in the street. It was very cold. I listened to the noise inside the bar where it was warm. The men were still laughing.

It must have been some time that I stood there because I became very cold. I was trying to think of some place to go; I knew I should have to find some place that was warm, but I couldn't think of one. I couldn't think.

When the taxi stopped by the lamp post, I moved out of the way so that whoever was inside could get out. But nothing happened for a minute. Then the door opened and a voice called to me.

"Barney—"

I looked up, and the voice called again, "Barney, come in here. I've been looking for you." It was Fern's voice.

I went over to the open door and looked inside. Fern was sitting in the corner. "Get in," she said. "I've been looking all over."

There was a fire burning, but I was still very cold; I couldn't get close enough for it to warm me. I sat in a chair drawn up to the fireplace and there was a small table beside the chair. On the table were cigarettes and an ash tray and a bottle of cognac, and a glass filled with brandy-and-soda. It stood there.

"Drink it," Fern said.

"I don't drink."

She picked up the glass and put it in my hand. "Drink it," she said again. "You're shivering. It will be good for you."

I drank it. She nodded and went into the bedroom. In a moment she came back again and her arms were heaped high with bedclothes. She went over to the window-seat and began making up a bed. I knew that she was doing it for me, and that didn't seem right. It didn't fit into the picture. The brandy warmed me; I could feel the cold being pushed down and down. I poured another drink into the glass.

The bed was made now; she came over and put her hand on my forehead. "You have a temperature. Your bed is made. It's time to sleep now."

No sleep, not anymore. "Fern, I love you."

Her hand was cool on my forehead. She ran it up

and through my hair. "I know."

"I got twisted some place—before. I got a wrong idea. I thought that you were to blame—you and I, both—for Sheila. I thought it was because of us that she did what she did. That was wrong, but I kept thinking and thinking about it and I got twisted." I looked around the room; it was familiar, but off key somewhere. "The picture's still wrong."

"It'll come right." She took my hands, and I stood up and she led me across the room to the window-seat. With her aid I got my clothes off, but all the time I was wondering.

"It's not right," I said, once. "I shouldn't be here." But she didn't answer.

Then I was lying on the window-seat under the covers and she was bending over me.

She kissed me. "Good night," she said. Then, "Why are you crying?"

There were tears on my face; I felt them now. I hadn't known that I was crying before.

"I love you, Fern."

"I know," she said. "Don't cry, Barney. It will be all right."

She kissed me again, swiftly. "Good night, my dear." She went into her bedroom and closed the door.

I couldn't sleep. Shadows flickered on the wall, cast by the fire. Every now and then the fire popped and crackled. Once, a log shifted as a burnt end gave way. It made a rustling sound. It was as if the fire were alive, the only alive thing left.

I got up and put on my clothes and went over and sat by the fire. It was dying; there was no flame now, only a reddish glow. When that is gone, I thought, that will be the end. That will be the signal for the end. I sat hunched over the fire and watched it die.

There was no glow left; it was all gone. There was no light in the room at all except the little pale ray that filtered underneath her door. It settled in a small pale pool at the foot of her door, like a pool in which a child might wade.

My feet took me across the room and stopped in the place where the light fell upon them. I looked down at my feet. I stood still and looked at the light on my feet.

The door had opened and the light was full on me now. I raised my head. Fern was standing in the doorway looking at me. She was in her nightgown and she was looking at me curiously, but she was not afraid. Behind her the reading lamp shone over her bed.

She held out her arms to me and I went into them. For a little moment we stood pressed together. That was all. Then the long, slow walk to the bed. Only that little moment, and then the slow walk with what I knew at the end of it.

She sank down on the bed and raised her head to look at me. She didn't seem surprised when my fingers gathered at her throat; she might almost have expected it. A little questioning look, a smothered protest, and then a sigh as my hands tightened. No more.

Even as they glazed, her eyes considered me wonderingly. There was no reproach in them. Only at the end, when her mouth opened wide and the tongue fell out, was there anything that might have been called reproach.

And then I was completely spent. I fell across her body into an exhausted sleep.

The cold woke me. For a moment I lay stupidly, conscious of nothing but the cold. Then the stiffness, the unresponsiveness of the body upon which I was lying struck through me, and I sprang away and to my feet.

I looked down at her, and the backs of my knees seemed to disintegrate. My legs buckled, and I held on to the bedpost to keep myself from falling. Then, slowly, I backed out of the room.

Even in the dark, with the door to the bedroom closed, I found my way quickly to where the bottle of cognac had been left on the little table. I jerked the cork out and held the bottle up to my mouth and tilted it. The brandy ran down my throat and over my face. I only took it down to breathe and then, immediately, I drank again.

The bottle was empty. It lay on its side on the little table. I knew I must leave now. I had a date to keep. My clothes were on; my overcoat was lying there on the couch; there was nothing to wait for. I was late as it was.

I put on my overcoat and looked for my hat. I couldn't find it. It must be—to hell with it! I had to get going. I felt my way across the room until I found the doorknob in my hand, and I turned it and went out into the hall. I pulled the ivory-colored door shut behind me.

There were the stairs, slanting down. I started to climb down, holding to the banister. The stairs were very steep and I was in a hurry. I was months overdue and time was pressing. The stairs slanted abruptly—

I couldn't remember.

I was out in the street. It was cold and the street lamps were going past me. And time was passing with the street lamps; I could see the months slipping by— one—two—three—four. Fast. I was running. Running—

Someone shook me. I sprang to my feet and it was Tommy. I recognized the Highland Hotel. REAL BEDS TWENTY-FIVE CENTS.

"There's a guy downstairs," he said, "who wants—"

I brushed him aside and went down the steps, through the lobby and up the street. I didn't look at anyone. I went into a place on First Avenue and pounded on the bar. "Give me a double Scotch. I'm in a hurry."

John came in almost immediately. "Come on," he said. "We'll have to get your hat."

So much time lost.

We sat in Fritz's. John looked at me and cleared his throat. "I want you to take the eleven o'clock shuttle and meet me—"

I rose to my feet. "Why?"

"Don't you want me to help you? Don't you want another chance?"

"For Christ's sake, no," I said.

When the two men entered Madame Céleste's, I knew the time had come. I got up and left the place quickly; I didn't stop to look over in the corner where Pete McCord was. I ran down the steps and out the door and hurried to the subway.

I came at last to the shuttle and William and Mary was there waiting for me, as I knew he would be. I nodded to him and he smiled and looked at me with his penetrating black eyes. As he turned to throw himself at the cops, the shuttle door slammed shut.

I ran to the window and pounded on it. "Here!" I called. "Here!"

The cop saw me and pulled his gun. He leveled it at me. I pressed my forehead against the shuttle window and waited. There was a spurt of flame ...

Twenty-Eight

I opened my eyes and found that I was looking at the feet of a crowd of people standing around me. There was a pounding in my ears, *clatter clatter bang bang bang*. I'd been hearing it for a long time without being really aware of it. Now I recognized it as the subway.

I put my hand to my forehead and felt the warm blood there, and I was very glad. I'd kept my date. I struggled to my feet and listened to the shuttle pound along its way to the Grand Central, and I saw the people in the car shrink back from me. I didn't mind. I supported myself against an upright and felt the warm, tangible blood where the bullet had creased my forehead, and I was glad.

The date was May the twentieth, nineteen forty-two again, and maybe it had never been anything else. That didn't matter. It was all over, anyway, and I was glad.

When the shuttle slid to a stop and the doors opened, I was the first one on the platform. I looked through the blood streaming over my eyes and saw them down at the other end. Two of them, both in uniform. They saw me at the same time and they shouted and started to run.

I called, "There's no hurry. I'm coming," and walked down to meet them as I would have gone to meet a couple of friends.

THE END

William O'Farrell Bibliography
(1904-1962)

NOVELS:

Repeat Performance (1942)
Brandy for a Hero (1948)
The Ugly Woman (1948)
Thin Edge of Violence (1949)
Causeway to the Past (1950)
The Snakes of St Cyr (1951; abridged as *Lovely in Death;*
    reprinted in the UK as *Harpoon of Death*, 1953)
These Arrows Point to Death (1951)
Walk the Dark Bridge (1952; reprinted in the UK as *The
    Secret Fear*, 1954)
Grow Young and Die (1952)
The Devil His Due (1955)
Wetback (1956)
Gypsy, Go Home (1961)
The Golden Key (1963)

As William Grew
Doubles in Death (1953)
Murder Has Many Faces (1955)

SHORT STORIES:

Smart Dog (*Collier's*, April 12 1941)
I Could Go for You, Janie (*The American Magazine*,
    January 1942)
Wrong Turning (*Collier's*, May 2 1942)
Marks on a Leash (*Good Housekeeping*, June 1944)
Under Control (*Collier's*, February 27 1943)
The Rivals (*Cosmopolitan*, August 1947)
Exhibit A (*Ellery Queen's Mystery Magazine*, January
    1955; *The Saint Mystery Magazine*, September 1964)
The High, Warm Place (*Ellery Queen's Mystery Magazine*,
    October 1957)

The Girl on the Beach (*Ellery Queen's Mystery Magazine*, April 1958)

It Never Happened (*Manhunt*, June 1958)

Over There—Darkness (*Sleuth Mystery Magazine*, October 1958; *Ellery Queen's Mystery Magazine*, November 1964)

One Hour Late (*Manhunt*, April 1959)

Hi, Killer (*Mercury Mystery Magazine*, April 1959)

Long Drop (*Alfred Hitchcock's Mystery Magazine*, June 1959)

In a Tranquil House (*Alfred Hitchcock's Mystery Magazine*, October 1959; *The Saint Mystery Magazine*, August 1965)

The Girl in White (*The Saint Mystery Magazine*, December 1959)

Lady of the Old School (*Ellery Queen's Mystery Magazine*, September 1960)

Death and the Blue Rose (*Manhunt*, December 1960)

The Hood Is a Bonnet... (*The Saint Mystery Magazine*, December 1961; *Ellery Queen's Mystery Magazine*, October 1966, as "With Blue Ribbons on It")

Death Among the Geraniums (*The Saint Mystery Magazine*, April 1962)

A Plague of Pigeons (*The Saint Mystery Magazine*, August 1962)

A Paper for Mr. Wurley (*Ellery Queen's Mystery Magazine*, July 1963)

Philosophy and the Dutchman (*The Saint Mystery Magazine*, January 1965)

With Blue Ribbons on It (*Ellery Queen's Mystery Magazine*, October 1966; *The Saint Mystery Magazine*, December 1961, as "The Hood is a Bonnet...")

William O'Farrell was born William Buchanan Farrell in St. Louis, Missouri, on November 24, 1904, moving with his family to Pittsburgh in 1915. At age 16 he dropped out of school to work on the *Pittsburgh Post*, then in 1922 began traveling around Europe,  eventually becoming a Merchant Seaman. Around 1936, O'Farrell settled in Santa Monica where he first became an actor before turning to writing. He is best known for the 1942 novel *Repeat Performance*, which was filmed in 1947, but he also wrote for TV shows such as *Perry Mason, Thriller* and *Alfred Hitchcock Presents*. O'Farrell won an Edgar in 1959 for his short story, "Over There, Darkness" which was turned into an *Alfred Hitchcock Presents* episode starring Bette Davis. He died in Los Angeles on March 27, 1962.